LOVEBIRDS

Praise for Lisa Moreau

The Butterfly Whisperer

"[A] fast and easy read, very lighthearted...The sex was written with taste and beauty, definitely romantic."—*Artistic Bent*

"*The Butterfly Whisperer* is a lovely heart-warming story of two women who come back into each other's lives after ten years and find that the feelings they once had have not changed...The town of Monarch was wonderful and I loved the characters inhabiting it...There was a warmth and a feeling of community and I wanted Jordan to see that these things were more important than her Hollywood lifestyle." —*Kitty Kat's Book Review Blog*

"*The Butterfly Whisperer* by Lisa Moreau is a lovely romance with a bunch of my favourite themes all in one book. It has friends becoming lovers, an ice queen gets thawed, and it's a second chance love story. It even has the right amount of delicious angst to keep the pages turning...I had a great time reading it and I'm looking forward to seeing what Lisa Moreau has in store for us next."—*The Lesbian Review*

Love on the Red Rocks

"This was a lovely read, immersive and beautiful. Thoroughly recommended!"—*Inked Rainbow Reads*

"When I read this book I had no idea it was a debut novel because it was written so well. The story had me hooked from chapter one."—*Les Rêveur*

"*Love on the Red Rocks* by Lisa Moreau is a very nice book for the author's first novel. It was engaging and entertained me as a standard romance novel kind of way. The best thing about this book, it is full of likable, fun characters." —*The Romantic Reader Blog*

Picture Perfect

"This is a witty, entertaining and thoroughly enjoyable light-hearted romance. It's extremely well written and edited, a wonderful and well developed cast of characters, excellent dialogue, extremely funny at times and with a warmth and humor throughout. It's my first from this author but definitely won't be my last, I thoroughly enjoyed it."—*Lesbian Reading Room*

"*Picture Perfect* has a light, breezy feel to it, making it an excellent beach read. It's sweet, sexy, and a lot of fun with characters I enjoyed and a romance that gave me a happy sigh!"—*The Lesbian Review*

"This novel makes me think summer read, lying on the beach, with book in one hand and Mai Tai in the other. Another great novel by Lisa Moreau. Her novels just keep getting better and it leaves me desperate for what comes next. 5 Stars." —*Les Rêveur*

By the Author

Love on The Red Rocks

The Butterfly Whisperer

Picture Perfect

Lovebirds

Visit us at www.boldstrokesbooks.com

LOVEBIRDS

by
Lisa Moreau

2018

LOVEBIRDS

ISBN 13: 978-1-63555-213-3

This Trade Paperback Original Is Published By
Bold Strokes Books, Inc.
P.O. Box 249
Valley Falls, NY 12185

First Edition: November 2018

CREDITS
EDITOR: SHELLEY THRASHER
PRODUCTION DESIGN: STACIA SEAMAN
COVER DESIGN BY TAMMY SEIDICK

Acknowledgments

I read a quote once that said, "Don't write what you know. Write what you love." That stuck with me and it's something I've always adhered to. If you've read any of my other books, you know I love nature and small, quaint towns, which is odd considering I've always lived in large metropolitan concrete cities. I feel most at home strolling through a forest, communing with pine trees, colorful butterflies, deer, and any wildlife that doesn't devour or bite me. So, when I was contemplating the subject for this book, how could I not go with my favorite fowl: lovebirds? I also wanted the setting to be in the charming California town of Ojai (Oh-Hi) which is nestled in a picturesque valley—a place I frequent often. Of course, there's a lot more that goes into outlining a novel than subject and location, but that's always where I seem to start. I hope you enjoy reading *Lovebirds* as much as I enjoyed writing it.

A special thank you to:

Sandy Lowe for your excellent input in my book proposal and the trillion things you do every day to make Bold Strokes Books run smoothly.

Radclyffe for making yet another one of my dreams come true by publishing my novel.

Shelley Thrasher for being the best editor a writer could ask for. I consider myself very lucky to be paired with you.

Everyone at Bold Strokes Books. Literally. Everyone.

Dena Blake, fellow BSB author, for reading 70% of my manuscript, giving me excellent feedback, and letting me know it didn't suck.

Judi, my beautiful girlfriend, who gives me space to write, never complains, and is always supportive. I especially appreciate and admire you for going outside of your comfort zone to do practical research for this book when I wasn't able to do so. It was enormously helpful. I'm so lucky you're my girl.

For Judi

You raise my oxytocin level more than anyone I've ever known.

CHAPTER ONE

Soup Swap

No one wants bird poop in their salad.

That's what Emily Wellington's girlfriend, Gretchen, always said about the Little Bird, a quaint, outdoor café across from the ocean in Santa Monica. True enough, but it was still Emily's favorite restaurant. The place was surrounded by bird feeders that attracted calliope hummingbirds, American goldfinch, and song sparrows. It was like dining with feathered friends, which were preferable to most humans.

Emily shifted in her seat, tugged on her collar, and glanced around the café. It was like a million-watt spotlight beamed down, considering the table was right in the epicenter. That wasn't good when it came to tornados, earthquakes, or restaurant seating. Emily preferred out-of-the-way corner locations, anyplace where she could blend into the scenery like a chameleon. To take her mind off being center stage, she replayed the strange voice message she'd received from Gretchen that morning.

First, it was odd she'd suggested they meet at the café for lunch, considering the bird-poop threat and the fact that it was Monday. Lunch was every Tuesday and Thursday, date nights Monday and Friday, and lovemaking Saturday night. This impromptu lunch would throw off their entire schedule, which was unheard of. And even weirder was that Gretchen had ended by saying, in a terse tone, "We need to talk." Normally, that'd mean Emily was about to get dumped, but she knew better. They fit together like peanut butter and chocolate. Emily's mouth watered. What she wouldn't give for a Reese's peanut-butter cup. Instead, she slipped a straw into her mouth and gulped down unsweetened, watered-down tea, which was a sad substitute.

There was only one thing this unscheduled lunch could be about: D-Day. Two years ago, Emily had made a promise to her parents and Gretchen, and now it was payback time. She'd racked her brain all morning trying to come up with an excuse to postpone the inevitable, but she had nothing. She closed her eyes, took a deep breath, and reveled in the lullaby of a sparrow: three short, clear notes followed by a buzz and ending in a trill. If anything could calm her nerves, it was a songbird. She probably could have sat there all day allowing the symphony to wash through her if it weren't for someone loudly clearing their throat.

Emily's eyes popped open. A stunning woman with deep-blue eyes and shoulder-length golden hair stood beside her table. She had the milky complexion of a snowy owl, and despite well-defined arms that suggested she lifted weights, the woman moved as gracefully and confidently as a peacock when she shooed a bluebird off the table. Instinctively, Emily sucked in her gut. The woman had the proportions of a Malibu Barbie. Emily, on the other hand, would be Barbie's distant cousin who never got invited to the Dreamhouse for a pool party.

"Well?" The woman rhythmically tapped her foot, which probably wasn't to the tempo of a bird song.

Momentarily confused, Emily silently stared until she realized the woman had most likely been speaking for quite some time. Tuning people out was one of her talents, especially when birds were around.

"What?" Emily asked.

The woman sighed and looked as though she was resisting a dramatic eye roll. "Would you like to order now?" She pronounced each word precisely and raised her voice as though Emily might be deaf.

"But what about—"

"Jill, your waitress, is on a break, and I'll be taking over your table." The woman's left eyebrow shot up. "Sooo?"

"Oh. No. I'm waiting on someone."

"Right. Your girlfriend."

"How'd you know that? Wow. Just how gay do I look?" Emily chuckled.

The woman turned redder than a male cardinal. "I didn't mean...I just...um...I'll check back later." And with that she was gone.

Emily grabbed a spoon and studied her reflection. Short chestnut hair, brown eyes, khaki shorts, red plaid shirt, hiking boots. What about that screamed lesbian? It wasn't like she was carrying a golf club, and her rainbow keychain was tucked into her pocket, not even visible.

When the waitress cleared her throat again, Emily jumped in her seat, causing the utensil to clang to the table.

"Christ. You scared the crap outta me. You're as quiet as a dead three-wattled bellbird."

"A what?"

"The bellbird is the world's loudest bird. It can be heard almost a mile away, so the fact that it's *dead* would then make it the quietest. Get it?"

The woman blinked rapidly and didn't even crack a smile. No one ever got her bird humor.

"Yeah. Whatever. I just wanted to say that I don't have anything against lesbians."

"Okaaay."

"There's no reason to say anything to my manager. I'm one myself. A lesbian, I mean."

"I didn't plan to."

The woman's jaw muscles clenched. She peered down at Emily with squinty, suspicious eyes and looked like she was about to grab her by the collar with both hands. It was amazing how she could pull off stunning centerfold and scary biker chick all at once.

"I haven't seen you here before," Emily said. She usually didn't strike up conversations with strangers, but something about this woman piqued her interest. She didn't look like the waitress type.

The woman paused, one of those long, uncomfortable silences that made Emily want to crawl under the table. Finally, she said, "I've been here a couple of months. I work the night shift, but I'll be taking over the lunch run for Jill."

"Oh, right. She mentioned she was going on vacation next week. I'm Emily, by the way."

"Sydney."

"You'll see me here a lot. It's my favorite lunch spot."

"Really? Even with all these birds flying around?" Sydney ducked when a hummingbird whizzed past her head, so close her hair swayed in the breeze.

"That's the best part. I own a bird magazine. *The Tweet*. Maybe you've heard of it?"

Sydney stared, stone-faced, like a flawless marble Aphrodite statue. She was about as enthralled with that revelation as she was with Emily's bellbird joke.

""It's okay," Emily said. "Most people aren't into birding. Where'd you work before?" Emily held up a finger. "Wait. Don't tell me. You're a wannabe actress slumming as a waitress, right?"

"No."

"Musician?" Sydney shook her head. "Dancer?"

"Not exactly."

"What then? I know people. Maybe I could help." That was a lie. Emily knew no one. If she wasn't sitting in her cramped two-person office, she was looking through binoculars. But she was curious as to the beautiful waitress's aspirations.

Sydney's eyes, the color of the Mediterranean, shifted back and forth. "I should just concentrate on this job for now. I really can't fuck it up again."

Again? Sounded like Sydney had issues holding down a position.

"Well," Emily said, not wanting to push the issue, "I'll give you a little tip about waitressing. Be nice no matter how cranky the customers are."

"Right. Oh, hey. Here comes your girlfriend." Sydney pointed to a fast-approaching Gretchen.

"How'd you know—"

Sydney sped away before Emily could finish her sentence.

Gretchen hooked her bag on the back of the chair and lightly patted Emily's shoulder. "Sorry I'm late," she said, breathless. "The Rasmussen audit went long."

Emily pointed at Sydney's retreating back. "Do you know her?"

Gretchen slid into the chair and ran fingers through long, frizzy brown hair. "No. Why do you ask?"

"She recognized you."

A flash of something, maybe worry or anger, crossed Gretchen's face. She grabbed a menu, eyes darting around like a nervous squirrel. "How about mushroom soup?"

"Gretchen, look at me."

Gretchen sighed dramatically and focused on the space above Emily's head. And there it was, the telltale sign of lying—no eye contact. Emily's heart beat faster than a hummingbird's wings. Oh my God. Maybe she *was* about to get dumped. Maybe Gretchen and the waitress where having an...

"An affair? Is that why you wanted to meet me here?"

"What are you talking about?" Gretchen batted her eyelashes and looked about as innocent as a convicted felon.

"You and Sydney!"

"Who the hell is Sydney?" Gretchen's voice rose two octaves.

"Our waitress!"

Gretchen burst out laughing. After several minutes, she said, "I barely even caught a glimpse of her, and you think we're having an affair?"

"But...she knew I was waiting for my girlfriend...and...she's a lesbian and...she recognized you..." All that information seemed incriminating in Emily's head, but saying it aloud sounded ridiculous.

"I'm not sleeping with the waitress." Gretchen chuckled in a way that made Emily feel like a moron. "Now where's this Sydney person? I'm ready to order."

Gretchen signaled Sydney, who was beside their table in a flash with a pad and pen.

"Mushroom soup?" Gretchen asked Emily.

Emily scrunched her nose and scanned the menu. "It's too hot. A Cobb salad sounds good."

"You're slouching again," Gretchen said.

Emily sat upright and lifted her chin. Sydney shot Gretchen a go-to-hell look, the kind Emily wished she could do sometimes. It always made her feel like a kid when Gretchen corrected her posture. She was right, though. Emily wasn't the most poised person.

"I heard the soup is really good here," Gretchen said.

"Where in the world did you hear that? And since when are you so hot for soup?" Emily chuckled at the unintended pun, which apparently went over everyone's head. "Get it? Hot? Soup?"

"We'll take two mushroom soups," Gretchen said, completely ignoring Emily.

"Right away." Sydney gathered the menus and sped away before Emily could protest.

Whatever. She didn't want to waste time changing the order. The sooner she got this lunch over with, the better.

Emily took a deep breath. "I know why you wanted to meet."

"You do?" Gretchen's forehead wrinkled, which always happened when she was worried about something.

"I realize it's been almost two years." Sydney placed a bowl of steaming soup in front of Emily. "Wow. That was fast."

"Let's dig in," Gretchen said brightly. She was awfully excited about mushroom soup.

Emily gulped down a spoonful. "Now about—"

"Take another bite. A big one." Gretchen sat motionless, observing Emily like a specimen under a microscope.

Emily did as instructed, with Gretchen watching her every move. After she swallowed, Gretchen frowned and peered into the bowl. Had she seen a bug fly in there or, worse, a bird dropping? Suddenly, Emily wasn't very hungry. She pushed the bowl aside.

"Eat more," Gretchen demanded.

"Why? You haven't even touched yours."

Gretchen huffed, grabbed a spoon, and vigorously stirred the thick liquid. She grunted and signaled Sydney, who rushed to the table. Sydney looked as though she were about to say something when a woman sitting beside them screamed like a banshee. She took something out of her mouth and plunked the object into her bowl. Gretchen sprang to her feet, pushed Sydney aside, and thrust her hand into the woman's soup. She whirled it around a few times, grabbed the object, and clutched it in her fist.

"What the hell's going on?" Emily jumped up. Why was her girlfriend's hand covered with a stranger's tomato soup?

Fire blazed in Gretchen's eyes as she pointed at Sydney, red sauce dripping from her fingertips. "You idiot! I told you mushroom, not tomato."

The manager, in a suit two sizes too small, rushed to the table. "What happened?"

Gretchen wagged her finger, causing drops of tomato juice to dot Sydney's white shirt. "Your idiot waitress just ruined the most important moment of my life!"

Emily nervously looked around the restaurant, all eyes on them. She wanted to shrink to the size of a mouse and scurry into a hole. She'd been taught never to make a scene. Her own mother's hair could be on fire, and you wouldn't hear a peep out of her.

Sydney's eyes narrowed, fists clenched. "You switched it at least five times yesterday. I had to keep crossing it out and rewriting the order."

"I want her fired," Gretchen demanded.

"I'm not losing my job over your stupid idea. Who the fuck proposes to someone with mushroom soup? You should have done it during a Dodgers halftime like every other moron in this city who thinks love lasts a lifetime."

Wait...what had Sydney said? Gretchen was going to propose?

The manager pointed at Sydney. "You. Behind the counter. Now."

"Un-fucking-believable." Sydney shot invisible death rays at Gretchen and stalked away, yelling over her shoulder, "And I'm not an idiot!"

The manager attempted to wipe Gretchen's dripping tomato hand with a napkin, which did nothing but make a bloody mess. "I'm so sorry, miss. There's no charge, of course. Can I bring you another bowl?"

Gretchen shook her head. "It's too late. The damage is done."

"I'm terribly sorry," he said and headed straight toward Sydney.

Emily lowered herself into the chair, knees suddenly wobbly. "You're going to ask me to marry you? With mushroom soup?"

"This isn't how I planned it. I spent an hour explaining my idea to our idiot waitress yesterday."

Gretchen plopped into her chair and shot Sydney a dirty look. Emily blinked wildly, still not comprehending what was happening. Marriage? That seemed so...permanent.

Gretchen dipped the ring in her water glass and wiped it on a napkin. She scooted her chair closer and focused on Emily. "We've been together for five years now, and it seems that the next reasonable step in our relationship is that we get engaged."

Gretchen grabbed Emily's hand and slipped a diamond ring on her finger. Emily's gaze jumped from the sticky, red-from-tomato-sauce ring to Gretchen's expectant expression. Emily waited for more words to come, but none emerged. She'd never been proposed to before, but wasn't it supposed to be in the form of a question and weren't you supposed to wait until *after* the woman accepted to put the ring on her finger? But then again, wasn't Emily's response inevitable? She and Gretchen were perfect for each other. Both were practical, responsible, and had the same values. Gretchen was right. It was the next reasonable step.

"Well?" Gretchen asked, concern filling her brown eyes.

"Yes. Of course I'll marry you."

Gretchen smiled and looked as though she were about to kiss Emily, but refrained. She wasn't one for public displays of affection. "I think we should make the announcement tomorrow night at your parents' dinner party."

Emily nodded, knowing that everyone would be ecstatic.

"So what do you think?" Gretchen motioned toward the ring.

"It's so…big. And beautiful."

The diamond was huge, probably five carats. Too garish for Emily's taste, but she certainly couldn't complain. It must have put Gretchen, or rather her parents, back over ten thousand dollars. She guessed this meant she needed to get Gretchen a ring now. She certainly couldn't afford something this expensive.

"You don't seem very excited," Gretchen said.

"I am! I'm just surprised. Actually, I thought you were going to talk to me about the magazine." Emily chuckled nervously.

"That's second on my agenda." Gretchen pulled a stack of papers out of her bag and shoved them at Emily. "As your accountant I must tell you that *The Tweet* is in serious trouble."

Emily had no idea what she was looking at, but all those negative numbers couldn't be good. She knew her business was losing money, but was it *that* bad?

"You're headed toward financial ruin. And need I remind you that you're nearing the deadline."

Two years ago, Emily had quit a high-paying marketing-manager position to start a bird magazine, despite horror-filled gasps from Gretchen and their parents. She'd promised that if she couldn't make a success of the publication in two years, she'd shut it down and go back to the corporate world. But that was the last thing Emily wanted to do. *The Tweet* was everything to her.

"If it weren't for Owen..." Emily scowled.

"You can't blame him," Gretchen said adamantly.

Actually, she could.

"And now that we're getting married, you need to think about our future," Gretchen said. "You've had your fun. Now it's time to grow up and get a real job."

A real job? Emily had worked harder at the magazine than she ever had in marketing. It never felt like work, though, since it was her passion. Gretchen never had understood Emily's love of birds. She'd tried to explain it to her many times, but it was like talking to a potted plant. She hadn't comprehended one word, not that Emily could blame her. Most people thought birding was for nerds.

"You promised. Remember?" Gretchen flashed a stern expression.

Emily lowered her head, the glint from her diamond ring momentarily blinding her. "I know. Maybe you're right."

It would be devastating, but closing the magazine would be the responsible thing to do, and Emily was all about being responsible. In fact, quitting her job and starting *The Tweet* was the only irresponsible thing she'd ever done.

CHAPTER TWO

Pole Power

Click-click-click.

That's what Sydney Cooper heard when she turned the ignition on her eleven-year-old Ford Fiesta.

"Come on, baby. Don't do this to me now." She wiped a bead of sweat from her forehead and cranked the engine again, with no success.

"Fuck." Sydney banged the heel of her hand hard against the steering wheel.

It'd been one hell of a day, and the last thing she needed was a dead battery. Sydney glared at the Little Bird Café through her bug-stained window. She couldn't go back in there and ask for help, not after getting fired thanks to that dreadful couple. She couldn't believe that Gretchen woman had called her an idiot. That had stung worse than getting canned.

Sydney rolled down her window when Jill tapped on the glass.

"Are you okay? I saw what happened." Jill eyed the inside of Sydney's car disapprovingly.

Due to a break-in last month, the passenger window had been smashed, the CD player ripped out, and the carpet and seat were stained. It wasn't like she lived in the safest LA neighborhood.

"I'm fine."

That was a lie, but Sydney certainly wasn't going to say otherwise, especially to someone as put-together as Jill. She was a fifty-something rich widow who worked as a waitress because she thought it was "fun." She had houses in Beverly Hills and Palm Springs and a cabin in Ojai

Valley, and she was going to Europe soon on vacation for a month. Some people had all the luck.

"You know," Jill bit her bottom lip, "you really shouldn't yell at the customers or, God forbid, use the F-word. You might have a bit of an...anger problem."

Sydney stuck her tongue inside her cheek to keep from pouncing on Jill like a Tasmanian devil. She really didn't want a speech right now about her temper. She'd heard it all before.

"Riiight. Well, I don't want to keep you from work." Sydney nodded toward the café.

Jill stood upright and said, "Good luck. You'll need it." She'd whispered that last part just loud enough for Sydney to hear.

After Jill disappeared into the Little Bird, Sydney sat back in her seat and fumed. Monica would throw her out of the apartment for sure this time. Sydney had barely been able to come up with her half of the rent for months, and she certainly couldn't do so now. Maybe Sydney's mom had been right after all. Maybe she was a loser.

Sydney grabbed her phone and pressed the speed dial. "Hey. It's me."

"Hi," Monica said, breathless. "What's up?"

"My battery is dead again. I thought maybe you could pick me up."

"Sorry, but I'm running out the door for work. Did your shift end early?"

"Um."

"Syd?"

"Wellll."

"Christ. You got fired again, didn't you?"

Sydney could picture Monica standing in their 4x4 pink-painted kitchen with a hand on her hip, smoke practically coming out of her ears.

"I know...I know...but it wasn't my fault."

"You should stop screwing around with crappy jobs and come back to the club."

"No way." Sydney vigorously shook her head.

"Cruz said you were the best pole dancer he's ever had. He'd hire you back in a minute."

"The last thing I want is to entertain sleazy, drooling, drunk men and the occasional seedy lesbian. No matter how much they pay me. It's demeaning."

Hopefully, Sydney hadn't just insulted Monica, considering she was Leave It to Beaver's top dancer. Actually, Sydney was grateful for the five years she'd worked there. It had gotten her out of her mom's house, and she'd met Monica, who introduced her to pole dancing, which had changed her life in ways she'd never anticipated.

"Fine," Monica said and blew out a strong puff of air. "I'll get Victor to jump-start your battery, but he can't do it until late tonight."

"Tell your muscle-bound boyfriend thanks. And don't worry. I'll find a way home. I'm a survivor."

"All right, tough girl, but how do you plan to pay your half of the rent?"

"I'll figure it out."

"If you need me to loan—"

"No...no. I can handle it." The last thing Sydney wanted was a handout.

"Whatever. I gotta run. Later."

After quitting Leave It to Beaver three years ago, Sydney had gotten fired from so many two-bit jobs she'd lost count. Most times it was because of her so-called "bad attitude," but there were always extenuating circumstances that weren't her fault.

"Enough," Sydney said to herself.

No more crappy jobs.

No more hateful customers.

No more being broke.

She knew exactly what she wanted to do with her life. And this time she wouldn't take no for an answer.

Sydney opened her wallet and frowned at a lone five-dollar bill. That wouldn't get her very far in a taxi, and she didn't have much more than that in her checking account. She got out of the car and stuck her thumb in the air. Hitchhiking probably wasn't the safest thing to do, but with her good looks she usually nabbed a ride within minutes and always had a can of mace in her backpack in case anyone tried to get fresh.

An hour later, Sydney wound her way through a courtyard, behind manicured bushes, inside a gate, and stood in front of PowerBar,

Beverly Hills's hottest women's pole-dancing studio and where her dream job resided. It'd taken her days to find the place the first time she'd heard about it. It was tucked away with no signs in sight, like a dirty little secret. Not the way Sydney would have done it if this were her studio.

Most people thought pole dancers were strippers or even prostitutes. What Sydney loved about it, though, had nothing to do with getting men hard but just the opposite. She wanted to teach classes that empowered and liberated women and to help them get in touch with their bodies through physical expression. After all, pole dancing had saved her life years ago.

Sydney examined her white shirt splattered with tomato soup. It looked like she'd been in a gang fight. Damn that Gretchen. It wasn't bad enough she got Sydney fired, but she had to wag her finger around spraying soup everywhere. Oh well. She didn't have time to go home and change. She grabbed the steel handle and yanked open the heavy wooden door.

Sydney nodded at a tall, lanky woman wearing enough bling to blind ten people, strode purposefully to the main desk, and stood behind someone talking to the receptionist. Sydney wasn't one to eavesdrop, but she couldn't help but overhear their conversation.

"I can't do *that*," the woman said.

Sydney cringed at the word *can't*, which wasn't in her vocabulary.

"I have no upper-body strength." The woman rolled up her sleeves and attempted to flex. "Plus, isn't it for younger women? I'm not in my twenties anymore. I have at least ten extra pounds on me. They're practically…naked." She whispered the last word, as though it were obscene.

Sydney couldn't stand by and listen to this nonsense any longer. She loudly cleared her throat, which prompted the woman to turn around.

"Sorry to interrupt," Sydney said, "but I've been pole dancing for years, and while those are typical reasons why someone wouldn't try it, I have to say that they're not altogether accurate."

"Oh, really?" The woman's tone oozed cynicism and a little irritation.

"First, the lack of clothing has to do with the fact that dancer's legs, arms, and stomach need to be exposed in order for skin to grip the pole. It's a safety concern. And it doesn't matter how strong you are, your age, or even your size. There are maneuvers that anyone *can* do."

The woman chuckled. "You don't know me, honey. I have two left feet. I'm just here picking up my daughter. She's into this stuff."

"I know several routines you'd be amazed that you could accomplish. The more you do it, the stronger you get. There's no judgment, no competition. Everyone goes at their own pace."

The woman leaned close to Sydney and whispered, "Just between us, it is something I've always wanted to try. You really don't think I'm too old or thick around the middle?"

"Not at all. More than anything, it's about letting go and trusting yourself." Sydney pulled out her business card and handed it to the woman. "Why don't you give me a call? I give private lessons in the comfort of your home."

The woman studied the paper. "Hmm…I might just do that, Sydney Cooper."

Sydney watched the woman walk away, knowing full well she'd probably never hear from her. Too bad. She was just the type of person Sydney wanted to help.

Sydney leaned across the receptionist's desk. "Hi. Is Sue here?"

"She's finishing a class and should be right out. Oh, there she is." The receptionist pointed down the hall.

When Sue, PowerBar's owner, met Sydney's eyes, her wide smile dropped. She approached and cocked her head. "You? Again?"

"Just checking to see if you have any openings."

"Since the last time you asked two days ago? No."

What an exaggerator. It had been at least four days.

"If you'd just give me a chance to show you what I can do, I'm sure you'd—"

"Sydney, as I've said before, you don't have the…qualifications I need." Sue eyed Sydney's tomato-stained shirt and shook her head slightly.

Qualifications, my ass. What you really mean is I'm not posh enough.

Sydney bit her tongue, literally, and paused to reel in her rising temper.

"All I'm asking is a chance to demonstrate my skills. You have no idea how good I am. Sue, working at PowerBar is my dream." Sydney batted big baby blues and flashed a pleading expression.

Sue rubbed her forehead like she had the worse migraine ever and drummed her fingers on the desk. This was a good sign. She'd never done that before. It was always an immediate no.

"All right, listen. I do have an opening, and we're having auditions at the Ojai Women's Festival." Sue reached across the reception desk, grabbed something, and handed Sydney a piece of paper. "Fill out this application, bring it with you, and I'll let you audition."

Sydney's heart ballooned to the size of the Goodyear blimp, her lips curling into a smile. She couldn't even remember the last time she'd been this excited.

"You won't regret this. You'll see. I'll knock your socks off."

Sydney rushed out of the studio before Sue could change her mind. She'd lost a job today, but she'd just gained a lifeline. Now all she had to do was find a way to Ojai, the small valley town two hours from LA, and come up with enough money to pay for a hotel. She'd figure it out. Nothing would stand in her way.

Sydney glanced at the application she was clutching, her heart suddenly deflating.

Crap.

Question number five could not only stand in her way but completely obliterate any chance she had.

CHAPTER THREE

Where the Lovebirds Are

Emily's stomach soured the moment she walked into the Little Bird Café and heard that crackly, grating voice. *Owen.* Backstabbing, con artist, lower-than-the-lowest-slug Owen. He was sitting at a corner table, yapping to someone. Owen ran *For The Birds* magazine and was Emily's biggest competitor, but that's not why she despised him.

Jill approached with a menu. "Table for one?"

"Yeah. As far away from *him* as possible." Emily pointed.

Jill grinned and led her to the opposite side of the restaurant. With Owen's big mouth, everyone within a fifty-mile radius knew they were mortal enemies.

After taking a few deep breaths to calm her nerves, Emily perused the lunch specials, when she saw mushroom soup recalling Gretchen's proposal from the day before. It hadn't been very romantic, but Gretchen wasn't the mushy type, not that Emily needed hearts and flowers. Fairy-tale romances were for kids. Who wanted to be swept off their feet anyway? That sounded kinda dangerous. Yes, they were the perfect couple, except maybe for the bedroom, but that was Emily's fault. It wasn't something she and Gretchen ever discussed, of course—that would be far too embarrassing—but it was abundantly clear that Emily was incapable of having orgasms. Actually, she could have orgasms, but only when alone.

Chills ran down Emily's spine at the snap, crackle, and pop directly behind her. She knew that sound all too well. Owen had cracked his knuckles, just one of his many annoying habits.

"What a rock! You getting hitched?"

Emily glanced over her shoulder at the life-sized rat with beady pink eyes, long nose, and yellow, crooked buck teeth.

"That's none of your business."

"What'd you say?" Owen walked around the table and tilted his left ear forward.

Emily rolled her eyes. He always made a point of reminding her about his hearing loss. No matter what he said, it wasn't her fault.

"I said that's none of your business."

"What's that about beeswax?"

"I didn't...oh, never mind. What do you want, Owen?"

"Testy, aren't we?"

"I'm trying to figure out what to order," Emily said as she studied the menu.

"Who's a hoarder?"

Emily closed her eyes and sighed.

"Still sore about losing out on the blackbird story, I see," Owen said with a smirk.

Emily's eyes popped open, her heart beat wildly. "I didn't *lose* out on the story. You stole it!"

"Such strong words from a pretty little lady."

Jill approached Owen from behind. "Would you like some dessert, Mr. Reynolds? We have a nice pecan pie today."

"That *is* my favorite."

Funny how Owen had heard every word Jill had said, but when Emily spoke he was suddenly deaf. Jill winked at Emily and led the rat away.

Emily wasn't a violent person, but she'd give anything for a rock-hard dinner roll to sling into the back of his meaty head. She'd spent months doing research on the tricolored blackbirds and a week writing an in-depth article, only to have Owen snatch the printed copy off her desk when Cole, Emily's assistant, wasn't looking. Cole should have known better than to let Owen into the office when she wasn't there, but she couldn't blame him. He was an innocent kid tricked by a bitter old man. Emily had been shocked and appalled when Owen printed her story, word for word, in his magazine.

She'd reported him to the authorities, but there was no way to prove she'd written the article instead of him. It was his word against hers. Owen's magazine had gained national attention because of the story and an award from the California Fish and Game Commission. They listed the tricolored blackbird as an endangered species since the extensive research proved that the population had plummeted 64 percent in the past six years. That article could have secured her magazine's future, but instead, Emily was now facing closure.

Emily glanced around the café for Jill but spotted Sydney instead. Despite the mix-up yesterday, it was nice to see her. She looked even more beautiful today. Emily signaled Sydney, who stared a full minute before she finally crossed the room.

"Can I get the Cobb salad?"

Sydney's jaw dropped, eyes widening. "Are you kidding?"

"Uh...no. Am I supposed to order the mushroom soup again?" Emily chuckled.

"Unbelievable. What sort of sadist are you? You're sticking the knife in even farther?"

Emily tilted her head. "What?"

Sydney's eyes narrowed into two dark slits. "If this doesn't beat all. You and your girlfriend didn't have enough fun crucifying me yesterday?"

"You're the one who screwed up. And isn't *crucify* a little strong? I know Gretchen was mad, but—"

"Forget it. I have bigger and better things to deal with than you and your fiancée." Sydney turned and marched away.

What the hell was that about? Emily shook her head and grabbed her cell phone when it rang.

"Hey, Cole. I'll be in the office in—"

"Oh my God! You're not gonna believe the call I just got." Cole sounded frantic, from excitement or panic, Emily wasn't sure.

"Fran's Fig Farm in Ojai has a flock of *Agapornis canus* who are eating her crops, and she wants to know what to do about it. Can you believe it?"

"Wait a second. Take a deep breath and slow down. Now what's this about?" Emily couldn't have heard correctly.

"*Agapornis canus*. In Ojai!"

Emily chuckled. Cole was a nice kid who'd make a damn fine birder one day, but he still had a lot to learn. "Relax and check the *Sibley Guide*. It's on the bookcase behind my desk."

"I don't need to check anything," Cole said, sternly. "I know it's gray-headed Madagascar lovebirds. And at least twenty of them are eating Fran's figs."

"That's impossible. They wouldn't be in Ojai." Emily paused. "Unless...no, it couldn't be."

"But what if it is?" Cole asked, reading Emily's mind.

"What did this Fran person say exactly? Did she describe the birds?" Emily clutched her cell phone.

"She said some have green backs and wings, gray heads, and black markings on the tail."

"Male Madagascar lovebirds," Emily whispered. "What about the females?"

"She described them, too. Entirely green with dark-green backs and wings, and lighter gray-colored heads."

Emily gasped. "Are we the only ones she called?"

"I think so. She saw a copy of *The Tweet* at the grocery store and thought we might know how to stop the birds from eating her fruit. She didn't sound very happy about the situation."

"Call Fran back right now, get the address, and tell her I'll be in Ojai tomorrow."

Tingles rippled up and down Emily's spine, goose bumps appearing on her arms. This story could save her magazine. Emily disconnected and pulled out her laptop. She needed to book a hotel room quick.

"What's in Ojai?"

Emily whipped around to see Owen standing behind her. *Crap.* Hopefully, he hadn't overhead her conversation. The last thing she needed was him acing her out of the story.

"Geez, Owen. Stop creeping up on me. You're freaking me out."

"It's a free country."

Emily snorted. "Original comeback."

"You seem pretty excited about going to the valley."

"Aren't I allowed to take a vacation?" *Did that sound convincing?*

"You ordered the crustacean?"

Emily stared, expressionless. "Have you ever seen shrimp or lobster on the menu? I said vacation."

"This darn thing." Owen fiddled with his hearing aid. "It's pretty hot there this time of year."

Emily connected to a travel site and focused on her laptop. Maybe if she ignored him he'd leave...or not. After a few minutes, she looked up at him again. "Why are you still here?"

Owen rubbed his stubbly chin. "Seems like an odd time to take off, with your press deadline coming up and all."

"Don't you have anything better to do than concern yourself with my life?"

Owen cracked his knuckles and displayed an evil grin. "You have fun now, you hear?"

Emily shuddered as he slithered away. She returned her attention to the laptop and frowned. Her search for Ojai hotels resulted in no availability. That couldn't be right. The small town wasn't exactly a hub of activity. Emily logged into another site but with the same results. She even searched surrounding towns with no luck.

"Are you ready to order?" Jill placed a glass of water on the table.

"This is crazy," Emily mumbled to herself.

"Is something wrong?"

"I need to go to Ojai tomorrow, and all the hotels are booked."

"Oh, you won't find anything right now. A women's festival is going on. The place will be packed for weeks."

Ugh. Emily would sleep in her car if she had to, but a room with electricity and running water would be preferable.

"If you need a place to stay I have a cabin in Ojai," Jill said.

"Really? Could I rent it out?"

"Sure. I'll be in Europe for a month and won't need it. I gotta warn you, though, it's not very fancy."

Relief washed over Emily. "Anything will be fine. Thank you so much, Jill. You're a lifesaver." Emily took out her checkbook, scribbled an amount, and handed it to her.

"Whoa. You don't have to pay that much."

"Well, I'm not sure how long I'll be there, and trust me, it's worth it."

Jill paused but then tucked the check into her apron pocket. She wrote something on a pad and handed it to Emily. "Here's the address. And my email."

"What's this say?" Emily squinted at Jill's illegible handwriting.

"Reeves Road. It's close to Meditation Mount in the hills."

"Sounds nice. I've never been to Ojai."

"You're in for a treat. It ain't called California's Shangri-la for nothing," Jill said. "It's not very big, but it's picturesque and surrounded by the Topa Topa Mountains. It attracts nature lovers, artists, writers, and those new-age hippie types."

"I thought it was farmland."

"Oh, it is. It's a growers' paradise. Citrus, avocado, fig, apples, olives—you name it, it's there. Ojai is also famous for the *pink moment*."

"What's that?"

Jill smirked. "You'll see. It's usually a peaceful, serene place, but with the women's festival going on, there's no telling what it'll be like. My cabin is about two miles outside of the hubbub, though, so you should be okay. What are you heading up there for, anyway?"

"I'm going to Fran's Fig Farm. Maybe you know where it's located?"

Jill shook her head. "Honey, you must have that wrong. You ain't going there."

"Um...yeah, I am. She called *The Tweet* about needing some help." Emily didn't want to mention the Madagascar lovebirds. If the news got out, every birder this side of Texas would be in Ojai.

"If you're looking to buy Fran's figs, you can get those at the farmers' market out on Highway 150. No one goes to her farm."

"Why's that?"

"Just trust me on this one." Jill chuckled. "Now, the key is under a potted plant on the porch. Hopefully, the place has everything you need. I'm unplugging while I'm gone, but I'll try and check my email once or twice."

"Don't bother. I'll be fine. And thanks again."

Everything was falling into place. Now all Emily had to do was locate and photograph the Madagascar lovebirds, which shouldn't be too difficult considering she knew exactly where to find them.

❖

Sydney covered her ears as three police cars raced down Hill Street. She and Monica had lived in the neighborhood for years, but she'd never get used to the ear-splitting sirens. Unfortunately, it was a common occurrence in the crime-ridden area.

"So then what happened?" Monica asked and followed Sydney into the grocery store.

"Emily had the gall to give me her order. Can you believe that?"

Monica snatched a basket and walked to a display of latex condoms. She grabbed two boxes and tossed them into the basket. "Maybe she didn't know you got fired."

"Her girlfriend was the one who told the manager to can me. She knew." Sydney followed Monica down the chip-and-dip aisle.

"You're sure worked up over this woman." Monica peered at Sydney sideways. "Maybe you have a little crush on her."

"I don't even know her," Sydney said, irritated.

Monica stopped. "Ew, look at these weird chip flavors. Cappuccino. White chocolate. Hey, these look yummy." She grabbed a bag of wasabi ginger. "Is she cute?"

"I dunno. I didn't notice." But Sydney did know. Emily was adorable, with big, brown expressive eyes, a dainty nose, and pouty lips the color of Red Hots, the spicy, cinnamon candy. And she was way nicer than her girlfriend. If Sydney was the type to have crushes, Emily would certainly qualify, but the last thing she wanted was a girlfriend... an *engaged* girlfriend.

"Then why are you blushing?"

Sydney put her hands on her cheeks, embarrassed that they were warm.

Monica shot her an I-told-you-so smirk. "When was the last time you had a date?"

"I don't need a date. Besides, relationships never last." Just ask Sydney's mother. She'd been married five times.

"That's not true. Look at me and Victor." Monica grabbed a bottle of Scope.

"I don't think two months equates long-lasting. Speaking of which, hot date tonight? Condoms, chips, mouthwash."

"No. I'm working."

That explained the black lace tights, see-through beaded mini-dress, and leather boots. Normally, wearing an outfit like that outside of the club would be trashy, but in their neighborhood it was the norm. Sydney shuddered at the memory of donning that getup for five long years.

"What were you doing at the café anyway?" Monica surveyed the wine and snatched a bottle.

"Picking up my last paycheck. Not that it amounted to much. It'll barely pay my gas to Ojai."

"I don't know why you're so hot to teach a bunch of Beverly Hills bitches when you could be making big bucks at the club."

Sydney didn't bother trying to explain. Monica wouldn't understand since she actually enjoyed baring it all for sleazy guys. Sydney would be forever grateful to Monica for teaching her pole dancing, but she was growing out of the friendship. There had to be more to life than living in a run-down apartment in the worst part of town, struggling to pay bills, and working at jobs she hated.

"Why don't you just teach private lessons?" Monica asked.

"The clients aren't steady enough. I need a full-time job."

"What about Robin's studio? She's been trying to hire you."

"PoleCat? No way." Sydney huffed. "I wish she'd stop calling me about it."

"You've never even been there. Maybe it's nice."

"It's in South Central LA. How nice could it be?"

Monica stopped in the middle of an aisle and put her hands on her hips. "Well, excuse me. When did you get so high and mighty? Need I remind you that's where *we* live."

"I just…I want something better."

Monica took two pizzas out of the freezer and put them in the basket. "So, where are you gonna stay in Ojai if you're broke?"

"Well…" Sydney glanced around to make sure no one was listening. "Jill, a waitress at the Little Bird, has a cabin there."

"Oh yeah? She's letting you use it?"

"Yes. She just doesn't know it." Sydney smirked.

Monica stopped in her tracks. "You're gonna break in?"

Sydney put her hand over Monica's mouth. "Geez, just tell everyone in the store, will ya? Maybe there's a cop in aisle three who didn't hear you. It's not breaking in per se. It's more like…borrowing."

"I didn't think you had it in you." Monica chuckled and slapped Sydney on the back. "There's that seventeen-year-old badass girl I remember."

For some reason, that crack didn't sit well with Sydney. She'd like to think she'd matured the past eight years. Okay, so she should probably call Jill and ask her permission, but what if she said no?

Technically, it *was* breaking and entering, but it wasn't like it was a felony. She wasn't going to steal anything. Jill would be in Europe for a month and wouldn't know anything about it. Ignorance is bliss, right?

"So when's the audition?" Monica placed her items on the counter and didn't bat an eye when the checkout guy ogled her cleavage.

"In a couple of weeks, but I'm driving up there tomorrow. I can practice my routine and...well...get other stuff done." Sydney was tempted to tell Monica about the one thing that could prevent her from auditioning but changed her mind. No one needed to know about her private business.

They both jumped when two booming gunshots rang out.

"Whoa. That one was too close for comfort." Sydney craned her neck and peered outside.

"Probably the Tongan Crip," Monica said, referring to one of the many LA street gangs.

Sydney ducked when more shots were fired. She glanced at the checker, who hadn't so much as flinched, his eyes still glued to Monica's breasts.

Ugh. She needed to get out of this neighborhood...and fast.

Chapter Four

Meet the Parents

Emily frowned when her doorbell rang. Who could that be? She had way too much to do before leaving for Ojai in the morning. She didn't have time for company. She opened the door, surprised to see Gretchen standing there, looking like she was dressed for the Academy Awards.

Oh God. What did I forget?

"Aren't you ready?" Gretchen pushed past Emily and eyed the suitcases and birding equipment. "What's all this for?"

"I was about to call you." *Great. Lie to your girlfriend.*

"What's going on?" Gretchen placed her silver handbag on the counter. She was awfully dressed up. Hopefully Emily hadn't overlooked an anniversary or birthday.

Emily grabbed Gretchen's hand, guided her to the sofa, moved the spotting scope and binoculars aside, and said, "You're gonna wanna sit for this."

Gretchen crossed her arms over her beaded, black dress. "I'll stand."

"Okay, but don't say I didn't warn you." Emily took a deep breath, excitement bubbling inside her like a caldron. "I'm going to Ojai. There's—"

"Ojai? Why? When?"

"Remember last year when I told you about the flock of gray-headed lovebirds supposedly spotted in Pasadena? And the year before that in Orange County?"

"No. Oh wait…those Moroccan things?"

"Madagascar."

"Whatever."

"Well, Fran claims the birds are in…get this…Ojai!"

"Who the hell is Fran?"

"She owns a fig farm or something. That's not the point." Emily paused. She wasn't explaining this very well. "I'll start from the beginning. There's an aviary in San Diego where they care for exotic species that have been hurt or maimed. Two years ago, during a fire there, several of the birds escaped."

"I remember when that happened. It was sad. They said the ones who flew away didn't survive."

"Exactly! Except maybe the Madagascar lovebirds not only survived but thrived." Emily swept her arms out. "For the past two years, the birds have supposedly been sighted in Southern California, but no one's ever photographed them."

"What's so special about lovebirds? You can go to Petco and buy all you want." Gretchen rested her fists on her hips.

"These aren't like the African ones we saw on the Discovery Channel, Gretch. These are rare birds found only on Madagascar. There's never been a sighting in the wild in the US. This story is legendary in the birding world. Every birder in the West has been trying to track them down. If this is true—"

"Wait a second." Gretchen held up a hand. "What do you mean *if*? You're not even sure these birds are in Ojai?"

"Well, I can't be one hundred percent certain until I see them myself. But if it's true, this will be the only flock of Madagascar lovebirds in the wild within nine thousand miles of here." Emily placed her hands on Gretchen's shoulders and looked directly at her. "If I can find and photograph the lovebirds, this story would save *The Tweet*."

Gretchen glared, pursed her lips, and paced—as much as one could do so in a living room filled with birding equipment. After a full minute she stopped and faced Emily head-on.

"I thought you agreed to shut down the magazine." It wasn't a question.

"I know, but this is a huge exposé."

"Yeah, yeah…I get it." Gretchen waved her hands. "Gray-bodied Moroccan lovebirds."

"That's gray-headed Madagascar."

"Am I supposed to plan our wedding all by myself while you're traipsing God knows where? And we're supposed to be at your parents' right now announcing our engagement."

Crap. That's what Emily had forgotten.

"You could come with me. We can plan the wedding from Ojai." Emily took Gretchen's hand.

"I can't take off right now. This is a busy time of the year. How long will you be gone?" Gretchen sat on the sofa, looking deflated.

"I'm not sure. Listen, let's do FaceTime right now with our folks."

"You want to announce our engagement via video?" Gretchen looked horrified.

"I have so much to do before I leave tomorrow. I don't have time to drive to Beverly Hills right now." Emily grabbed her cell phone and sat beside Gretchen. "It'll be fine. I'll text Dad and tell him to get everyone together in front of the computer."

Within minutes Emily and Gretchen saw four heads scrunched together on the screen, everyone talking at once.

"Why aren't you here?"

"What's going on?"

"Why is your condo so messy?"

And on and on.

"Everyone. Can I have your attention, please?" Emily attempted to speak over the barrage of voices, without much success.

Emily drew her head back when her mother's Botoxed cherry-red lips filled the screen.

"Are you sick?" the lips asked. "You haven't been swimming in a lake, have you? You could have one of those brain-eating amoebas."

Emily sighed. "No, Mom. My brain is fine. And could you back up? All we see is your mouth."

Emily's father must have taken control of the laptop because everyone's faces reappeared.

"Gretchen, why are you on this video thingie?" Gretchen's mother drew her eyebrows together.

"We have an announcement to make, Mom," Gretchen said. "We were going to do this in person, but Emily is going to Ojai tomorrow."

Christ. That started a whole other line of questioning.

"Why Ojai?"

"Can you pick up some oranges?"

"Did you know your father won a golf tournament there in 1972?"

There was only one way to shut them up.

"We're getting married!" Emily shouted.

Gretchen shot Emily a dirty look while everyone else froze for five full seconds. Suddenly, the parents shrieked at ear-splitting volumes and congratulated each other. After all, they were the ones who'd gotten Emily and Gretchen together. The fathers were doctors at the same hospital, and after some intervening from the mothers, Emily and Gretchen were set up on a blind date. It had been decided, probably even before they'd met, that they would marry. It was "meant to be," as Emily's mother always said.

Gretchen squinted. "What's Dad doing?"

Gretchen's father was in the background talking on his cell phone.

"He's making arrangements with the country club," Gretchen's mom said.

"Isn't that something we're supposed to do?" Emily whispered to Gretchen.

"Might as well let him do it. He has connections."

Gretchen's father slipped his phone into his pocket and yelled, "The club is reserved for October fifteenth."

The moms squealed and clasped their hands together.

"You mean October of next year, right?" Emily asked.

"This year," the two moms said in unison.

"That's four months away! We can't plan a wedding that fast."

"The wedding consultant makes all the arrangements, silly," Emily's mom said. "We'll get Patrice. She's fabulous."

"I'm already on it." Gretchen's mother pressed a button on her cell phone.

Geez. Did she have the woman's number on speed dial? How long had they been anticipating this wedding?

Emily peered at Gretchen. "October seems so...soon. Don't you think?"

"If everything can be planned by then, why wait?"

Unfortunately, Emily didn't have a good response, at least not one that didn't sound callous.

"Sweetheart." Emily's mother's lips filled the screen again. "Does this video thing add ten pounds, because you're looking a little weighty." She whispered that last part, like that'd help soften the blow.

"Don't ignore your inner fatty unless you want to look like a balloon in your wedding photos."

Emily's mom was a die-hard fitness freak and Pilates instructor. Ever since Emily could remember, her mother had monitored her food intake and daily exercise. In their household, sugar was a four-letter word, so much so that when Emily was a kid she'd frequently misspell it on tests by writing *suga*. Her mom had many annoying sayings, like "diet like a beast, look like a beauty" and "sweat plus sacrifice equals success." The *inner fatty*, as her mom called it, was the part of Emily that'd allowed her to gain almost fifty pounds by the time she'd graduated high school.

"My weight is within normal range," Emily said, not even trying to hide her irritation.

"It's best to be under target, dear. That way, if you're bloated you'll still be at your goal. I just want you to be healthy."

Emily suspected her mother's concern had little to do with health but more about outward appearances.

"Why are you going to Ojai?" Emily's father asked.

Emily could have hugged him for changing the subject.

"I'm going to track down a birding story." Emily smiled.

"I thought you were shutting down that magazine."

Okay, maybe she wouldn't have hugged him after all.

Gretchen's mother chimed in. "Isn't the two-year deadline here yet?"

"This is a major story, Mom," Gretchen said. "It's rare Moroccan—"

"Madagascar lovebirds," Emily said.

"If this story doesn't pan out, Emily will close the magazine for good and go back to her marketing position." Gretchen turned and looked directly at Emily. "Right?"

She felt like someone had turned up the heat two hundred degrees. Five pairs of unblinking eyes focused on her. They weren't going to let up, and she *had* made a promise.

"Yes," Emily said. "If I don't get the story, I'll close *The Tweet*."

A hard lump formed in her throat, so big she couldn't swallow without considerable pain. She had to find those lovebirds. Her future depended on it.

CHAPTER FIVE

Two's a Crowd

Emily opened her sunroof and breathed in the scent of citrus as she drove down a shady, orange tree–lined road. Ojai was even more picturesque than Jill had described. When she turned a curve she was greeted with a breathtaking sight: mountains, which towered at least five thousand feet, surrounded green, rolling hills of perfectly manicured crops as far as she could see. This would be the perfect spot for a wedding, not that Gretchen or their parents would go for it. They required something more extravagant. By the time they'd finished the video chat, the entire ceremony had been planned. Every time Emily had opened her mouth to make a suggestion, someone cut her off. Eventually, she just gave up and sat there like a tree stump.

Emily was still shell-shocked about getting hitched so quickly. She was content, though, with the idea of marrying Gretchen. She felt comfortable having her future mapped out. The unknown could be risky. Look at *The Tweet*. It was dive-bombing faster than a magpie.

Emily adjusted her Bluetooth headset and called Cole. "Hey, have you heard from Fran?"

"Sorta."

"Text me her address. I'm driving right now and can't write it down."

"I don't exactly have it."

"Why not?"

"She said to meet her at Bud's Burrito 'n Bait Shop at seven."

"Why there?"

"I'm not sure. Em, she's kinda difficult."

Why did everyone have it in for Fran? She couldn't be that bad. "I've dealt with challenging people before." After all, look who Emily's parents were.

"Can you get me the number of the aviary in San Diego?" Emily asked.

"You're not gonna tell them about the lovebirds, are you?"

"Of course not. No one knows about this but you, me, and Fran. Let's keep it that way."

Emily heard typing, which probably meant Cole was googling the place.

"I got it," he said. "Want me to patch you through?"

"That'd be great. Thanks, Cole."

After a few rings, a man answered. "Littleton Aviary."

"Hi. My name is Emily Wellington and I own *The Tweet* magazine."

"Hmm. I don't believe I've heard of it. But we do subscribe to *For The Birds*."

Emily gritted her teeth so hard she was sure she'd cracked a molar. "I was wondering if Mr. Littleton was available."

"Speaking. What can I do for you?"

"Oh. Great. I'm interested in finding out more about the fire that happened a few years back."

"What about it?"

"Well, I was specifically looking for information about the Madagascar lovebirds that escaped that night."

Mr. Littleton released a deep, baritone laugh that seemed to last forever. "I wish I had a dime for every birder who's called about that. Don't tell me you're looking for them, too?"

"No. Not exactly." Emily was a terrible liar, but she wasn't about to tell him there'd been another sighting. "Do you think the rumors may be true? Could the lovebirds have survived?"

"Not unless you believe in miracles. I had those birds since they were young. They'd never even lived in the wild. Sadly, I don't see how they would have survived, especially not for this long."

"What was wrong with them? Why were they at the aviary?"

"Probably an animal attack. They had scars on their throats and heads. Had some wing damage, too."

"So as far as you know, the sightings have never been verified?"

"Nope, and I don't expect they ever will be. This rumor has gotten blown way out of proportion. Kinda like Bigfoot." Mr. Littleton released a hearty laugh.

"Thanks for your time," Emily said and disconnected. She didn't want to get discouraged, but maybe Fran, and everyone else, was mistaken. No. Emily had to trust her instincts, and every cell in her body believed that the Madagascar lovebirds were in Ojai.

Emily slowed when the speed limit dropped to thirty-five at the city limits. She wasn't one to break rules, not in driving or anything else. She took in the surroundings as she rolled through town. It looked like a quaint place, with gift shops, vegan cafés, and used bookstores. Emily leaned forward, amazed at what she saw a block ahead. Hundreds, or maybe even thousands, of women crammed into a park filled with tents and music stages. Obviously, this was where the Ojai Women's Festival was being held. Emily closed the sunroof in an attempt to mute the noise and slammed on her brakes when a group of partygoers stumbled into the street. They had on bikini tops and the shortest shorts she'd ever seen. Emily wouldn't have the guts to wear something like that in the privacy of her own home, much less in public. She shook her head and continued down the highway, glad when she'd passed the madness.

A couple of miles out of town, she turned down Reeves Road, which was a charming, winding path that led straight to the cabin… or at least, she thought it was the cabin. A beat-up car was parked in the driveway, and Jill had said it wasn't fancy, but from the outside the two-story structure looked amazing. No *Little House on the Prairie* log cabin here. She parked and eyed the number on the porch railing. Yep, this was the right place.

Emily opened the door, stretched her legs, and took a deep breath. The air was fresh, earthy. The cabin bordered a lush green sycamore and pine forest. Hopefully she wouldn't be in Ojai long, but she couldn't have asked for a more beautiful setting. She grabbed her binoculars and peered up at a black cottonwood, almost sixty feet tall. Perched on a branch was an American kestrel with a russet-colored back and double black stripes on its white face. When Emily heard the distinctive whistle of a black phoebe, she scanned the tree until his little black head and white belly were in view. She mentally thanked him for the warm welcome.

Emily could have stood there all day bird-watching, but she wanted to unpack and head into town to meet Fran. After she grabbed her suitcases and walked up the steps onto the porch, she saw a huge potted plant in a purple container, which was where Jill had said the key was located. Great. Just Emily's luck it looked like it weighed a hundred pounds. She strained to tilt the plant and peered down but didn't see anything underneath. She grabbed both sides of the tub and lifted, almost knocking her back out in the process. Still no key. Emily was sure that's where Jill had said it was hidden.

What was she supposed to do now? She couldn't break in. She wouldn't even know *how* to break in. Maybe if she jiggled the door handle it'd magically open. She put her hand on the knob and twisted, shocked to find it unlocked. A mixture of immense relief and concern filled her. It didn't matter how low the Ojai crime rate was. Not locking your door wasn't safe.

When Emily stepped through the doorway, she dropped her bags and glanced around the semidarkened room. After her eyes adjusted, she saw a big-screen TV mounted on the wall, leather couch and chairs, fireplace, and gorgeous hardwood floors. A spiral staircase wound to the second floor, which was probably where the bedroom was located. She inched through the living room and into a dining area that featured a massive, very expensive-looking chandelier hanging over a glossy walnut table. *Wow*. Emily would have to upgrade the description of this from cabin to mini-mansion. She pushed open the saloon-style swinging doors into the kitchen, which was well stocked with an impressive array of shiny appliances Emily had no idea how to use. The only thing she knew how to make were Pop-Tarts, and even then she usually burned them.

Goose bumps suddenly appeared on her arms, and a prickly sensation ran up and down her spine. An unsettling sensation rested in the pit of her stomach, along with the uncanny feeling that she wasn't alone. Weird. Being in a strange place was doing things to her imagination. She shook off the odd sensation and opened the refrigerator, which was completely empty except for a carton of almond milk that had probably expired months ago. Grocery shopping would be high on her priority list. Emily shut the door and shivered again, with an even stronger awareness that someone else was in the cabin.

"Hello? Is anybody here?"

Real smart, Emily. It's not like a burglar would respond. Basically, all she'd done was give him a heads-up so he could reload his pistol. She walked around the island in the middle of the kitchen and stopped, her breath catching in her throat. A glass filled with a disgusting green liquid sat next to a blender. She placed her hand on the cup. It was still cold, which meant someone had recently prepared the concoction. Oh my God, she *wasn't* alone. A vagrant or thief or murderer must have broken in. That's why the door had been unlocked. Emily needed to scram, and fast, so she could call for help.

"Crap," Emily whispered when she heard a noise, which sounded like someone running down the stairs. Frantically, she scanned the surroundings for a weapon. She'd never be able to lift the espresso machine, which looked like it weighed as much as the potted plant. Where were all the sharp knives? Or even a frying pan or spatula, something she could throw at the guy. As the footsteps grew louder, Emily's heart almost beat out of her chest. It sounded like they were headed straight for the kitchen. Emily's eye caught her sparkling, humongous ring. She could poke his eye out. Surely Gretchen would forgive her for any damage done if it saved her life. Emily snagged the revolting avocado-colored drink and squatted behind the island. She was shaking so much she had to hold it with both hands to keep it from sloshing everywhere.

Adrenaline coursed through her when she heard the kitchen doors swing open. She jumped up, screamed "ahhh," threw the drink into the intruder's face, jabbed her ring at him, and assumed a karate pose. Emily had never done karate before, but she'd seen *The Karate Kid* at least a dozen times and mentally patted herself on the back for the last-minute brainstorm. In all the commotion it took a few moments to comprehend what she was seeing. The intruder wasn't a man at all, but instead a woman, and not just any woman…it was the cranky waitress from the Little Bird.

"What the fuck?" The woman—wasn't her name Sydney—wiped green gunk from her face and went cross-eyed when she stared at Emily's ring, which was two centimeters away.

Emily lowered her arm, unsure of what was happening, but then pointed her ring at Sydney again. Just because Emily had met her at the café didn't mean she actually knew her. She was still an intruder. Sydney wiped her face on her sleeve. "Emily? What the hell are you doing here? And why the fuck did you just throw my drink on me? Christ, would you look at this?" She examined the front of her shirt. "First, your girlfriend gets tomato soup all over me, and now this. I spent all my money on those ingredients. Well? Aren't you going to say anything?" Sydney put her hands on her hips, looking a lot like the Jolly Green Giant.

Emily had so many questions she didn't know where to start. "You!" Weak start, but at least it was something.

Sydney tried unsuccessfully to push Emily's hand away. "Get that thing outta my face."

"Don't make a move. You don't want to be on the receiving end of this."

Sydney held out her wet shirt, which had probably soaked her to the skin. "You gonna blind me with your ostentatious diamond?"

"I'm just protecting myself."

"From what?"

"You! You're a burglar…an interloper…a criminal."

"You're the intruder, not me." Sydney walked to the sink and splashed water on her face.

"I paid Jill yesterday to rent this cabin, and she didn't say anything about you being here."

Sydney took her time washing her hands and drying them. Finally, she turned around and leaned against the counter. "Jill invited me to stay here while she's out of the country."

"That doesn't make any sense. Why would she rent the place to me?"

Sydney shrugged. "Maybe she forgot."

Emily finally lowered her ring finger, which was still pointed at Sydney. "You're bluffing."

"Hey. I'm just telling you like it is. She offered it to me after you and your girlfriend got me canned."

"I'm going to email…wait…you were fired?"

"Oh, like you don't know." Sydney rolled her eyes.

"Wow. I'm sorry. I didn't want that to happen." Emily rubbed her forehead. "Ohhh, so that's why you were so hostile at the café yesterday."

"So you see, I belong here and you don't." Sydney pushed off the counter, breezed past Emily, and went into the living room.

"Wait a second. I'm not going anywhere," Emily said, following close behind. "I'm emailing Jill to see what she has to say about this."

Sydney grunted. "Good luck with that. She never checks messages when she's out of the country."

"So what are we supposed to do?"

"I'm staying. You're leaving." Sydney stomped up the stairs.

"That's what you think, buster!"

Buster? Sydney was anything but. She was a head-turning babe with the most perfect features of anyone Emily had ever met—even with disgusting green stuff all over her face—which was all the more reason Emily needed to get this mix-up straightened out. And fast.

Sydney burst into the bedroom and ripped off her shirt, changed, and sat on the edge of the bed. The last thing she needed was a complication, especially from the woman who'd gotten her fired. Well, technically it was Emily's girlfriend, which was the same thing…sorta. Sydney could BS her way through anything, but she'd be in big trouble if Jill checked her email. She'd be hard-pressed to come up with a story to refute the fact that she'd broken into the cabin, which, by the way, had been ridiculously easy. Sydney couldn't believe where Jill had hid the key. What a dunce. She was probably the type to use her birthdate as her computer password. Some people had no street smarts.

Sydney stood and bolted out the door. She didn't have time to fret about Emily. She needed to unpack her car and get the pole set up. She had a lot to accomplish and only a week and a half to do it. When Sydney got downstairs, Emily was standing in the same position as when she'd left her.

"Still here, I see," Sydney said.

"I'm not going anywhere. I emailed Jill."

"Where's your fiancée?"

Sydney walked to the window and peered outside. She spotted a white truck, with someone sitting in the driver's seat, parked across the street. It was the same vehicle she'd seen when she first arrived, at least five hours ago. Who would sit in their car for that long?

"Gretchen? She's not with me."

Sydney turned and faced Emily. "She doesn't care if you shack up with another woman? Especially the one who so-called ruined the most important moment of her life?"

Emily opened her mouth but then snapped it shut, big brown eyes filled with fear. Sydney had her now. This little arrangement would never fly.

"Why don't you just drive into town and rent a nice little bed-and-breakfast?" Sydney asked.

Emily threw her shoulders back and straightened her posture. "First, I'm not leaving when I've already paid for the cabin, and second, there aren't any hotels available. Not with the women's festival going on."

Damn. Sydney hadn't thought about that. Still, though, she needed privacy to prepare for the audition. Emily had to go.

Sydney grinned and rubbed her palms together. "Great. Hope you don't mind sharing a bed."

Emily's eyes jumped to the ceiling. "How many rooms are up there?"

"A bedroom, a bathroom, and an office." Sydney winked and leered at Emily seductively.

"I'm not falling for your scare tactics," Emily said but took a shaky step backward. "I have an errand to run, and when I come back I expect you to be gone." She grabbed her bag and was out the door.

Heat flooded Sydney's cheeks. No one was going to tell her what to do. She'd been pushed around by her mom almost her entire life, and vowed it'd never happen again. Sydney opened the front door and watched Emily drive away in a luxurious navy BMW. Hopefully that errand consisted of finding a place to stay. Considering what she was driving and the gargantuan diamond on her finger, she could afford a hotel. If Sydney couldn't stay in the cabin, she'd have to sleep on a park bench.

Sydney went to her car, popped the trunk, and hoisted out a long box. Thankfully, Monica had loaned her a portable pole so she could get lots of practice in before the audition. She rested the box against the car and glanced over her shoulder. The white truck was still there, and the driver was staring right at her. From what she could tell it wasn't anyone she recognized. This guy was up to no good. She could feel it. After slamming the trunk shut, Sydney strode purposefully toward him. He immediately rolled up the window, started the vehicle, and screeched his tires as he sped away. Sydney stood in the middle of the road and watched the disappearing taillights. Who the hell was that guy, and what did he want?

CHAPTER SIX

Farmer Fran

Emily stopped on the side of the road and googled Bud's Burrito 'n Bait Shop, since she had no idea where she was going. Seemed like an odd combo for a store. Hopefully they didn't actually sell food and minnows in the same place. Once the address was programmed into her GPS, she merged back into traffic and headed down Highway 33 to Meiners Oaks, a suburb of Ojai.

Tingles rippled down Emily's spine. She was about to get the lowdown on the lovebirds. This would be the most amazing thing she'd ever experienced, not to mention the fact that it would save *The Tweet*. The magazine would get national attention after this. Emily smiled to herself, thinking about the conniption fit Owen would have. Everything was falling into place...except for the cabin. Emily hated that she'd argued with Sydney. She never butted heads with anyone—except Owen—but the woman was beyond stubborn. Hopefully after some time and space, she'd be more reasonable and scram. Gretchen would never sanction such a living arrangement, even for a few days.

Emily turned down a narrow gravel road and slowed when rocks pinged her car. Within a few yards, she turned on the headlights, everything suddenly dark from the forest of overhanging trees. This was certainly an out-of-the-way place for a store. Who'd drive this far for burritos and/or bait?

The sound of rushing water prompted Emily to stop. She rolled down her window and searched for the source, delighted to see a small, trickling waterfall. What a beautiful place. She grabbed binoculars out of the glove compartment and scanned the trees, spotting California quail and killdeer. Emily's heart lurched. Perched on a branch was a great horned owl. It had a bulky body, white throat, and distinctive ear tufts. This was a good sign. Owls are thought to bring good luck, and that's exactly how Emily felt about meeting with Fran, which reminded her she'd better get moving. She always prided herself on never being late.

A half mile later the glint from a tin building caught Emily's eye. It was Bud's Burrito 'n Bait Shop. After parking between two muddy, beat-up-looking trucks, she got out of the car and climbed rickety steps, assaulted by a nauseating fishy scent when she creaked open the screen door. The store was packed with fishing poles, scads of colorful lures, a tank filled with minnows, and an aquarium jam-packed with creepy, crawly things.

Emily eyed an elderly man with a white, stubbly beard peering at her suspiciously from behind the counter. She approached and held out her hand.

"Hi. I'm Emily."

The man gave her a limp handshake. "Bud. Pleased to make your acquaintance. What can I do fer you?"

Or at least that's what Emily thought he'd said since his speech was slurred due to a toothpick dangling out of the corner of his mouth.

"I'm supposed to meet someone here named Fran."

"Over there." Bud pointed.

Emily spotted a burly-looking woman wearing tattered, dirt-stained overalls and a lopsided straw hat. Fran looked to be over six feet tall and probably weighed close to three hundred pounds. She had one hand jammed into her pocket while the other stuffed a burrito into her mouth. If it hadn't been for large bosoms, Emily would have sworn Fran was a man. She could care less what the woman looked like, though. All that mattered were the lovebirds.

Emily practically skipped across the store. "Fran? I'm Emily. Oh my goodness. It's so nice to meet you. This is all so amazing. When my assistant got your call, I just couldn't believe it. I was sure he'd gotten it wrong. But no, he said Madagascar lovebirds."

Fran stood motionless, sporting the best poker face Emily had ever seen. She took another bite and chewed in slow motion, never taking her eyes off Emily.

"Listen to me. I'm just going on and on. So where exactly are the lovebirds?" Emily gazed up expectantly at the towering woman.

Fran blinked three times and looked at Emily as though she were an unidentifiable insect. "Want a burrito?"

Food? Who cared about food when rare birds were nearby? Emily let her gaze follow Fran's finger, which pointed to a handwritten menu next to a mounted scaly fish head.

"Uh...no, thanks. I'm good. So, about the birds. How many are there? Did you get photos? When did you first see them?"

Fran shook her head and put her burrito down on the germ-ridden counter next to a worm-filled container. "I'll tell ya 'bout those harebrained birds. They're eating all my figs!"

"That's a real shame," Emily said, trying to sound sympathetic.

"I called so you could tell me how to get rid of 'em."

Emily gasped and placed a hand over her heart. "You don't mean..."

"I ain't talkin' about shootin' 'em. I want 'em off my property!"

"Phew. That's a relief."

"If you can't help me I'll find somebody who can." The skin on Fran's sun-damaged, leathered face turned bright red.

"No! I'm your woman." The last thing Emily needed was Fran spreading the word about the lovebirds.

"Well? What you gonna do about it?" Fran picked up the burrito and took another bite.

"I can come out to your farm right now and—"

Fran shook her head. "Ain't no one invited to my place."

"But...how am I supposed to see the birds?"

Fran tilted her hat back and scratched her stubby, black hair. "We seem to have our wires crossed, missy. You tell me how to git those things off my land, and I do it."

"Riiight, but—"

"No buts about it. Now I'm leaving tomorrow afternoon for Santa Paula. Meet me back here Wednesday at noon with a solution."

"But that's a week away!"

Emily was tempted to grab Fran's arm as she turned but decided physical force wasn't the smartest idea, especially when the woman had several inches and many pounds on her. Fran tipped her hat to Bud and walked out of the store.

Well, damn. What was Emily supposed to do now? She couldn't get to the lovebirds if Fran didn't allow her on the farm, and she certainly didn't want to wait around a week until she got back. Emily shook her head and walked to the counter.

"Problem, little lady?" Bud asked, the toothpick still dangling out of his mouth.

"Big one. How well do you know Fran?"

Bud jutted out his lower lip. "'Bout as well as anyone, I suppose."

"Do you know where her farm is located?"

"Yep."

Emily paused, silently urging him on. Finally, she asked, "Could you tell me?"

"Nope."

Getting information out of Bud was like pouring molasses.

"Because?"

Bud took the toothpick out of his mouth and flicked it in the trash. "Fran isn't what you'd call a people person. She don't allow no one on her land except fer a few workers."

"I'm sure I could google it," Emily said more to herself than to Bud.

He shook his head. "Wouldn't do that if I was you. She'd have you behind bars for trespassing before you could say Bud's Burrito 'n Bait Shop."

Emily threw her head back and blew out a breath. She looked at Bud and attempted a weary smile. "Thanks."

Emily got into her car and looked at her cell phone when it rang. Shoot. It was Gretchen. Emily had forgotten to call her when she'd arrived.

"Hey, Gretchen."

"I thought you were dead!"

Talk about jumping to the worst conclusion possible.

"I'm fine. Sorry I didn't call, but it's been nonstop since I got here."

"Did you meet with that Fran lady?"

"Yeah. It didn't go as expected. She's leaving town for a while, so I can't look for the lovebirds until Wednesday."

"You're not staying there all week, are you? We have a wedding to plan."

"I want to try and contact her again tomorrow before she leaves. I'll be home as soon as I can."

Gretchen sighed into the phone. "So how's the cabin?"

Emily's heart rate increased. Should she tell Gretchen about Sydney? Probably not. No point in upsetting her when Emily was sure Sydney would most likely be gone soon.

"Great. Listen. I'm driving and trying to concentrate on the road." That wasn't a complete lie. It *was* a curvy lane.

"Where are you headed?"

"The grocery store to pick up a few things."

"Okay. Well, call me tomorrow."

"Will do. Have a good night."

Emily disconnected. Was it weird that she and Gretchen rarely said "I love you"? She knew Gretchen wasn't the mushy type, but sometimes it'd be nice to hear. Even a shortened version like "love ya" wouldn't kill her to say. It wasn't like Emily was any better, though. In fact, she'd probably only uttered it twice in the five years they'd dated. It wasn't that she didn't feel it. Emily was sure she loved Gretchen…at least pretty sure. She had no comparison since Gretchen was the only woman she'd ever dated. But what else could it be if it wasn't love?

❖

Emily struggled to open the cabin door while holding two bags of groceries. Once inside, she was surprised to see the living room filled with boxes. She glanced around but didn't see Sydney, so she gently kicked the largest one, which was at least six feet long. Whatever was inside must have been heavy, considering it didn't budge. She put the bags down, squatted, and read the mailing label on one of the items. If that was Sydney's address it certainly wasn't in a good part of town. Emily carefully lifted the top flap and peered inside. What a strange assortment of items: gloves, measuring tape, leveler, and a product called Dry Hands. Emily looked in another box, which was filled with a stack of *Dummies* books. Before she could clearly see the titles, someone slapped her hand.

"Excuse me," Sydney said. "Do you make a habit of going through others' belongings?"

"Sorry." Emily stood upright, grabbed the grocery bags, and bolted to the kitchen, sure her face was bright red. What was she thinking? She wasn't the snooping type. She'd let her curiosity get the better of her.

Sydney burst through the swinging doors like a torpedo, gritting her teeth. "My stuff is off-limits, you hear? Did you...see anything?"

"No," Emily lied.

"Good." Sydney's shoulders visibly relaxed.

Obviously, she didn't want Emily to know what was in those boxes, which made her even more curious. Emily swept her gaze down Sydney's body—her perfectly toned, scantily clad body. A fitted tank top clung to a trim, hard stomach, and shorts displayed muscular, long legs. Come to think of it, were those even shorts? They were high enough up her thigh to be considered underwear. Sydney showed more skin than Emily did when she showered. Maybe a slight exaggeration, but not by much.

"What?" Sydney looked down at her shirt. She'd obviously caught Emily staring.

"Could you put some clothes on, please?"

"What do you call this?" Sydney pointed at her tank top.

"They're unmentionables!"

Sydney snorted. "Unmentionables? Are you sixty?"

Emily busied herself unpacking groceries and tried not to notice the way Sydney's shirt hugged perfectly rounded, uplifted breasts. Inwardly, Emily groaned when she pulled out two cantaloupes. She wouldn't be eating those any time soon.

Sydney sat on a stool and glared at Emily with sparkling blue eyes. "Did you find a place to stay in Ojai?"

"I told you I'm not going anywhere. I'm the one who paid for the cabin, remember?"

Guilt instantly clenched Emily's insides when she appreciatively eyed Sydney's tan, toned arms resting on the counter. Ogling hot, hard-bodied women when she was engaged wasn't allowed. She forced her eyes upward to see Sydney practically drooling over the cantaloupe.

"Are you hungry?" Emily asked.

Sydney's eyes shot upward. "No."

"You can have one." Emily used a celery stalk like a pool cue to roll a melon toward Sydney.

"I said I wasn't hungry." Sydney jumped off the stool.

They both looked at the phone when it rang.

"No!" Emily yelled when Sydney reached for it. "It might be Gretchen. My cell died so I gave her this number."

"You didn't tell your fiancée you're shacking up with me?" Sydney grinned.

"We're not shacking up."

"Let's make a deal. You leave tonight and I'll let you answer it."

"That isn't a deal. It's a bribe, you intruder."

They both lurched for the phone, arms and legs pushing and kicking. Sydney pinned Emily's left wrist down. She was so strong, Emily couldn't budge. When Sydney placed her free hand on the receiver, Emily pinched her thigh hard.

"Ow." Sydney released her hold and rubbed a red spot on her leg.

Emily grabbed the phone. "Hello? Gretchen?"

"Uh, no. This is Monica. I'm looking for Sydney."

"It's for you. Someone named Monica."

Sydney gripped the phone when Emily thrust it at her. "Hey, Monica." Pause. "No one. Just an annoying creature." Sydney shot Emily a dirty look.

Emily opened the freezer and filled it with frozen dinners. Maybe Monica was Sydney's girlfriend. She was probably a wafer-thin runway model. Sydney probably didn't date chubby girls. Emily sucked in her gut and pulled on the waistband of her jeans. Maybe her mom was right. Maybe she did need to go on a diet.

"Addressed to me?" Sydney asked. "What's it say?" Pause. "Well, open it."

After a few seconds, Sydney turned ghostly white, closed her eyes, and rubbed her temple. "Seriously? Jesus Christ. I can't catch a break."

Emily quickly looked down when Sydney caught her staring.

"I gotta go." Pause. "I don't know what I'm gonna do. I'll figure something out. Bye." Sydney stood motionless and stared at a blank wall for several seconds.

"Problem?" Emily asked.

"No." Sydney responded without even looking at her and walked out of the kitchen.

❖

Sydney lifted the biggest box in the living room and dragged it upstairs, glad to have something physical to do to take her mind off her problems. She made several more trips until all the items were in the bedroom before she collapsed on the bed. How could she owe nine hundred dollars to the state? She should have never let Monica open that envelope. This wouldn't have happened if Sydney hadn't been so stubborn. She'd been sure she could do her own income taxes without any help. Boy, had she been wrong. How was she supposed to come up with that kind of money?

Sydney had always prided herself on being independent. She'd been able to get herself out of any jam, but she'd certainly done a bang-up job this time. Unemployed, broke, in debt, and let's face it—she was a squatter. Maybe she should just head back to LA, look for a waitress job, and forget about the PowerBar audition. Who was she kidding anyway? They'd never hire someone who lived on the other side of the tracks.

Sydney sat up and put her hand on her growling stomach. She hadn't eaten anything all day. She should have accepted that cantaloupe, especially since Emily was the one who'd ruined her energy drink.

"Damn pride," Sydney uttered.

"What?"

Sydney jerked her head up to see Emily standing in the doorway.

"Are you eavesdropping?"

"No. Just passing by. Why do you get the bedroom?" Emily eyeballed the surroundings. "Where am I supposed to sleep?"

"How do I know?"

"You don't have to be so snippy," Emily said. "You're not the only one with problems, you know."

"Worried about missing a weekend sale on Rodeo Drive?"

Emily puffed out her chest. "Not that it's any of your business, but I don't shop there. What makes you think you know me?"

"Gargantuan diamond ring, BMW, and you said you own a fashion magazine."

"It's *birds*. As in, you know…" Emily wildly flapped her arms.

Sydney stifled a giggle. Emily looked pretty cute when she got riled up. Feet firmly planted on the ground, big brown eyes glaring, and a sweet-looking face that attempted to pull off ferocious without much success.

"And it's a magazine that's quickly going down the tubes, particularly when a very large, not-so-nice, burrito-eating farmer is standing in my way. So don't you dare think you know me." Emily turned and disappeared down the hall.

Sydney couldn't help but grin. Emily was annoying but awfully cute and had loads of chutzpah. She closed the bedroom door, locked it, and stuffed the books in the closet—in a back corner so Emily wouldn't find them. Next, she opened the long box and ran her hand down a smooth silver rod. If anything could make her feel better, it was pole dancing.

Thirty minutes later, Sydney had erected and secured a portable pole in the middle of the room. After doing a series of stretches, she clicked on some music, grabbed the rod just above her head, and pranced around it several times. She put her back against it, circled her hips, and slid down. As Sydney moved to the music, thoughts filled her mind.

I'm not smart enough. I can't hold down a job. I'll always be broke. I'm such a loser.

Sydney froze mid-turn. How many times had she told a student to pay attention to their thoughts the moment they stepped onto the dance floor? Something about moving one's body always brings up insecurities and fears. Sydney would never forget her first lesson with Monica. Her mind had been filled with nonstop babble the entire time. She'd told herself she couldn't possibly twist around the pole and hold herself up, at least not without landing hard on her ass. And forget about mastering more difficult moves like gracefully climbing. She'd been sure her arms and legs couldn't hold her up.

Somewhere in the middle of the lesson, Sydney had become conscious of the negative self-talk. At first, she tried to ignore it, but when that didn't work, she acknowledged the thoughts, let them go, and focused on the joy of the dance, and surprisingly it *was* joyful. After some practice, Sydney had even conquered a move she never thought possible. She'd never felt so proud and empowered before.

Sydney grabbed the pole with both hands, so hard her knuckles turned white. She refused to let cynical thinking dissuade her from going after her dream. She'd go to that PowerBar audition and blow them away.

Chapter Seven

A Rat in Ojai

Emily hypnotically stared at the bloodred numbers on the digital clock. Three-fucking-fifteen a.m. She flipped her pillow, brutally punched it, and turned onto her side.

"Ow! What the hell is that?"

Something hard had poked her in the ribs. Luckily it hadn't punctured a lung. The pull-out sofa bed in Jill's office sucked. It was like sleeping on a wooden plank topped with a layer of nails. She bolted upright and winced when a sharp something-or-another pinched her ass. Emily hated confrontation more than anything, but enough already. Any sane person would have challenged Sydney hours ago.

She bolted out of the medieval torture device, stomped down the hall, and banged on Sydney's door. What the hell was going on in there? Thunderous thuds and music blared at ear-deafening volumes. Was she doing jumping jacks to Rihanna or whoever the hell was straining her vocal cords? When she had no response, Emily tried to turn the knob, but it didn't budge. Had Sydney locked the door? Did she think Emily would break into the room in the middle of the night and strangle her? Actually, considering everything, that wasn't such a bad idea.

Emily was usually an even-tempered person, except when it came to Owen, but this really burned her up. She'd paid a lot of money for the cabin and was stuck sharing it with an annoying, disrespectful woman who was in *her* bedroom. After knocking until her fists were numb, Emily gave up and went downstairs. Maybe she'd have better luck sleeping on the couch...or not. It was certainly more comfortable, but she couldn't escape the noise.

Emily looked at the clock. Three thirty a.m. She'd wanted to be up by eight to figure out her Fran problem. If she fell asleep right this second, she'd get four and a half hours, and if she nodded off at four a.m. she'd get only four hours. Emily spent the next ten minutes calculating how much sleep she'd get, dependent on when she dozed, each scenario worse than the last. She covered her ears with two throw pillows and grumbled four-letter obscenities normally not in her vocabulary.

❖

Emily's eyelids fluttered open as the sun streamed in through the curtains. The clock slowly came into focus after she rubbed itchy, swollen eyes. She'd slept approximately three point four hours, which was just enough to make her cranky as hell. She swung her legs off the couch and sat upright, head spinning. It would serve Sydney right if Emily banged on her door right now when she was probably asleep. She'd knocked at least three separate times last night, with no response. Anyone with even an ounce of human decency knows that you open a door when someone knocks. Instead, Emily opted for a long, hot shower, but not without making as much noise as possible, hoping she'd disturb Sydney.

After dressing, Emily headed into the kitchen for some breakfast. She rummaged through cabinets, aware that Sydney hadn't bought any groceries. As thin as she was, she probably ate twigs. Emily grabbed a box of strawberry Pop-Tarts, paused, but then ripped open a package. She could diet later. Today she needed a carb boost. While the pastry was in the toaster, she chewed on her lower lip and surveyed what might be a coffeemaker...or part of a NASA rocket. Emily pressed a few buttons and tapped it with her palm, but nothing happened. Even though she desperately needed a java jolt, she lost interest when the Pop-Tart ejected. Sugar trumped caffeine every time.

Perched on a stool at the counter, Emily opened her laptop. She broke off a piece of pastry and shoved it into her mouth, burning her tongue. You'd think she would have learned that lesson as a kid. Obviously, she still didn't have much patience, at least not when it came to Pop-Tarts. Emily clicked on her Google mail, hoping to see an email from Jill, but found nothing. Hopefully, she'd reply soon, and Emily could kick Sydney to the curb. She was sure she'd made up the story about Jill inviting her to stay in the cabin.

Emily groaned when she saw ten emails from her mother, all with subject lines about fitness. For laughs, Emily opened one titled *Lose 10 lbs in One Week!*

> *Hey Sweetie,*
>
> *Boy, do I have the solution for you. It's the Baby Food Diet! Everyone at the fitness center is doing it. You eat jars of baby food and lose a ton of weight. You have a wedding coming up, you know. Check into some Pilates classes in Ojai, too. Remember: you're not going to get the butt you want by sitting on it.*
>
> *Love, Mom*

Emily shifted on the stool. What was wrong with her butt? Okay, so it wasn't as perfect as Sydney's, but she was probably a carbon copy of her mother, all about eating healthy and exercising. As though on cue, Sydney shuffled into the kitchen wearing the scanty outfit from the night before. Christ, she even looked sexy with her hair in disarray and half asleep. All the more reason to hate her.

Sydney went directly to the space-age-looking machine and fiddled with it. Within minutes, the mouthwatering aroma of coffee filled the air. She poured a cup, closed her eyes, and took a sip. Emily watched, impatiently waiting for Sydney to open her eyes. Bitching someone out required their full attention. Sydney took another drink and released a deep, guttural moan, which sounded terribly sensual. Emily let her gaze drift downward to the worse place possible: Sydney's breasts. Could they look any more perfect? They probably weren't even real.

Finally, Sydney opened her bloodshot eyes, and Emily was ready to pounce.

"Do you have any idea how many hours I slept last night because of you?"

Sydney stared for what seemed like an hour. Finally she said, "Don't talk to me until after I've had my coffee." She spoke slowly, with a voice that sounded like she was in the early stages of laryngitis.

"You wouldn't be so tired if you hadn't stayed up all night making so much noise. Just what were you doing in *my* bedroom?"

"Do you hear that sound coming out of your mouth? That's talking."

"You kept me up all night! I slept three point four hours. Did you not even consider that someone else was in the cabin? And why didn't you answer your door?"

Sydney pressed two fingers against her temple. "I can't handle this many words in the morning. Seriously. You're giving me a migraine."

Emily shook her head. Trying to reason with someone like Sydney was impossible.

"You have no regard for anyone else. Just like my mother. I bet you even eat baby food for breakfast." Emily grabbed her mouse and clicked hard on the *x* to close out her email.

"Why do I feel like that isn't a compliment?"

"Have you ever done the baby-food diet?"

Sydney placed her cup on the counter, looking suddenly awake. "I can afford to buy adult food, you know."

"I didn't mean it that way. I meant to lose weight."

"Oh." Sydney rubbed her eyes. "God, no. Who would do that?"

"My mom. She's a fitness freak. Her biggest regret in life was having an overweight daughter."

Ugh. Why did Emily just say that? Especially to someone as sublime as Sydney. Being the size of a Hefty trash bag wasn't one of her finest accomplishments.

Sydney pointed. "You?"

"Yeah...well...I lost it in college."

"How much did you lose?"

"Let's drop it."

"Come on. Tell me."

"You're suddenly chatty for someone who doesn't like words in the morning."

"Please?"

Surprisingly, Sydney actually sounded sincere, and her blue eyes filled with what looked like compassion.

"Fine," Emily said. She lowered her chin and practically whispered. "Fifty pounds."

"Wow. That's amazing. You should be proud of yourself."

Proud? Try ashamed.

"I shouldn't have allowed myself to get that big." Emily stared at her computer, hoping Sydney would drop the subject.

"Maybe you were rebelling."

Emily looked at Sydney. "What do you mean?"

Sydney moved closer and rested her elbows on the counter. "It sounds like your mom was strict with eating and fitness, right? Well, it would only be natural for a kid to want to do the opposite of what they're told."

"I do remember feeling empowered when I'd sneak candy bars behind her back. I felt in control, even though I was doing something that wasn't good for me."

"You were a little rebel."

Emily was surprised when Sydney smiled. She really should do that more often. It made her look even prettier...and a hell of a lot nicer.

Emily grunted. "Hardly. I've always followed the rules, except when it came to starting my magazine."

"The fashion...I mean, bird one?"

"Yeah. It wasn't exactly the plan, according to Gretchen and our parents. So what do you do aside from waitressing? I get the feeling that isn't your passion."

"It's so not. I'm a pole-dancing instructor. Well, I will be soon." Sydney's eyes sparkled and she beamed.

Emily couldn't have possibly heard correctly. "You mean...you're a stripper?"

Sydney looked like Emily had just kicked her in the shin. She hadn't meant it to be mean, but seriously? Sydney was an exotic dancer?

"You're just like everyone else." Sydney crossed her arms over her flimsy cotton shirt. "We're not all strippers, nor do we take our clothes off."

"Sorry, but...pole dancing sounds so...so..."

"So what?" Sydney put her hands on her hips.

"Well...you know. Is that what you were doing last night with all the loud music?"

"If you don't like it you can just move out. In fact, right now would be an excellent time to do just that." Sydney rushed out of the kitchen.

Wow. Talk about snarky. It was a perfectly reasonable question. Sydney had to go and blow it just when they were actually getting along. Emily took another bite of Pop-Tart, which was now cold, and concentrated on her laptop. She had more important things to worry about than Sydney.

After typing Fran's Fig Farm in the Google search bar, Emily found the website. It was filled with tons of fig facts, photos, and harvesting techniques…everything except what she wanted: an address. Fran was certainly private. Why wouldn't she want anyone to find her farm? Was Ojai a hotbed for fig thieves? Well, Emily could outsmart the elusive farmer. She connected to Dun & Bradstreet and within minutes had located Fran's company.

"Aha!" Emily said to herself. "I've got you now." Or not.

It was listed as a private business with a blank address. Damn. Emily stared into space, fingers poised on the keyboard. The information had to be somewhere. She could ask the townspeople, but they'd probably be as helpful as Bud had been. Suddenly, Emily had a lightbulb moment. Gretchen could help. She knew all about this stuff since most of her clients were privately owned businesses. Emily grabbed her phone and sent Gretchen a text. Within minutes, she responded and suggested an online research company. After typing in the web address and paying a small fee, Emily had Fran's address. She smiled and mentally patted herself on the back. Sherlock Holmes had nothing on her. Now all she had to do was get to Fran before she left for Santa Paula.

Sydney slammed on her brakes. Emily had annoyed her so much she hadn't realized she'd been speeding. Normally, she could care less what people thought about her, so why would a bird-watcher affect her? Not that Sydney wanted to admit it, but Emily's opinion of her did matter, which was probably what made her madder than anything.

Sydney answered her cell phone when it rang. If she'd looked at the display first she would have let it go to voice mail. "Hello?"

"Hi. This is Robin. We worked together at Leave It to Beaver."

"Hey. What's up?"

"I was wondering if you'd reconsider coming to work at my fitness studio, PoleCat."

"Well, to be honest I have an audition with PowerBar." Sydney sat up a little straighter in her seat.

"The one in Beverly Hills? Nice. I'm sure you'll get the job, but if not give me a call. I'd still be interested in talking to you about a position."

"Thanks, Robin. I'll do that," Sydney lied.

Considering Sydney was unemployed she probably should have jumped at the opportunity, but she had her sights set on something bigger and better. Robin seemed nice enough, but Sydney had driven by her studio once and wasn't very impressed. It was in a bad part of town in a run-down building that needed repairs and a paint job. She could only imagine what the inside looked like.

When Sydney passed the site of the women's festival, she slowed, hoping to spot the PowerBar tent, which was where the auditions were being held. All she saw, though, was a sea of women—most of who were probably lesbians, not that Sydney cared. She wasn't beyond having an occasional one-night stand, but relationships were off-limits. She couldn't think of one couple who'd ever stayed together more than a few months, including her own mother. So many stepfathers had crossed Sydney's path that she couldn't keep them straight. Nope. That wasn't for her. She didn't want to rely on anyone but herself.

Sydney stopped at a red light and eyed a white truck behind her. It was the same one that had been lurking around the cabin yesterday. Was she being followed? She'd certainly associated with some shady people in the past but didn't think she had a stalker. When the light turned green, Sydney floored it and took a series of sharp turns, the truck staying close behind. She needed to lose this creep...and fast. She slowed at a yellow light and then sped up right before it turned red, forcing the white truck to screech his tires as he stopped.

"Take that," Sydney said to herself.

She pulled into a vegan restaurant and got out of the car, hoping they had some cheap breakfast options. She had walked halfway across the parking lot when the white truck pulled up beside her.

What the hell?

She should probably run inside and call the police, but curiosity got the better of her. When the driver rolled down the window she glared at a man with bloodshot eyes, a pasty complexion, and white fuzz on top of his head.

"Look, chump. I know you've been following me. What gives?" Sydney asked.

"I have a proposition for you." He smiled, displaying yellow, crooked teeth.

"Not interested." Sydney spun around.

"Not even for a thousand dollars?"

Sydney stopped and turned back.

"Thought that might grab your attention." He waved five one-hundred-dollar bills in the air. "Why don't you hop in, and I'll tell you all about it?"

Sydney huffed. "Do you think I'm an idiot? We talk inside."

She strode into the restaurant and found an empty table. Normally, she wouldn't give the time of day to a guy like this, but the money he'd flashed had piqued her interest.

The man entered the restaurant, spotted her, and slid into the booth opposite her.

"What's all this about? And who *are* you?" Sydney asked.

"Shh. Not so loud." The guy glanced around and cracked his knuckles. He leaned over the table, so close Sydney could smell a mixture of Old Spice and sweat. "You're staying at the cabin with Emily, right?"

"Do you even have to ask? You're not very good at undercover work. I saw you staking the place out."

His pale face turned beet red. "Are you a friend of hers?"

"What's it to you?"

"I'm gambling that you're not. I saw you two at the Little Bird Café the other day, and you both seemed less than friendly."

"Look, buster, just spill it. What do you want?" Sydney was losing her patience.

"I want you to snoop on Emily for me."

"Did Gretchen hire you? Trust me. We're not having an affair. We don't even like each other."

"What I want is simple. Find out what bird story Emily is working on. If you tell me what she's doing here, I'll give you five hundred dollars. And if I get the story instead of her, I'll give you another five hundred." The man cracked his knuckles and smiled widely.

Seriously? He'd pay a thousand dollars for a story? About *birds*? They weren't exactly talking about another Watergate here.

"Wait a second. Let's back up. Who are you, and how do you know Emily?"

The man peered over his shoulder, as though to make sure no one was listening. He'd obviously seen one too many spy flicks. He waited a few beats and whispered, "My name is Owe…"

"Owen?"

His left eye twitched erratically, lips set in a hard, thin line. He probably hadn't wanted to reveal his real name. Sydney wasn't working with a smooth operator here.

"It's Oswald."

Sydney snorted. "Right. *Oswald*," she said sarcastically. "Are you a bird-watcher, too? Do you own a magazine like Emily?"

Fear filled Owen's eyes as he stared at the salt shaker, probably trying to come up with a story. He really should have thought this through before soliciting her.

"You're Emily's competition, aren't you?" Sydney asked. "Geez. I didn't realize bird-watching was so cutthroat."

"Listen, girlie. Just concern yourself with why Emily is here."

Girlie? He was probably trying to be threatening, when really he was nothing but a clown in a suit.

"Why do I get the feeling there's more to this than a little healthy competition?"

Owen glared, pulled something out of his ear, and placed it on the table. Eww. It was a hearing aid with earwax caked on it. Sydney lost her appetite.

"See this? That's Emily's fault."

"I'm not following."

"She caused an accident that cost me my hearing in one ear. It's her fault I can't properly hear bird calls." Owen's nostrils flared. "She maimed me! Because of her, my magazine sales have gone downhill. She owes me!"

Ah, so he *did* own a magazine. Sydney held up her hands. "All right. Calm down, Owen."

"Oswald!"

"Whatever."

Owen pulled on his collar as though he were suffocating. After a long pause, he asked, "So, will you do it?"

"All I have to do is tell you what story she's working on?"

"That's it. Easy money."

"Why do you need me? Why not just follow her around yourself?"

"She knows my truck. She'd spot me in a minute, especially in this sea of women. Plus, I need to get back to LA. If you report something worth my time, I'll be here in a flash."

"How do I know I can trust you? What if I give you the information and never see you again? I want the five hundred now."

Owen stuck his hearing aid back in. "How do I know I can trust *you*?"

"You don't. We're both taking a gamble." Sydney paused. "I want a nonrefundable two-fifty now for my trouble, and the rest when I get the information."

Owen squinted, his beady eyes slits. "Nonrefundable?"

"You're asking me to befriend someone who doesn't even like me and play private detective. I deserve something for my time."

Owen sat back and crossed his arms. "All right, but you better come back to me with something."

Owen fished the money out of his pocket and gave it to Sydney. After they exchanged phone numbers, he left when she promised to contact him in a couple of days with an update.

Sydney sat motionless, amazed at her incredible luck. It wasn't enough to pay the income taxes, but at least she could eat. The thousand, though, would solve a lot of her problems. Of course, she'd have to rat Emily out, but it wasn't like they were friends. Besides, Sydney needed the money more than Emily needed a story. It was just freaking birds. It wasn't like it was anything important. The only problem now was how she could make her roomie think her attitude had done a one-eighty without causing suspicion.

CHAPTER EIGHT

Emily's Fake Friend

Emily passed Bud's Burrito 'n Bait Shop on her way to Fran's Fig Farm, determined to strong-arm her way in if need be. Sitting on her butt—her less-than-firm butt, according to her mother—in the cabin for a week until Fran got back wasn't an option. Emily followed the GPS instructions, turning down several dirt roads before coming to a halt at a closed gate with an incredibly large padlock attached. A looming sign overhead read Trespassers Will Be Prosecuted, and the barbed-wire fence was lined with yellow caution tape, making it look like a crime scene. Emily got out of the car and waved away the dust that had yet to settle. She peered over the gate at an empty field split in half by a long, straight gravel path. This called for her high-powered Avalon 20x50 binoculars. With those suckers she could see three miles away.

Emily grabbed the field glasses out of her trunk and rested her elbows on the hood of the car, not wanting to take the time to set up the tripod. Immediately, she spotted a small white house in front of what looked like several acres of trees. She scanned to the right and froze. She'd recognize that overall-clad physique anywhere. Fran was standing next to a pile of tree branches stuffing them into a wood chipper. Hopefully there weren't any lovebirds on the twigs. Emily shuddered. Fran didn't seem to be a fan of the feathered friends, and Emily wouldn't put it past her.

She lowered the binoculars and considered her options, which were dismal. Ramming her car through the gate wasn't a possibility, nor was attempting to squeeze through the barbed-wire fence. Knowing Fran, it was probably electrically charged. And even if Emily could get through the gate somehow, she'd have to walk at least a mile to reach the house. Her only option was to sit on her horn in hopes that Fran would hear and come to see what all the ruckus was about.

Emily looked through the binoculars again, a chill running down her spine at the sight of Fran still cramming branches into the wood chipper. Maybe she'd seen *Fargo* one too many times, but she had a sudden urge to bolt. She slumped and glanced upward at the no-trespassing sign. Yes, she should scram. Breaking the law wasn't an option. Emily got into her car and sped away, hoping Fran hadn't seen her spying.

On a whim, Emily pulled into Bud's Burrito 'n Bait Shop. Since her farm visit had been a bust, maybe she could at least get a little more insight from Bud. A wave of nausea washed over her as the scent of burritos mingled with minnows assaulted her nostrils. She resisted pinching her nose when she spotted Bud. Had he even changed clothes or moved a muscle from yesterday? He looked like an exact replica, toothpick hanging out of his mouth and everything.

Emily approached the counter and flashed the best smile she could muster. She'd learned long ago that a little kindness goes a long way. Too bad she couldn't remember that when it came to Sydney.

"Howdy do, little lady." Bud tipped his faded, weather-worn cowboy hat. "What brings you back so soon?"

"I was wondering if maybe you could tell me a little more about Fran."

Bud scratched his scraggly chin. "Why you so interested in her?"

"I'm…I'm a…a fig investor." *What the hell is a fig investor?* "I'd like to learn more about her…um…farming techniques."

Bud peered at Emily hard. "A fig investor, you say?"

"Yeah. I'd like to…well…invest in the farm. You know, to make money for both of us. But I can't likely do that unless she lets me onto her property."

Emily lied about as well as the Pope. Luckily, Bud actually seemed to buy it.

"Well, what is it you're wantin' to know?" he asked.

"Does Fran have any family?"

"Nope."

"Friends?"

"Nope."

"Favorite activity?"

"Nope."

Emily took a deep breath. "Work with me here, Bud. Isn't there anything you can tell me about Fran that would help?"

Bud took the toothpick out of his mouth and flicked it a few times between his two front teeth. "Well, there is one thing Fran loves. More than figs. More than her farm. More than anything."

"What's that?" Emily asked, brightly. Finally she was getting somewhere.

"Conway Twitty."

Who?

As though reading the question in Emily's eyes, Bud said, "He's a country 'n' western singer. Fran is the president of his North American fan club."

He has a fan club?

"She has every album he's ever made. Her dream was to go to Twitty City in Tennessee, but they stopped giving tours."

"Huh. Well, that's unexpected. I thought you were going to say her favorite thing was a pet or truck or something. So, this Conway Twitty guy...is he still alive?"

"Nope. He died in the '90s. Fran could tell you the day, year, and probably the time."

Well, that wasn't much help. How could a dead country-western singer help her reach Fran?

❖

Sydney turned a corner in the Nature's Bounty grocery store and spotted Emily standing in the aisle holding a can. Maybe it was the lighting or the quirky, confused expression on her face, but she looked awfully cute. Not in an overtly sexy, put-it-all-out-there way like the women Sydney had worked with at the club, but a unique kind of pretty. If they had met under different circumstances, Sydney probably would have hit on her, not that Emily would have given Sydney a second look. They were in totally different social classes.

Sydney approached and lightly tapped Emily's hip with the shopping cart.

"Oh. You." Emily's face fell.

The chilly reception wasn't surprising. Sydney had a lot of backpedaling to do to get on her good side.

"Stew in a can?" Sydney scrunched her face.

"I'm in dire need of some comfort food." Emily put the item back on the shelf and scanned the selections.

"Rough day?"

"You could say that. And rough night." Emily peered at Sydney sideways.

"Oh. Right. I...uh...I owe you an apology."

Emily's head jerked toward Sydney, a what-the-hell expression on her face.

"I'm sorry about the loud music and not responding when you knocked." Surprisingly, she'd actually meant that. It had been rude and Sydney *was* the squatter, whereas Emily had paid for the cabin—not that she'd ever admit that.

"Hmm." Emily cocked her head and seemed to weigh the sincerity of the apology. "So what are we supposed to do about this rooming situation?"

"Considering there aren't any other places available, maybe we should make the best of it."

Emily snorted. "You certainly changed your tune."

Too much too soon? Sydney better scale it back a bit so as not to raise suspicion.

"It's not what I'd want," Sydney said adamantly. "But we don't seem to have any other choice."

"At least not until Jill responds to my email and I find out you're lying." Emily sulked and studied the label on a can. "Would you look at this? Fat-free, organic, vegetarian stew? Where's the real food?"

"You *are* in a health-food store, you know. I thought you already went grocery shopping."

"I did, but I was craving something else."

"Not this." Sydney grabbed the can and placed it back on the shelf. "If you'll buy the ingredients I'll make you my world-famous stew."

"You don't look like the type that would have a stew recipe," Emily said. "And you're seriously going to cook for me? Why are you being so nice?"

Sydney spotted a boy about ten years old wearing soiled clothes two sizes too big. He glanced around nervously, fear etched across his face. It was a look Sydney knew all too well. He was alone, desperate, and had just done something he shouldn't have, considering the extra-lumpy jacket he was wearing.

Emily snapped her fingers in front of Sydney's face. "Hello? You're totally ignoring me. I knew this nice thing couldn't last."

"Shh...would you be quiet for a second?"

"What?" Emily glanced around, letting her gaze land on the boy. "You know him?"

"Yes and no."

Sydney walked toward the kid, with Emily following. When he spotted them, he turned and started to run, but Sydney grabbed his arm.

"I'm not going to hurt you," she said.

The kid tried to wiggle out of her grasp with no success.

"What the hell are you doing?" Emily asked.

Sydney ignored the question. People like Emily wouldn't understand. She'd probably been raised in a life of luxury, never having to worry about when or where the next meal appeared. Her parents had undoubtedly tucked her into bed each night and kissed her forehead. She'd probably been loved.

"This isn't the way," Sydney said. "Trust me. Now why don't you hand over the items?"

The boy gazed up at her with a panic-stricken expression. When she let go of his arm, he unzipped his jacket and pulled out two cans of beans. Sydney snatched them and put them back on the shelf. She took out a fifty-dollar bill, thanks to Owen, and held it up.

"This is yours, if you promise me something."

The boy never took his eyes off the money and was practically drooling.

"Don't ever steal again. Hey, look at me."

The kid's eyes shot upward.

"Do you want to go to jail?"

He shook his head.

"Good, because it's not a nice place. You think you're hungry now? All you'll get is stale bread and dirty water. You'd be better off eating the cockroaches and rats running around in the cell."

Both Emily and the kid gasped.

"Do I have your promise?"

"Yes ma'am," the boy whispered.

"Go buy yourself something healthy to eat, and if I ever catch you stealing again I'll call the cops."

He took the money and ran.

"Wow," Emily said. "You just gave him fifty dollars. That was so nice."

Sydney shrugged. "He needed it more than me."

"Do you think he'll steal again?"

"I dunno. I hope not."

"What did you mean when you said that you knew him but didn't know him?"

That was something Sydney had no desire to explain. She rushed down the aisle and yelled over her shoulder, "If you want stew for dinner, we need to get moving."

Emily sat on a stool in the kitchen and watched Sydney expertly slice carrots. "You sure I can't help?"

"Positive," Sydney said without looking up.

"Good, because I'd probably cut my fingers off. I'm not much of a cook."

"No?" Sydney glanced at Emily. "Oh. You probably have a maid who takes care of that."

"I think you're under the erroneous impression that I'm rich."

Sydney scooped up the carrots and put them in a pot on the stove. "You like garlic?"

"Love it."

Sydney grabbed a couple of cloves and began dicing. "Where'd you grow up?"

Emily paused, knowing the reaction that'd elicit. "Beverly Hills, but—"

"Ha! I knew it. You said your mom is a Pilates instructor. What does your dad do?"

"He's a brain surgeon."

"Ha, again."

"No ha," Emily said, irritated. "I've been supporting myself since college. My parents don't give me a cent."

"Wait a second." Sydney put the knife down and faced Emily. "Isn't your last name Wellington? As in…Wellington Hospital?"

Emily shifted in her seat. "Well. Yes."

"Oh my God. An entire medical center is named after you."

"Not me. My father. You act like having wealth is a sin. I do believe you were the one who just gave fifty dollars to a stranger. You must be doing okay."

"Things have just recently picked up in that area." Sydney resumed slicing and dicing.

"What do your parents do?" Emily asked.

Sydney turned her back and scrubbed potatoes in the sink. Emily had a feeling that was more about ignoring the question than having spick-n-span veggies. Avoidance seemed to be her specialty. After several long moments, Sydney turned around and began peeling the potatoes.

"My mom has had a variety of jobs. And I never met my dad." Sydney spoke in a monotone voice without taking her eyes off the spud.

"I'm sorry. Did he pass away when you were a baby?"

"No. Maybe. I dunno. My mom doesn't even know who he is. I mean, my dad could be one of many men. She was popular." Sydney shot Emily a quick glance.

"Ah. So it was just you and your mom?"

"And about fifty stepfathers. Slight exaggeration, but not by much." Sydney threw diced potatoes into the pot and faced Emily. "I'm going to take a shower. The stew should be ready in a couple of hours."

Emily had a feeling there was a lot more to Sydney's life story, and it probably wasn't a pretty one.

A few hours later, they were sitting at the dining table with two big bowls of stew, garlic bread, and a bottle of white wine. Emily was amazed at how scrumptious everything tasted but even more astonished that she was actually having fun.

"Mmm. This is sooo good. Where'd you learn how to cook? Did your mom teach you?" Emily regretted the words the moment they were out of her mouth. She had a feeling the woman hadn't been much of a role model.

"No. YouTube videos." Sydney shoved a spoonful into her mouth.

Emily had never seen anyone eat so fast before. It was as though she hadn't had a bite all week. Emily was half expecting her to lick the bowl when she finished.

"Seriously?"

Sydney swallowed and took a sip of wine. "Yeah. I swear you can find anything on YouTube."

Emily snuck glances at Sydney as she ate. Golden locks framed a stunning, makeup-free face. She didn't even need a stitch of blush or eyeshadow to look amazing. *Damn her*. Emily ran fingers through short, chestnut hair. Maybe she should let it grow out a little. Perhaps some highlights, too. She looked down at her stomach. And shed a few pounds. Okay, a lot of pounds. But then again, what would be the point? She'd never be a blond-haired, blue-eyed beauty.

"Is something wrong?" Sydney asked. "You're not eating."

"Just taking a breather. It's really amazing."

"Thanks," Sydney said and wiped her mouth with a napkin. "So, what brings you to Ojai?"

Emily thrust a potato into her mouth, hoping to buy some time. She chewed slowly and took several gulps of wine. Finally, she said, "Vacation."

"Without your fiancée?"

Emily took another drink. "She couldn't take off."

"How long are you staying?"

"I'm not sure. You?"

"A couple of weeks. I have an audition."

"Really? For what?"

"Pole-dancing instructor, which is *not* a stripper."

Emily cringed. "Sorry about that. I didn't mean to be insulting before. It's just that I've never known anyone who did *that*. Who's the audition with?"

"PowerBar. It's a fitness center in Beverly Hills." Sydney smiled, a full-on, heart-stopping smile that made her face light up. "Maybe you've heard of it?"

Emily shook her head.

"Not surprising. It's behind bushes and gates, hidden from the public. That's one of the things I want to change. Pole dancing isn't anything to be ashamed of."

Sydney spoke animatedly and with feeling, sounding very

different than when she was talking about her mom. Obviously this was a subject she was passionate about. Emily could relate. It was how she felt about her magazine.

"Tell me what you love about it," Emily said, surprised she actually wanted to know.

"So many things. It's about getting out of your comfort zone and accomplishing something you never thought possible. It's a huge self-esteem booster." Sydney stared into space and said, "It's like...having an orgasm."

Emily spewed wine across the table, which resulted in a mini-coughing fit. Sydney jumped up and patted her on the back.

"Are you okay?" Sydney asked through a chuckle.

Emily cleared her throat and downed an entire glass of water. She took a deep breath, reveling in the aroma of coconut—her favorite scent. It must have been coming from Sydney, maybe her shampoo or soap. After regaining her composure, Emily was very much aware that Sydney's hand was on her arm—her warm, sturdy hand that sent tingles through Emily and settled in the pit of her stomach. Emily wiggled free and motioned for Sydney to sit back down. At the other end of the table. Far away.

"Sorry about that," Emily said, hoarse. "Now what were you saying about...um..."

"Orgasms."

Emily gulped. "Right. That."

"In pole dancing, you have to relax and let go. When you're doing a move that you've never done before, it can be scary. If you try to stop yourself or hold back, you'll fall. You have to give up control, let go of the reins, and just go for it. It's the ultimate release."

Maybe that's why Emily couldn't have orgasms with Gretchen. She was a control freak. Letting go wasn't easy, though. It made her feel vulnerable, exposed, and who wanted that?

"Interesting," Emily said, desperately wanting to change the subject.

"Maybe you should try it some time."

Emily's eyebrows shot upward and she gulped. "Orgasms? Oh, I've had plenty of those. Like hundreds...no, I'd say thousands. Like almost every day. Yes. I'd say daily...at least...yes."

Sydney grinned and scratched her head. "Actually, I was talking about pole dancing."

"Oh." *Crap.* "Oh, no. I could never do that." Emily vigorously shook her head.

"Why not?"

How in the world could Emily explain it without actually having to be honest? Pole dancers were seductive, sensual, and physically fit— like Sydney. Emily would never describe herself as sexy, and no way in hell would she ever wear those skimpy outfits. Nope. She'd never be comfortable doing something like that in a gazillion years, something Sydney would never understand.

"It's just not really my thing," Emily said and pushed her chair back. "I'll do the dishes since you cooked, and then I'm hitting the sack. Can I trust you to be quieter tonight?"

"Yes. I promise. How's the sofa bed in Jill's office?"

"Great if you like sleeping on a bed of very sharp nails." Emily gathered the dishes and carried them into the kitchen.

Sydney pushed through the swinging doors. "Maybe we could share the bedroom. You know. Take turns."

Emily was so shocked she almost dropped the bowls. She put everything in the sink and faced Sydney. "What in the world got into you since this morning?"

Sydney's gaze dropped to the hardwood floor. "Just trying to be fair."

"Well, you won't hear any arguments from me. I'll gladly take the bed tonight."

"I'll just grab some stuff out of my…our…room and get out of your way."

Talk about a switch. Whatever the reason, Emily was just happy they weren't arguing and that she'd get a good night's sleep. She did feel a little guilty about not coming clean to Gretchen, but she needed a place to stay until she got the lovebird story. Personally, Emily didn't see anything wrong with having a roommate, even if she was a hot pole dancer. It wasn't like they were going to have an affair.

CHAPTER NINE

Pop-Tart Talk

Had Emily died and gone to heaven? If angels hand-made mattresses, it would surely be this one. She rolled over, pulled the sheet under her chin, and snuggled into the warmth of the most comfortable bed ever. Burying her face into the pillow, she took a big whiff, coconut filling her senses. Maybe she hadn't died at all but instead was lying on a deserted tropical island with a piña colada in one hand and Hawaiian Tropic suntan oil in the other. Coconuts. Emily loved the smell of coconuts. Where had she detected that aroma before?

Suddenly, she bolted upright. Sydney! Nervously, Emily glanced around, half expecting to see Sydney lying beside her...naked. She wasn't sure why she'd pictured Sydney nude, but there it was. After realizing she was alone, Emily fell backward and shook her head as though to knock sexy Sydney images out of her brain. Gretchen was the one she should be thinking about, not her housemate. Gretchen was also...well, no...she wasn't actually sexy. She was stable, secure, trustworthy, which was exactly what Emily wanted in a girlfriend. Physical attraction went just so far.

Strange grunting noises coming through the vent caused Emily to sit upright again. Was a wild pig downstairs? She got out of bed and tiptoed down the stairs, the sound growing louder with each step. Emily stopped midway and peered over the railing, surprised to see Sydney sitting on the couch ranting and raving.

"Argh! I'll never get this! Grrr."

"Hey, are you okay?" Emily asked, bounding down the remaining steps.

Sydney appeared startled and stuffed whatever she was looking at under an afghan. Something was definitely up, something Sydney didn't want Emily to know about.

"What's under there?" Emily pointed.

"Nothing," Sydney said, looking nervous and terribly uncomfortable.

Emily walked around the couch and sat on the armrest. "Then why don't you show me?"

"You're awfully nosy."

"Just curious. It's obviously something you're not happy about."

Sydney's lips turned upward into a wide grin, which wasn't the reaction Emily was expecting.

"What...uh...what are you wearing?" Sydney asked with a sparkle in her eyes.

Emily looked down at her PJs and let her shoulders slump. *Crap.*

"Are those little birds?" Sydney looked like she was about to burst out laughing.

"They're lovebirds, thank you very much." Emily jutted her chin out. "We don't all sleep in provocative lingerie, you know."

"Are you insinuating that this is provocative?" Sydney motioned to her outfit.

"The way you wear it, it is."

Emily regretted the admission, but for Pete's sake, could Sydney look any sexier in the baby-blue tank top that made her gorgeous eyes pop even more than usual and the leg-revealing blue and white polka-dot shorts?

"I seriously don't mean to laugh," Sydney said, still smiling. "You look adorable. Really."

Emily sneered, flung a pillow at Sydney, and marched into the kitchen. The navy PJs, which were covered with pink lovebirds, were intended to inspire Emily. They symbolized her goal. When she'd packed for the trip, she hadn't expected to model the outfit in front of a pole dancer.

One of the swinging doors creaked open, Sydney halfway into the kitchen. "You gonna throw anything else at me?"

"Probably." Emily opened several cabinets, looking for those damn Pop-Tarts. She needed something sweet.

Sydney walked into the kitchen and rested a hip against the counter.

"Ahh. Here they are." Emily held up the box and smiled. "You probably don't eat these, do you?"

"You toast. I'll pour the OJ."

They sat on stools opposite each other at the counter and chowed down. It was actually nice eating breakfast with someone. Even when Gretchen stayed the night, they'd go their separate ways early the next morning.

After a few minutes, Sydney asked, "Are lovebirds your favorite?"

"No one has ever asked me that before," Emily said, wondering why Gretchen or her parents had never inquired. But then again, they hadn't been supportive of that particular interest. "Yes. As a matter of fact they are."

"Why?" Sydney took another bite of a strawberry Pop-Tart.

Emily smiled, recalling the first time she'd laid eyes on her beloved pets. "When I was twelve my dad came home with two rosy-faced lovebirds. My mom had a fit, but he did it to cheer me up. And—"

"Why'd you need cheering up?"

Emily's pulse quickened. She didn't like thinking about that time, much less talking about it. "Remember when I said I was overweight? Well, let's just say kids can be cruel." Not to mention mothers.

"You mean you were teased?"

"Uh-huh. A lot." Emily met Sydney's eyes, which were filled with an unexpected compassion. She didn't think someone so fit would understand body-shaming. "Anyway, I had Bogie and Bacall...that were their names...for ten years. They were my best friends. I guess that's when my affection for birds began."

Sydney stretched, opened the fridge, and grabbed the orange juice. She poured some into Emily's cup and put the carton on the counter. That was nice. Emily hadn't even noticed her glass was empty.

"Why lovebirds and not an eagle or something more majestic?"

"They're amazing," Emily said with a wide grin. "They're one of the few animals on earth who mate for life. They have high levels of oxytocin, the love hormone, and spend their days preening and snuggling with each other. When they're separated from their partner, they have erratic behavior and become sullen. And many die within days from what's known as the heartbreak syndrome. That's what happened to Bogie. He was completely healthy but then died two days after Bacall did."

Sydney eyed Emily, clearly skeptical.

"And if they're separated and then reunited they feed each other to reinforce their bond. How sweet is that? They have deep, loving relationships just like humans."

Sydney snorted and rolled her eyes.

"What's that supposed to mean?"

"Mating for life. What a fairy tale."

"You don't believe in happily-ever-after, I take it?"

"God, no. I've never known anyone whose relationship lasted more than a few months."

"You included?"

"I've had plenty of girlfriends, some who were a lot of fun, but long-term doesn't happen in real life."

"I'm going to have to shatter your theory, Miss Grumpy Pants."

Sydney chuckled and mumbled to herself, "Grumpy Pants?"

"Gretchen and I have been together for five years. In fact, she's the only woman I've ever dated."

Sydney raised an eyebrow. "You two spend your days snuggling, and when you're separated you become depressed? You're not together now, and you don't seem very *sullen*."

"For your information, we..." Actually, she and Gretchen weren't the snuggling type, and Emily hadn't really missed her all that much. In fact, it'd been kind of nice to have time to herself.

"...we have an adult relationship," Emily said. "We don't spend every moment together, and we respect each other's space."

Sydney grunted. "Doesn't sound like you have much of that oxytocin hormone flowing."

Anger burned in the center of Emily's chest. "Are you insinuating we're not in love? We're getting married, for Christ's sake. Our relationship is stable, reliable, and secure." Emily nodded once and crossed her arms.

"Sounds like you're describing your accountant, not the love of your life."

Actually, Gretchen did do Emily's taxes, but she certainly wasn't going to mention that now. "How dare you—"

"Okay...okay. I'm sorry. You're right." Sydney waved her hands.

Still steaming, Emily wasn't quite ready to accept an apology. "Just because you've never dated anyone longer than a few months doesn't mean—"

"I said I was sorry. Really."

Emily opened her mouth but then snapped it shut when her laptop rang with an incoming video call. "This is Gretchen. *Please* don't make a sound."

Sydney grinned. "You still haven't told her that we're shacking up?"

"Just...shush." Emily shot Sydney a dirty look, which made her smile grow even bigger.

To get Sydney out of the camera's line of sight, Emily pulled the laptop directly in front of her. After she accepted the call, Gretchen and Emily's mother appeared on the screen. Gretchen's hair was in disarray, her normally pale complexion scarlet, and she appeared to be frazzled, which was very unlike her. Emily's mother, on the other hand, looked the same, wearing a three-hundred-dollar designer yoga outfit, a blinged-out headband, and freshly applied makeup with an overabundance of cherry-red lipstick. Emily had never seen her mother without makeup, which begged the question of whether she went to bed every night all dolled up. Emily would bet her pricy Audubon bird cam that she did.

"Hey, you two. Gretch, are you okay?"

Gretchen peered at Emily's mother out of the corner of her eye and flashed a strange expression. Enough said. The workout queen was giving her a hard time, probably about the wedding plans. Here Emily was, having a leisurely breakfast with Sydney, leaving Gretchen to deal with her mother. She should be ashamed.

"Hello, darling." Emily's mother elbowed Gretchen out of the way, her clown face filling the screen.

"Emily, is that a Pop-Tart?" Horror filled her mother's eyes.

Emily pushed the plate out of view and ignored the question. "Mom, you can back up. You don't need to be two centimeters away from the camera."

Anger flashed across her mother's face right before she made some grunting noises and sat back, both women coming into view again.

"We're having a bit of a disagreement," Emily's mother said. "I think we should order a minimum of two hundred invitations but—"

"Good Lord! We don't know that many people," Emily said.

"Think about it, Emily Gail." Her mom meant business. She'd used her middle name. "We could fill that many seats with just hospital personnel, not to mention your guests."

Shouldn't they all *be our guests?*

"We don't know anyone from the hospital, Mom. Our dads work there, not us."

Her mom looked as though someone had thrown ice water in her face, instantly freezing it in place.

"Your father's colleagues have known you two since you were kids." Emily's mom looked at Gretchen, then back at the screen. "You two were both born in that hospital."

A sarcastic "so what" was on the tip of Emily's tongue. Instead, she asked, "Gretchen, what do you think?"

"I had thought we'd have a small ceremony," Gretchen said, cautiously.

Emily's mother threw her hands up in the air. "I can't believe you two. We're paying for everything. Most couples would die to have a lavish wedding."

Lavish? There was no telling what else they were planning.

Her mother huffed and puffed for a full minute. "We can't settle this, or anything else, over this video thingie. When are you coming home? Haven't you found those—"

"I'll be back as soon as I can." Emily peered at Sydney over her laptop.

"You really do need to be here," Gretchen said adamantly. "Did that Farmer Fran woman let you onto her property yet?"

"I'm working on it. Listen, I need to go, but I'll talk to you both later."

Emily disconnected, closed her laptop, and attempted to avoid Sydney's glare.

"Who's Farmer Fran? I thought you said you were on vacation."

"I am." Emily took her glass to the sink and rinsed it out.

Sydney swung around on the stool. "Seems like an odd time to take off when you should be planning a wedding."

Emily blew out a puff of air and leaned against the counter. "All right. You win. I'm here for a...a fig story." Okay, so that was a lie, but she had to say something to appease Sydney.

"Did you say fig? I thought you were a bird-watcher."

"My magazine specializes in all sorts of nature-related material, including agriculture. We report on more than just birds." Hey, she wasn't so bad at this fibbing thing after all.

"Okaaay. So you're doing a story on someone named Fran?"

"Her figs. If I can get onto the property, that is. She's a bit difficult. You should see the place. There are no-trespassing signs everywhere."

"You've tried reasoning with her?" Sydney asked, surprisingly interested.

Emily nodded. "At Bud's Burrito 'n Bait Shop." When Sydney made an "eww" face, Emily said, "Don't ask."

"So break in."

"What? I can't do that." Could she? No, of course not. It was illegal.

"Why not?"

Sydney nonchalantly propped her elbows back on the counter. Emily couldn't believe how casual she was being about this whole situation.

"One word. Prison. I have no desire to dine on cockroaches and rats."

"Huh?" Sydney paused and then chuckled. "Oh. I was just making that stuff up to scare the kid. I've never been in jail. I don't know what they eat."

"Regardless, I'm not trespassing on anyone's property. Besides, I don't even know if there is a…a fig story, and I can't find out until I get access to the farm."

Sydney hopped off the stool. "Look. All you have to do is sneak in and check out her figs or whatever. I'll help you."

"Why would you do that?"

Sydney shrugged. "It's exciting, adventurous. This gets my heart pumping." She rubbed her palms together briskly.

"It makes me wanna barf." Emily breezed past Sydney, went into the living room, and sat on the couch.

Sydney followed and perched on the coffee table in front of Emily. "Don't you want to find out if there's a story? If so, you can work on Fran, but if not then you can go home and not have to deal with me anymore." Sydney smiled.

"You're just trying to get rid of me."

"Hey, it's your call. I'm just offering my assistance. And breaking-and-entering expertise."

"You sure you've never been in prison?"

"Come on. It'll be fun." Sydney lightly slapped Emily's knee.

Emily picked a thread on the afghan, deep in thought. She'd give just about anything to find the Madagascar lovebirds. She didn't like the idea of Sydney being there, but she didn't know a bird from a squirrel. She was just in it for the rush.

"Fran did say she was going out of town for a few days," Emily said, thinking aloud.

"That's perfect!" Sydney swooshed out her arms.

Emily looked directly at Sydney. "Are you *sure* we won't get caught?"

"Positive."

A hard knot formed in the pit of Emily's stomach. "When should we do this?"

"Tonight. At nineteen hundred hours we'll execute Operation Fig Find."

❖

Sydney trekked through the woods, far enough away from the cabin that she was out of earshot. She sat on a log and called Owen.

He immediately picked up. "It's about time you called."

"Hello to you, too," Sydney said sarcastically.

"What'd you find out?"

"Are you sure this is about a bird story and not a fig one?"

"What the hell are you talking about?"

"Emily said she's here about figs and that her magazine covers agriculture."

Owen grunted. "She's lying. Find out the real story or else no reward. Got that?"

Sydney's skin crawled. She didn't like this guy one bit. "I know the deal," Sydney said, not even trying to hide her irritation. "She's desperate to gain access to someplace called Fran's Fig Farm so—"

"That's where the story is, then."

"Yeah. I picked up on that. And—"

"So go to the farm and find out what's going on."

"If you would let me freakin' finish a sentence, I was going to say that we're going there tonight."

"Good. Report back ASAP," Owen said and hung up.

It irked Sydney that she was helping Owen and not Emily. She liked the cute bird-watcher. Sure, Emily had been testy when they'd first met, but she seemed like a genuinely nice person, and Sydney didn't encounter many of those types. If she didn't need the money so badly she'd tell this buffoon to get lost. But she did need it, desperately. And it was just a bird, or maybe fig, story. It wasn't like it was anything earth-shattering.

CHAPTER TEN

Bonnie and Clyde

"I'm not so sure about this," Emily said as she eyed the Trespassers Will Be Prosecuted sign.

Sydney forcefully shook the steel gate at the entrance of Fran's farm. Did she seriously think the humongous padlock wouldn't hold? Besides, Emily had already tried that yesterday.

"You don't understand," Emily said. "I'm a bird-watcher. The most dangerous thing I've ever done was tip my neck back too far looking through binoculars. I don't come from adventurous people. Breaking and entering isn't in my DNA."

If Gretchen and her parents could see her now they'd probably cancel the wedding and commit Emily to the nearest psychiatric ward.

"We shouldn't do this. I don't have a criminal mind." Emily looked at Sydney. "Are you listening to me?"

"I don't see any cameras," Sydney said, scanning the area. "Fran is threatening, but in a crude way."

Where's a paper bag when you need one? Emily was about to hyperventilate. She leaned her backside against the car and dropped her head between her legs, taking deep breaths in an attempt to slow a rapid heart rate. When she stood upright, Sydney was nowhere in sight.

"Sydney?" No answer. "Sydney? Where the hell are you?"

"Shh. Not so loud. I'm down here."

Emily heard a voice but couldn't see anything in the near darkness, especially since Sydney had insisted they dress in all black. It was a little unnerving how savvy she was when it came to planning the perfect crime.

"Where?" Emily whispered.

"To your left. Down the fence."

Emily squinted and tiptoed through the tall grass until she bumped into a dark form. "Don't disappear like that. You scared the crap outta me."

"Look." Sydney pointed to a hole in the barbed-wire fence. "We can fit through here if we lift this up."

Emily grabbed Sydney's arm when she reached out. "Don't touch that. What if it's electric?"

"Good thinking. Maybe you have a criminal mind after all." Sydney grinned.

"So you *were* listening. Like I was saying, we should just go. It's too dark to see anything anyway."

Sydney pulled a flashlight out of her bag and clicked it on. Unfortunately, she had an answer for everything. Still, though, Emily would never be able to spot the lovebirds in this lighting.

"What are you doing?" Emily asked when Sydney put her ear up to the fence.

"Listening for a current. I don't hear anything." Sydney shined the light on the ground, picked up a stick, and tossed it at the fence. "Nothing. It should be fine."

Should be? Emily needed more reassurance than that.

"Throw your backpack over the fence, and when I lift it up, climb through," Sydney said. "And be careful. The barbs are razor sharp."

Emily did as instructed and watched Sydney grab the wire. Did she seriously think Emily's ass would fit through that small opening? Emily sucked in her stomach, placed one foot through the hole, and ducked. Panic gripped her insides when she couldn't go any farther. It was as though someone had grabbed the back of her collar and was holding her in place. She was stuck straddling the fence, bent over in an awkward, uncomfortable position.

"I can't move," Emily said, fearfully.

"Hold on. Your shirt is caught."

"Oh my God. I'm about to fall over. My legs are shaking." Sydney yanked the material, but she was still frozen in place.

"I can't stand up anymore." Emily's legs trembled and her back ached. She visualized herself tumbling down, sharp points penetrating her skin.

Sydney wrapped one arm around Emily's waist. Wonder Woman

had nothing on Sydney. It was amazing she could hold up the wire with one hand and Emily with the other. If that wasn't enough, she also had the strength to bend down.

"Emily, look at me."

Slowly, Emily peeled her eyes open, not realizing they had been squeezed shut. Two sparkling sapphire crystals stared back at her. She'd never looked into Sydney's eyes from this close before. They were mesmerizing, hypnotic even.

"I won't let anything happen to you. I promise." Sydney's voice was confident, soothing.

Those eyes.

That voice.

Sydney would fix everything. Within seconds, she unhooked the snag and supported Emily until she was safely on the other side.

"Are you okay?" Sydney asked.

"Yeah," Emily said, feeling foolish for freaking out. "Sorry for being such a wimp."

"There's nothing to be sorry about. You're doing something you've never tried before. That takes bravery."

"Me? Brave?" Emily slowly smiled. "It is kinda exciting."

Maybe it was the adrenaline rush or the fact that she was safely on the other side of the fence unharmed, but Emily had never felt so alive before. It was as though every nerve ending in her body had been jolted awake. Who knew danger could be so much fun?

"Now you're talking like a daredevil," Sydney said. "Help me get through so we can find those figs."

Once they were both over the fence, Sydney shined a flashlight as they walked down a dirt road.

"How far is it?" Sydney asked.

"I'm not sure. Maybe a mile."

"What's so special about Fran's figs?" Sydney peered at Emily out of the corner of her eye.

"They're...um...big. Like largest in the world."

The world? I might as well have said the universe.

"Wow! So *Guinness Book of World Records* big?"

"Possibly. I'm not sure. That's why I need to see them." Emily silently prayed that Sydney would shut up already about the freakin' figs.

"So what's the deal with Fran? Why's she so private?"

Emily sighed. "I have no idea. She's not the warm and fuzzy type. Bud said she keeps to herself and isn't a people person."

"Bud?" Sydney asked. "Oh, from the bait place."

"Have you ever heard of Conway Twitty?"

Sydney pointed the light in Emily's eyes. "Talk about a conversation changer."

Emily batted the flashlight down. "Bud said Fran is obsessed with the guy. It's the only thing she loves aside from her farm. I dunno. I thought it might somehow help me get on her good side."

Sydney chuckled. "Good luck with that one."

After several minutes of silence, Emily asked, "Where do you live in LA?"

Sydney's footsteps faltered. "Probably no place you're familiar with."

"Try me."

"It's...uh...South Central."

Yikes. Not a good area. Sydney was right. Emily had never been there.

"You mentioned your mom before. Do you keep in touch with her?" Emily asked.

"What's with all the questions?" Sydney sounded irritated.

"Just trying to get to know you better."

Sydney took a deep breath and let it out slowly. "No. I don't communicate with her. I ran away from home when I was seventeen and haven't seen her since."

"Oh. Wow. I'm sorry."

Emily had a gazillion questions. Where'd Sydney go? Did she live on the streets? How'd she support herself? But she bit her tongue, knowing Sydney probably would be offended. Getting to know Sydney was going to be a slow process, and surprisingly Emily actually wanted to try it.

Suddenly, Sydney stopped and grabbed Emily's arm. "The house is up ahead. I see lights. We should skirt around the back in case anyone is there. Where are the fig trees?"

Emily peered through the binoculars that hung around her neck. "From what I can see, which isn't much, looks like behind the house."

Knowing she was so close to the lovebirds sent shivers down

Emily's spine. They went in a wide circle through an empty field, hid behind a wood chipper, and eyed a small, white house in desperate need of a fresh coat of paint.

"Maybe Fran didn't go out of town," Emily whispered.

Sydney turned off the flashlight. "Let's get a little closer."

"Hold up, Indiana Jones. What if we step on a cow patty or minefield or something? I can't see where I'm walking without the light."

"Just stay close to me." Sydney slipped her hand into Emily's.

Ahh. That felt nice. Pole dancing obviously hadn't given her calluses. Her skin was soft, warm, and reassuring. Emily probably would have followed Sydney anywhere. When was the last time Emily and Gretchen had held hands? Come to think of it, had they *ever*?

When Sydney stopped, Emily crashed into her backside, breasts pressed into firm muscles. Sydney tensed at the contact. This probably wasn't what she meant when she said to stay close. For once, Emily was glad it was dark, certain she was blushing. Having Sydney against her felt much too enjoyable. Emily took a big step back and dropped Sydney's hand.

"Why'd you stop?" Emily asked.

Sydney cleared her throat and took a moment to respond. Finally, she pointed and said, "Look."

Emily's jaw dropped. "Holy crap." She was staring at a sea of fig trees. How in the world was she supposed to find twenty Madagascar lovebirds in all that? She was a bird-watcher, not a miracle worker. Unfortunately, this meant Emily needed Fran to show her where they were nesting. She couldn't accomplish this mission alone.

They both shielded their eyes when a silhouette shined a mega-spotlight on them. Emily froze, terror shooting through her gut like a sharp, hot knife. It was Fran. She was sure of it. There went Emily's chance of ever gaining her trust. Not only that, but Emily was surely going to the slammer now. Cockroaches and rats, here she came.

"What are you two doing out here?"

That wasn't Fran's voice.

"Bud? Is that you?" The light clicked off, and Emily put a hand over her heart. "Oh, thank God, it's you."

"That still don't answer my question, missy."

"We...uh..."

"We broke in," Sydney said.

Emily gawked at her. "Geez. Way to cover."

"Sometimes it's futile to lie." Sydney shrugged.

Bud tipped his cowboy hat back and pinched his lips. "You tryin' to steal Fran's figs?"

"No, no. Of course not." Emily waved her hands.

"You said you're a…a"—*Please don't say it. Please don't say it*—"a fig investor."

Damn. He said it.

Sydney's head jerked to Emily. "Investor? I thought you were writing a story about humongous fruit."

They both stared at Emily with non-blinking, wild eyes, making her want to shrivel to the size of a housefly and scram.

"I think a better question is, what are *you* doing here?" Emily asked Bud.

"Fran has me check on her place when she's out of town."

"Oh." Emily ran trembling fingers through her hair, trying to ignore the fact that Sydney was still staring at her. "Look, Bud, we're not here to steal anything. All we wanted to do was look over the farm. I can't complete my assignment without doing so, and we both know Fran would never allow that."

Bud nodded in slow motion. "Yep."

Emily sighed. "I'm glad you understand. So this will be our little secret?"

"Nope."

"You're going to tell Fran we're trespassing?"

"Yep."

"You can't!"

Sydney placed a hand on Emily's shoulder, possibly to hold her back from decking Bud.

"Maybe we can reach an agreement," Sydney said, her voice much too calm considering the circumstances. "Obviously, this is important to Emily…for whatever reason…" Sydney shot her a weird look. "Is there anything we can do for you in exchange for keeping quiet?"

Bribery? Oh my God. How many laws were they going to break tonight?

"Well, there is one thing," he said.

"Anything. Just name it." Emily would restock his worm tank, fry burritos, and even gut fish if she had to.

"Git me a date with Fran."

"How's that?" Emily couldn't have heard correctly.

"I've been askin' her out for up to three years now, and she ain't a-budging."

"Wait a second. You're asking us to play matchmaker? With someone who hates people?"

"Yep."

"That's impossible." Emily shook her head.

"Now, now, nothing's impossible." Sydney held out her hand. "You've got yourself a deal."

Bud pumped Sydney's arm twice and said, "I'm holdin' you to that, young lady. Now you two better git going."

Emily opened her mouth to protest, but Sydney practically knocked the wind out of her when she grabbed Emily's arm and tore down the trail.

"Are you nuts?" Emily asked, trying to keep up with Sydney's quick pace. "You haven't met Fran. She's a scary woman. What makes you think we can get her to go out on a date when Bud's been asking for three years now? I don't have time to make a love connection. I'm here for a bird..."

Sydney stopped and looked directly at Emily. "Aha! I knew you were lying. World's largest figs, my ass. Give it up. What's all this about?"

"All right. Fine." Emily blew out a strong breath. "I'm looking for lovebirds."

"Yeah. So? What makes these so special?"

"All lovebirds are special. They're my favorite. Remember? I need to get into Fran's good graces so she'll show me where they're located."

"So what are you going to do?"

Emily shot Sydney a dirty look. "I guess the first thing I need to do is get Bud a date."

Sydney winced. "Sorry. I was just trying to help."

The sincerity in Sydney's eyes softened Emily. "It was my fault. I never should have agreed to trespass."

"But you did admit it was exciting." Sydney's smile lit up the night so much that Emily couldn't help but join her.

"Yes. It was." Emily grabbed Sydney's arm. "Promise me you won't tell anyone about the lovebirds. This is too important."

Sydney's gaze fell to the ground.

"Sydney?" Emily squeezed firm muscles.

"Right. Of course. Who would I tell?"

CHAPTER ELEVEN

Tutor Time

This was a first. Sydney never woke up at six a.m. She'd been so tired after the farm excursion that she went right to sleep, and on the couch no less, when it was her turn to take the bed. She yawned and stretched like a lazy feline, arms and legs pushed against the armrest. It was an ungodly hour, but she really needed to get moving. She had a lot to accomplish before the PowerBar audition.

Sydney sat upright and grabbed her phone to check messages. Geez. Was Owen impatient or what? He'd sent three texts late last night after she'd already gone to sleep wondering what she'd found out. Sydney typed a response.

Emily is doing a lovebird story. We got access to the farm but didn't find anything.

Owen immediately responded. *Lovebirds? She's lying again. Find out the real story or else no reward.*

Sydney tossed her phone onto the coffee table, feeling like a big, fat rat. This spying thing would be a lot easier if she didn't like Emily so much. Sydney had to look out for herself, though. That's the way the world worked. She bounded off the couch, slipped on gray sweats, picked up the box of books she'd taken out of the bedroom closet, and headed into the kitchen. After making a pot of coffee, she opened the sliding-glass door and stepped onto the deck. From this vantage point she could see when Emily went into the kitchen and would have time to hide everything. She'd barely been able to conceal the books when Emily caught her on the sofa yesterday morning.

After spreading the material out on the table, Sydney settled onto the bench. This was the absolute last thing she wanted to do. Why couldn't she just practice her pole routine? That was something she understood. Several sips of coffee later, she cracked open a book. Within just a few minutes, the words blurred, causing her to blink rapidly. This made no sense whatsoever. Was it even written in English? She turned a page, studied it a few minutes, then turned another one. It was all gibberish. She slammed the book shut and grabbed another one, which wasn't much better. Within seconds, her eyelids drooped. This was the most boring thing ever. She shook her head and gulped down more coffee.

"Wake the fuck up and get this stuff done," she mumbled to herself.

With posture as straight as that of a runway model, Sydney opened her eyes wide. It had probably been only a minute or two when her head bobbed and her forehead hit the book, jarring her awake. Obviously, she wasn't going to accomplish anything until she got some more shut-eye. That should teach her to get up so early. Sydney yawned and rested her head on the table. Just a minute or two of sleep and she'd be fine.

The next thing Sydney knew something tapped her shoulder. She jumped upright, glad to see it was Emily and not a bear...or maybe not so glad.

"What's all this?" Emily asked, eyeing the books.

"Nothing." Sydney threw herself over the table in a lame attempt to hide her dirty little secret.

"Then why are you acting like a lunatic?"

When Emily sat across from her, Sydney sat upright and tried to avoid eye contact.

"What's going on?" Emily's tone was laced with kindness, which made it even worse. The last thing Sydney wanted was pity.

"I'm studying," Sydney said, finally looking Emily in the eye.

Emily brightened. "For what?"

Sydney chewed on her lower lip. "For my...uh...my GED."

"But...that's for...oh."

"Right. My high school diploma."

Why did Emily have to be the one to find out that Sydney was ignorant? For some reason, she wanted Emily's admiration, not shame.

"I quit school my junior year when I left home. I never graduated. I know, I know. I'm a dummy."

"You are not!"

"The last thing I want is a pep talk, and I don't need you feeling sorry for me." Sydney bolted upright and walked to the railing, her back to Emily. She gazed out at the forest, desperately hoping Emily would retreat into the cabin and leave her alone. No such luck. Emily stood beside Sydney and stared at her profile.

"I didn't walk in your shoes, Sydney. I don't know what you went through in your life. I'm sure you did the best you could."

Sydney looked into Emily's beautiful brown eyes. She was perfect. Perfect complexion, perfect lips, perfect everything. She'd probably gone to the best, most expensive college that her doctor dad could afford.

"That's right," Sydney said. "You have no idea about my life." *And you never will if I can help it.* What would Emily think if she knew Sydney had worked in a seedy nightclub? She'd think stripper for sure.

"I'm not judging you. Not getting your high school diploma doesn't make you less than. And look what you're doing." Emily motioned toward the table. "You're working on getting your GED."

Sydney snorted and shook her head. "I don't understand one thing in those books. And they're *Dummies* books! What does that say about me?"

"You're really hard on yourself. It's been a while since you've been in school, and it *is* a lot to learn."

"This is worse than pity. Now you're humoring me."

"I am not! Oh my God. Could you be any more exasperating?" Anger flashed across Emily's eyes. She gripped the railing hard, muttered something to herself, and focused on the pine trees. After a few moments, she turned and looked at Sydney.

"Lord knows why I'm offering this, but maybe I could help you study."

"That's even worse than pity! That's charity!" Sydney said, throwing her hands up in the air.

Sydney breezed past Emily, stormed into the kitchen, and flew out the front door, wanting nothing more than to drive at dizzyingly fast, record-breaking speeds. She stood on the sidewalk and frowned. That couldn't happen when Emily's BMW was blocking her in.

Instead, Sydney did the next best thing and took off running. Luckily, she was wearing sweats and sneakers. It didn't take long before her heart pounded and her legs ached, but that didn't stop her. Maybe if she moved fast enough the motion would empty her mind and drown out her mother's irritatingly shrill voice, the one that would stab her in the heart when she was a kid.

You're not good enough.

You'll amount to nothing.

Run faster so she can't catch you.

You're a rotten kid.

Pump those arms harder. Go...go...go...

You're such an idiot!

Sydney's legs gave way, and she tumbled onto the ground, breathless. She grabbed a handful of grass and yanked, squeezing the blades in her palm. How could Sydney's mother still affect her? She hadn't seen the woman since she was seventeen. Sydney wiped away an angry tear, determined not to let her mother's words ever wound her again.

This wasn't going to be fun. Apologies never were. They required too much emotional sharing and, God forbid, maybe even a hug. Sydney creaked open the cabin door and peeked inside. Emily wasn't in the living room. Maybe she'd headed out for the day. She closed the door behind her and went into the kitchen. Not in there either. Hopefully by the time Sydney saw Emily again she'd have forgotten all about her little outburst. Sydney felt her shoulders slump when she spotted Emily on the deck, standing in the same place as when she'd stormed out like a cranky toddler.

Sydney attempted to check out her reflection in the microwave.

The last thing she needed was for Emily to see that she'd been crying. Now *that* would be embarrassing. She wiped her eyes and fluffed her hair. Ugh. She looked like crap. Did she have time to run upstairs and do damage control? It shouldn't matter what she looked like, but Emily was so adorable Sydney didn't want her to think she was a slob. Oh well. She might as well get this over with.

When Sydney slid the screen door open, Emily twisted around to face her. See? Adorable. Wind-tossed chestnut hair, glowing complexion, faded jean shorts that showcased smooth, pale skin, and salmon-colored T-shirt that hugged beautiful curves.

Sydney walked across the deck and nonchalantly rested a hip against the railing. "Sorry I blew up at you."

"Why did you?"

Of course Emily would have to ask the most difficult question. Sydney turned and faced the forest. It was easier to tell this to the trees than to Emily.

"I get a bit defensive when I think maybe my mom was right about the things she used to say about me."

"Did she call you a dummy?"

Sydney bowed her head. "That and more."

"She didn't hit you, did she?" Emily placed a hand on Sydney's arm.

Something about the sound of Emily's voice and the softness of her touch sent waves of warmth radiating across Sydney's chest.

"No." Sydney faced Emily. "I know the things she said aren't true, but sometimes they still creep up on me when I least expect it."

Emily gritted her teeth, her face bright red. Was she angry? Sydney thought she'd done a pretty good job of apologizing.

"I cannot believe some people," Emily said through tight lips. "You deserved better than that woman. I'm glad you left and never looked back."

Oh. Emily was mad at Sydney's mother. That was a first. No one had ever stood up for her before. Sydney felt an intense desire to wrap her arms around Emily, which was the weirdest thing ever. She wasn't a hugger. In fact, she couldn't even remember the last time she'd embraced anyone except in a way intended to lead to sex. Instead, she crossed her arms over her chest to keep from doing something foolish, not to mention embarrassing.

"You can do anything you put your mind to," Emily said adamantly. "And my offer from before still stands."

Sydney drew her head back. "Really? You'd help me study?"

"Of course."

"What do you want in return?" Sydney eyed Emily.

"What do you mean?"

"No one does a favor without wanting something in return."

Emily gawked at Sydney in seeming disbelief. "I don't know what kind of world you live in, but when I do a favor for someone it's not to get anything back. So, what do you say?" Emily motioned toward the stack of books.

Normally, Sydney would rather die than admit she needed assistance, but Emily's kind eyes and sincere tone made it easy to accept. Plus, she was screwed if she didn't pass the test.

"Okay," Sydney said.

"Good." Emily smiled and slid onto the bench.

Sydney sat unnecessarily close to Emily, so close she could feel the warmth from her body. It was comforting, reassuring. That was even weirder than wanting a hug. Sydney would have to check the calendar when she went back into the cabin. Undoubtedly she was PMSing, which always made her overemotional and a bit needy.

"When's your test?" Emily opened the science book.

"Monday."

Emily gulped and turned to face Sydney. Wow. Her eyes were beautiful. Sydney had always thought they were brown, but from this distance she could see shards of red and orange, which made them look more russet than boring brown.

Emily gawked. "As in day after tomorrow?"

"Nothing like waiting till the last minute, huh?" Sydney forced a chuckle, which came out more like an inhumane, crazed tremor.

"If you don't feel ready, why not just take it at a later date?"

Sydney shook her head. "I can't do the PowerBar audition unless I have a high school diploma. It's one of their prerequisites."

"When's the audition?"

"In a week. I'll find out the results of the GED on Tuesday. If I don't pass, then I can kiss my chance of ever working at my dream job."

"You'll pass."

Emily had more faith in Sydney than anyone she'd ever known, even more than Sydney herself. Sydney dropped her gaze to Emily's soft-looking, full lips. Did she use lipstick, or were they naturally a luscious shade of red? When Emily licked her lips, Sydney flicked her eyes upward. Hopefully she hadn't noticed Sydney staring.

Geez. Pull it together. Someone shows you a little kindness, and you go all gooey.

Sydney slid a few inches away from Emily and sat on her hands.

"What hangs you up the most?" Emily asked, her nose stuck in a book.

"Everything. How am I supposed to remember all these dates? Who the hell knows when the Boston Tea Party was? And don't even get me started on algebra. I'm totally lost there."

Emily looked at Sydney with those gorgeous russet eyes. "Have you ever heard of mnemonics?"

"No. What's that?"

"A device that helps with memorization. It helped me a lot through school."

"I'm up for anything. How's it work?"

"One method is to use rhymes. Like...'59 was the date when Alaska and Hawaii became new states. Or 1773 was the date of the Boston Tea Party, so just think '73 is heavenly tea."

"Oh. I get it. What are some others?"

"Let's see what else I can remember." Emily stared into space before her face lit up. "Ooh. This was one of my favorites. My very excited mother just served us nachos."

"What the heck is that supposed to mean?" Sydney pulled her eyebrows together.

"That's a way to remember all the planets. Look at the first letter of each word. Mercury, Venus, Earth, Mars, and so forth."

"That's cool. What else?"

"I'm here to help, not do all your work for you. You come up with one. How would you remember the properties of matter? Mass, density, volume, and weight."

Sydney gazed up at the clouds. "Umm...how about...models diet very well."

Emily laughed. "Excellent. And probably very true."

"This isn't so hard after all. But I still have a lot to learn."

"We have two days. Don't worry. You'll be ready."

We? Sydney had never been a "we" before. She liked the sound of it. It made her feel stronger, more confident, as though she and Emily could scale Mount Everest together. Sydney closed her eyes and shook her head. The next thing you know she'd be belting out "Climb Ev'ry Mountain." Okay. That just proved it. She was most certainly PMSing.

CHAPTER TWELVE

The Pink Moment

Emily placed both hands on Sydney's shoulders—her very firm, well-defined shoulders—and looked directly into her eyes—her stunning, anxiety-filled eyes. "You couldn't be any more prepared after cramming for two days straight. Did you get any sleep last night?"

Sydney shrugged. "A little."

"Just relax." Emily gently shook Sydney's shoulders and dropped her arms. "You've got this."

Emily wanted to wipe the concern from Sydney's eyes. She had a better chance of passing the test if she wasn't so stressed. More than anything, Emily wanted success for Sydney. She had a feeling this was about more than just the PowerBar audition. Not having a high school diploma undoubtedly fed into Sydney's feelings of inadequacy. If Sydney's mother was standing in front of Emily right now she'd… she'd…well, she wasn't sure what she'd do since she wasn't a violent person, but she'd certainly do *something* to the awful woman.

"How long is the test?" Emily asked.

"Seven hours. I better go. It's an hour's drive to Santa Barbara, and you never know about traffic on the 101." Sydney grabbed her bag off the kitchen counter and slung it over her shoulder.

"Hey," Emily said, which caused Sydney to stop halfway through the swinging doors. "Pudgy elves may demand a snack."

Sydney grinned, which lightened Emily's heart. "That's the mnemonics for the mathematical order of operations. Parenthesis, exponents, multiplication, division, addition, subtraction."

"Go get 'em." Emily smiled and watched Sydney leave with a swagger in her step.

Emily poured herself a second cup of coffee and looked at the clock. The test started at nine, which meant it'd be over at four, so Sydney wouldn't be home until five at the earliest. That was nine hours away. Emily rubbed sweaty palms on the legs of her lovebird PJs. Waiting that long would be torture.

Expertly balancing coffee, laptop, and cell phone in both hands, she went into the living room and settled onto the couch. This wouldn't be fun, but she really needed to call Gretchen since they hadn't talked all weekend. She'd want to know Emily's lovebird progress, and she had absolutely nothing to report aside from the fact that she was now a criminal who was being blackmailed by a burrito-and-bait salesman. Emily pressed the speed dial, Gretchen answering on the first ring and getting right to the point.

"How's it going?"

"No 'good morning' first?" Emily asked, trying to lighten the mood.

"Our mothers are driving me crazy. When are you coming back?"

Emily massaged her temple. "As soon as I can. I'll see Fran day after tomorrow."

Silence.

"Gretch?"

More silence.

"You still there?"

"Do you not want to get married?" Gretchen's voice sounded strained, like maybe she was near tears.

"Of course I do! This trip has nothing to do with us. Once I get the story I'll come home, and we can plan the wedding together, if our moms haven't already done so."

"Because if you don't want to—"

"No. I mean yes, I mean no, I don't not want to." Emily shook her head. "You know what I mean."

"Do you ever think about me?"

"Y-yes! A-all the time." *Since when do I stutter? It is the truth, isn't it?*

"Just hurry." Gretchen sighed into the receiver. "I gotta get ready for work."

"Okay. Have a good day."

Gretchen disconnected without saying good-bye. She was pissed and with good reason. Emily was a horrible girlfriend. Here she was having Ojai adventures and helping Sydney while her fiancée was all alone. She needed to get her act together, write the story, and hightail it back to LA. What Emily needed was a list. It always made her feel more organized. She opened her laptop and typed: How do you solve a problem like Fran? With fingers poised over the keys, she wasn't sure what else to put. First, she had to hook Fran and Bud up, or else he'd snitch, and then she needed to convince Fran to let her on the farm to get photos of the lovebirds.

Emily wrung her hands. She was screwed. She had no idea how to accomplish any of that. She could always contact the American Bird Conservancy to help, but then everyone would know about the lovebirds and Emily wouldn't get the scoop. She closed the document without saving it. Lists weren't all they were cracked up to be anyway.

Emily opened her email, her heart skipping a beat at the sight of Jill's name. She jerked her hand off the mouse as though it were a hot potato. Jill had finally responded to Emily's message. Just one click and she'd have the answer of whether Sydney had lied about the cabin. Emily stared at the screen until the letters blurred. She blinked several times, took a deep breath, and opened it.

Hi Emily. I was shocked to hear that Sydney is at the cabin. She was NOT invited. Please call the police and have them escort her out. I'll contact them about pressing charges. I'm so sorry for the inconvenience. I'll check my email tomorrow in case you have any issues. All the best, Jill

Emily's stomach soured. Sydney had lied. Maybe she *was* a criminal, considering the farm break-in. No. That was to help Emily, and they weren't planning to steal anything. Sydney was probably desperate for a place to stay in Ojai since no rooms were available. Still, though, she could have been honest about it. But then again, Emily would have kicked her out.

Listen to me. I'm making excuses for her. She should confront Sydney and see what she had to say for herself. She certainly didn't want to call the police and have Sydney arrested. Plus, she didn't want her to leave. Emily widened her eyes at the admission. She was actually having fun with the pole dancer.

Emily hit the reply button on Jill's email.

Hello Jill. Thanks for getting back to me. Things have changed since I last contacted you. Sydney has actually been a help to me, so if it's okay I'd like her to stay. I'm more than happy to pay extra if need be. Hope you're enjoying your vacation. Emily

Heat crept up Emily's neck. If Gretchen ever found out Sydney was not only staying in the cabin but that Emily wanted her to, she'd be crushed. Emily pressed send before she could change her mind.

As much pacing as Emily was doing, she'd probably have to buy Jill new hardwood floors. It was after six o'clock and Sydney still wasn't back yet. Emily rushed to the front door when she heard a car in the driveway, desperately trying to get an indication of how things had gone from Sydney's expression. The woman would be an excellent poker player. She wasn't giving anything away.

"Well? How was it?" Emily asked before Sydney even reached the porch.

"Long." Sydney sighed and sat on the top step.

Emily sat beside her. "Do you think you passed?"

"Hell if I know. It didn't seem too difficult, but…I dunno." Sydney looked like she'd just run a marathon, exhausted and ready to drop at any moment.

"Are you hungry?"

"Not really. God, it's going to kill me to wait until tomorrow to get the results." Sydney rested her chin on her fist.

Emily wished she could do something to help, but patience wasn't one of her strong points. She was just as anxious as Sydney. Not only did Emily want her to pass, but she felt invested in the outcome since she'd helped Sydney study.

They sat in silence for a while, watching cars drive by and enjoying a cool breeze. Suddenly, Sydney sat upright with a big smile on her face and took a bag out of her backpack.

"I almost forgot," Sydney said. "I found something that will help your Fran problem."

"You did? What?" Emily couldn't imagine what it could be.

"I stopped by a used bookstore after the test and ran across this." Sydney pulled out a book. "Ta-da!"

Emily furrowed her brow and silently read the title: *What's Cooking at Twitty City*.

"It's an out-of-print cookbook written by Mickey, Conway Twitty's wife." Sydney was as excited as a kid with a shiny, new toy. "You said Fran was his biggest fan. You gift this to her and she'll love you."

"This was thoughtful, but I think it'll take something more than a cookbook to get to Fran."

"Are you kidding?" Sydney's voice rose two octaves. "The bookstore owner said it's a rare find. You can't buy this anywhere. Not even on eBay."

Emily flipped through the cookbook. Texas fried steak. Hush puppies. Buttermilk biscuits. This probably wouldn't do anything more than clog Fran's arteries.

"Thanks. But I dunno."

"Oh ye of little faith." Sydney snatched the book out of Emily's hand and stuffed it back into the bag.

Emily shivered and wrapped her arms around her knees.

"Are you cold?" Sydney asked.

"A little."

Sydney looked as though she was about to put her arm around Emily's shoulders, but she refrained. What would it feel like to be in Sydney's arms? Probably safe, secure, and wonderfully soft. Suddenly, Sydney stood and reached her arms high overhead in a long stretch.

"Are you going in?" Emily gazed upward.

"I guess. How about you?"

Emily stood and smiled. "I'm heading to Meditation Mount to see *the pink moment*."

"What the heck is that?"

"It's something Jill told me about. You wanna go?"

"Mmm...I dunno."

"Come on. It'll be fun." Emily tugged on Sydney's shirt sleeve, not wanting their time together to end.

Sydney looked at her car, parked behind Emily's. "Am I driving?"

"If you don't mind. It's less than a mile away."

"I don't have a BMW, you know. And my car was broken into so the passenger side has cardboard for a window."

"Good gosh. My ass doesn't demand to be in a luxury seat. I don't care what you drive." Emily bounded down the steps and yelled over her shoulder, "Get a move on. We're going to miss it."

❖

Emily thrummed her fingers against her knee, opened her mouth, but then snapped it shut. She was probably resisting asking Sydney if she could drive faster. Sydney couldn't help but smile. Emily was cute when she got excited.

"Are you sure we're going in the right direction?" Sydney asked. They were driving down an extremely narrow, winding lane and had just passed a sign that said Dead End.

"Yes. Just keep going."

They drove up a hill, around a curve, and into a parking lot. Emily opened the door before Sydney came to a complete stop.

"What's the rush?" Sydney asked.

"We're going to miss the sunset." Emily marched down a dirt trail like a drill sergeant.

Sydney got out of the car and jogged to catch up. "I hate to break it to you, but we're facing east, not west. We can't see the sunset from this vantage point."

Emily ignored the comment as they walked down a path lined with a multitude of colorful flowers. After passing a pond filled with lilies and a trickling waterfall, they reached the end of the trail that had a spectacular view of Ojai valley.

Emily gasped, pointed over Sydney's shoulder, and said, "Oh wow. Look."

When Sydney twisted around she was awarded with one of the most gorgeous sights she'd ever seen. The Topa Topa Mountains looked as though they were airbrushed in a bright fluorescent pink. The setting sun in the west cast a colorful light on the mountains in the east. She could see why the locals called this *the pink moment*. They stood motionless, absorbing the beauty as the color transformed into shades of peach and lavender.

Sydney glanced at Emily, struck by something even more beautiful than the mountains. She looked breathtaking, sparkling eyes that reflected the sunset and full lips curved upward in a smile. Tingles rippled up and down Sydney's spine when their eyes met. She had an urge to place a soft kiss on Emily's lips and pull her close. Instead, she forced her eyes back to the mountains, which were now violet.

"This might be the most gorgeous thing I've ever seen," Emily said, gazing at Sydney.

For an instant, Sydney wasn't sure if Emily was referring to her or the sunset. Surely she meant the sunset.

"I've never seen anything like this in LA," Sydney said and sat on a nearby bench.

"Me neither. Gretchen lives close to the ocean and we've seen some beauties, but not this vibrant." Emily sat beside Sydney.

"You two don't live together?"

"No. But we will soon. In October." Emily's eyes darkened, her lips set in a hard, thin line.

"The wedding is in four months?"

"Yes." Emily slowly nodded and stared into space, seemingly lost in thought.

"You don't seem very excited." Sydney felt a sudden jolt of hopefulness. That was strange. Why should she care if Emily wanted to get married or not?

"Oh, I am! I mean…everyone is excited about it."

Sydney let her shoulders slump. Of course. Why wouldn't Emily be ecstatic about marrying Gretchen? "Everyone?" she asked.

"Our parents. They're the ones who set us up on a blind date. It's the perfect scenario, really. Both families already know and love each other. It's like it was meant to be."

"Don't you wonder what it would be like to date other women? You said Gretchen was the only one you ever went out with."

"Of course not!" Emily's eyes blazed, and she looked at Sydney like she'd just insulted her.

Sydney held up her hands. "Don't jump down my throat. I'm just asking. I didn't realize she gets your oxytocin flowing."

"It's not like that with us. We love each other, but we're not all googly-eyed. It's a comfortable relationship." Emily glared at Sydney like she expected her to say something offensive.

After a few moments, Emily asked, "So you're not dating anyone?"

Sydney crossed her leg and put her hands behind her head. "Nope. All I care about is pole dancing."

"Sounds lonely."

Sydney shrugged, not sure how to respond. Normally, she'd spout something about being a loner, but the past few days with Emily had actually been enjoyable.

"Well, it sounds like you really love it," Emily said. "I'm sure you'll get the PowerBar job."

"I hope so. I've been trying for years to get an audition."

"Why do you want to work there so badly? Surely there are other places."

"There's another club, PoleCat, that's been recruiting me, but it's in South LA. Not a very good part of town. PowerBar is the most respectable establishment in the area. If I got a job there it'd mean I was..." Sydney paused and shook her head. "Never mind. You wouldn't understand."

Emily placed her hand on Sydney's knee. "Try me."

Sydney stared at Emily's smooth skin and graceful fingers. Her touch felt comforting. She gulped and said, "It'd mean I was worthy."

Emily's expression softened. "You're already worthy, Sydney. That feeling should come from within and not because of where you work. You said that you want to empower women. Beverly Hills isn't the only place you can do that."

"Working at PowerBar would mean I'd made it. I'd be somebody. Not a penniless louse living in the slums." *Ugh. Why did I just admit that?* Something about Emily made Sydney say things she normally wouldn't.

"Is that why you broke into the cabin? Because you didn't have money for a hotel? I got an email from Jill."

Sydney jerked her head toward Emily, her face heated. "The jig is up, I guess."

"You didn't have to lie. You should have told me you couldn't afford a place to stay."

"And you wouldn't have thrown me out?"

"All right. I would have then, but we're friends now. Aren't we?" Emily gazed at Sydney, looking hopeful.

Sydney grinned. "Yes. We're friends."

That felt nice. Really nice. Sydney didn't have many of those. She looked at her phone when it chimed with an incoming text, her chest tightening when she saw it was from Owen. He was the last person she wanted to hear from.

"Is anything wrong?" Emily asked.

"Just no one I care to hear from anymore."

Sydney slid the phone into her back pocket and decided right then to cut Owen off. It wasn't worth selling out someone she cared about. The admission that she had feelings for Emily should have shocked her, but it didn't.

"So," Sydney said. "Can I stay until the audition?"

"Of course." Emily responded without hesitation. "I don't want you to leave."

Sydney's heart felt lighter than it ever had before. She wasn't sure if that was the result of having a roof over her head or because Emily wanted her to stay.

CHAPTER THIRTEEN

Disco Fever

"Any news yet?" Emily stood in the bedroom doorway.

Sydney frowned and shook her head. She'd been lounging on the bed the better part of the day with a computer perched in her lap waiting on the GED results.

"It's four o'clock. You'd think the scores would be available by now." Sydney scowled.

Emily sat beside Sydney and stretched out her legs. Being in such an intimate setting probably should have felt uncomfortable, but instead it seemed natural.

Sydney crossed her arms over a gray, cotton T-shirt and stared at the computer screen. "What if I don't pass?"

"Worrying about it is useless." Emily snatched the laptop, closed the lid, and hugged it tight against her chest.

Sydney sat upright. "Hey! Give that back."

"You've been staring at this thing all day. You need to relax."

"I need to know my results." Sydney glared.

"What do you usually do to unwind? Go for a walk or run maybe?"

Sydney grumbled something about Emily being a pain in the ass and pointed to a silver pole in the middle of the room. "I do that."

"Well, so…do that then."

"Let me check just once more."

Sydney reached for the laptop and jerked her hand back when she accidentally brushed Emily's breast. Her eyes widened and she jumped off the bed. Hopefully she hadn't noticed that Emily's nipples hardened from the contact and goose bumps appeared on her arms. She'd never had such an immediate reaction to a simple touch before.

"Fine. You win," Sydney said and slightly shook her body, as though to relieve tension.

Sydney closed her eyes and took a deep breath, releasing it slowly. When she whisked off her shirt and tossed it into the corner, Emily's eyes nearly popped out of her head. Sydney was practically naked! Granted, she was wearing shorts and a sports bra, but still. Emily should leave and give her some privacy, but she couldn't very well do that when her eyes were glued to Sydney's long, lean legs and rippled abs.

Emily's mouth went dry as she watched Sydney prance to the pole and grab it above her head. She rose on her toes and took two steps forward, looking more graceful than any ballet dancer Emily had ever seen. Without slowing down, Sydney placed her other hand on the rod and levitated off the ground, going around it at least three times. Talk about upper-body strength. Sydney whirled around in a fancy move Emily couldn't quite follow and proceeded to rest her back against the pole, put her hands on her knees, and squat several times with her legs spread. Her movements were elegant, flowing, and downright erotic.

Is it getting hot in here? Emily's pulse quickened and she tugged on her collar. Thank God no sexy striptease music was playing. Otherwise she'd probably hyperventilate. Emily really needed to scram, and she did try, but her butt seemed to be cemented into the mattress. In one swift move, Sydney turned upside down, released the pole, and held on with nothing but her legs.

Emily's jaw dropped. "Oh my God!"

Sydney righted herself and looked at Emily like she'd forgotten she was even in the room. "What's wrong?"

"You're amazing."

Sydney smirked and lowered her head, looking embarrassed.

Emily scooted to the edge of the bed. "I'm serious. I figured you'd be good. I mean, look at you." Emily waved her hands toward Sydney. "But you're like circus good. No. Olympic good."

"Thanks. I've worked hard at it. I could show you a few things if you'd like."

"On that?" Emily drew her head back and pointed at the pole. "No way." She crept back onto the bed.

"Why not?"

"There are so many reasons, I don't even know where to begin."

Emily would rather spend the day with Owen than take her shirt off in front of someone as perfect as Sydney, not to mention the fact that she'd embarrass herself silly by falling on her head. But Sydney didn't need to know any of that.

Emily opened the laptop. "How about we check to see if your scores are in?"

"You're totally changing the subject, but okay." Sydney sat beside Emily and crossed her legs. "You look. I'm too nervous." Sydney handed Emily a laminated card. "Here's my student ID. You have to type in the number."

Emily connected to the website and navigated to the test-results section. She jerked her head toward Sydney. "They're in."

All the blood drained from Sydney's face, and she closed her eyes. "All right. Let's have it."

Emily typed Sydney's name in the search bar along with her ID number.

"What's taking so long?" Sydney asked. "I failed, didn't I?"

"Hold on. I'm almost there." Within seconds, Emily beamed and said, "What's the opposite of failed?"

Sydney opened one eye. "You mean…"

"Look!" Emily turned the computer, knowing Sydney probably wouldn't believe it unless she saw it with her own eyes.

Sydney stared at the screen in seeming disbelief. "Oh my God. I passed? Really?"

"Congratulations. You have successfully earned your GED."

"Un-fucking-believable!" Sydney threw her arms around Emily's neck, which caused them both to tumble backward onto the bed.

One minute Emily was sitting upright, and the next she was lying on her back with Sydney's breasts pressed against hers, not that she was complaining. Who wouldn't want a hard-bodied pole dancer on top of her? Wait. That's not something she should want. She was engaged to…to…what was her name…Gretchen. That was it!

Get up. Move. Blink. At least take your hands off her ass. But all Emily could do was lie there and bask in the feel of Sydney in her arms. Surprisingly, she wasn't all muscle; she had a softness and warmth to her frame. Emily inhaled deeply, as much as she could do so with a pole dancer pressed against her, and smelled the scent of mouthwatering coconut. She had an insatiable urge to run her fingers through Sydney's golden locks to see if the aroma was coming from her shampoo. Luckily, she didn't do so but instead gazed into mesmerizing blue eyes, which—if Emily wasn't mistaken—were filled with desire. Sydney's breathing increased and she licked her lips, the space between them so still and silent that Emily heard the distant whistle of a bird.

Birds. That's what I'm here for. Not this. Emily jerked her hands off Sydney's ass and held them high in the air. The movement seemed to jolt Sydney back to reality.

"Oh my gosh. I'm sorry," Sydney said in a husky voice.

She jumped out of bed and hurriedly put her shirt back on. Well, that was disappointing. It seemed almost a sin to cover such an amazing body. Emily swung her legs over, stood beside Sydney, and resisted the urge to tell her that her shirt was not only inside out but also backward.

Emily wasn't sure what to say or do. Should they laugh about it or hug it out? God, no. Not hug. That's what had started all this. Well, she should do something other than stand there like an idiot shuffling her feet back and forth and staring at the bedspread.

Thankfully, Sydney made a move when she opened the nightstand drawer and pulled out a piece of paper and pen. Emily watched as she marked an *X* next to the high school-diploma question on the PowerBar application. She'd probably anxiously been waiting to do that for weeks.

"We should celebrate." Emily clapped her hands together.

Sydney's face lit up. "Let's go to the women's festival. There's a dance tonight."

"Dance? Absolutely not." Emily vigorously shook her head. "Rhythm isn't in my blood. Besides, I don't think my fiancée would like me going out with another woman."

"It's not a date. Come on. You have to go. You're the reason I passed."

"Thanks, but you're the one that did it."

Sydney placed both hands on Emily's shoulders and stared into her eyes. "I'm serious, Em."

Emily's heart lightened at the shortened version of her name. No one ever called her that. She liked it.

"I appreciate you helping me, and I'd really like to celebrate with you," Sydney said.

Sydney's striking, earnest eyes were like a magnet. Emily couldn't have looked away even if she tried, and strangely she had no desire to do so. In fact, she probably would have done anything Sydney had asked in that moment.

"Okay. I'll go with you," Emily said. "But I'm not dancing. I'll just watch."

Emily mentally kicked herself. *Great idea.* Sydney's dance moves were probably even sexier than her pole ones, if that was possible.

❖

Life was good. Sydney had her high school equivalency, an audition for her dream job, and a night out on the town with a beautiful woman. Granted, Emily wasn't *her* woman, but it was still nice, particularly when she was rocking snug black jeans, a white fitted V-neck T-shirt that displayed enticing cleavage, and black boots. In fact, Emily looked so hot Sydney had to force herself not to stare when she came down the stairs.

"Do I look okay?" Emily asked, rubbing her palms on her thighs.

"No. You look amazing."

The corners of Emily's mouth turned upward. "Really? I wasn't sure what to wear. I would have tucked my shirt in, but I look thinner with it out." Emily tugged on the bottom of her T-shirt.

Sydney grimaced. She hated the taunting a young Emily had endured, which must have been ten times worse with a fitness-freak mother.

"Come here." Sydney held out her hand, which Emily immediately accepted, and led her to a full-length mirror. She stood behind Emily and peered into her eyes in the reflection. "Now look at yourself and tell me you're not perfect in every way."

Emily gazed up and down her body. After a few moments, she appeared near tears, which wasn't Sydney's goal. Frantically, she racked her brain trying to think of something that would lighten the mood. Emily tucked in her shirt and smiled through watery eyes. She turned and planted a light kiss on Sydney's cheek, causing her stomach to flutter.

Emily leaned close and whispered, "Thank you."

Chills ran up and down Sydney's spine, and her skin tingled where Emily's lips had been. She displayed what was probably a goofy grin and placed her fingertips on her cheek. What was wrong with her? It was a G-rated kiss. She'd never been this affected by a woman before. Their little bed encounter earlier had left her breathless, and now she was acting like a doofus. She needed to get a grip.

"You're welcome," Sydney said and cleared her throat. "We better get going." She grabbed her keys and headed out the door, hoping the cool night air would slap some sense into her.

By the time they parked and were walking to the event it was almost eleven. Sydney covered her mouth in an attempt to hide a yawn. She'd been up since early that morning waiting for the test results.

"I saw that! You're tired. We should go back." Emily tugged on Sydney's arm.

"Nice try," Sydney said and stopped in her tracks. "Do you hear that?"

"You mean the loud, obnoxious noise coming from where we're heading? How could I miss it?"

"That's 'Dancing Queen.' I love disco music!"

"You weren't even born in the '70s."

"I know, but they played it at the…"

Emily raised an eyebrow. "At the what?"

"At a…uh…club I used to frequent."

Sydney had almost blown it. If she could help it, Emily would never find out she had worked at Leave It to Beaver.

"Come on," Sydney said. "This'll be fun."

When they walked through the entrance, Sydney felt like she was stepping into the past. She'd obviously been born in the wrong decade since she loved the strobe lights, silver hanging balls, and a multicolored, checkered dance floor. She couldn't help but sway her hips to KC and the Sunshine Band's "Shake Your Booty."

"Do you wanna dance?" Sydney yelled.

"What?" Emily leaned closer.

"Dance!"

Emily looked panic-stricken. Obviously, she needed to loosen up first. Sydney took Emily's hand and led her to the bar, which was a tad quieter. Emily sat on a barstool with Sydney beside her.

"What do you want to drink?" Sydney asked.

Emily paused for several beats and stared into space. Finally she said, "I'll take bottled water."

For that she had to think?

Sydney displayed her best you-must-be-kidding look.

"All right," Emily said, obviously getting the message. "Order me something fruity."

"Two Sex on the Beach?" Sydney told the bartender.

"Sex on the beach?" Emily asked.

"Trust me. You'll like it. I'm getting one, too, because sex is always better in twos."

Emily grinned and turned a pretty shade of scarlet. Sydney glanced down the bar, seeing someone who looked very familiar.

"You know her?" Emily asked, following Sydney's line of vision.

"That's Sue. She owns PowerBar."

"You should go schmooze with your future employer."

"You don't mind?"

"Of course not. I'll stay here and have sex alone." Emily took a sip of her drink, which the bartender had placed in front of her, and smacked her lips. "Ooh, that's good stuff."

Sydney smiled. She seemed to do that a lot around Emily. "I'll be right back." She walked around the bar and tapped Sue's shoulder. "Hi. It's nice to see you again."

Sue turned and cocked her head. "Do I know you?"

What the hell? Sydney had been in her studio begging for a job every week for the past several years. Maybe she was drunk, although she didn't appear to be tipsy.

"Um...it's Sydney. I'm auditioning on Sunday."

Sue threw her head back. "Oh, right. I'm sorry. I've seen so many women this week already."

Relief washed over Sydney. "That's okay. I understand."

"I do hate to be rude, but I *was* in the middle of a conversation." Sue motioned to a blonde sitting next to her wearing a perturbed expression.

"Oh. Right. I didn't mean to intrude. I'll just get out of your way."

Sue whisked around, putting her back to Sydney, and resumed her discussion. Feeling like a third wheel, Sydney slinked away with a weird sensation in the pit of her stomach. When she reached her seat, Emily was slurping down the last drops of her drink.

"Whoa. Slow down there, slugger. Something tells me you're a lightweight."

"That was sooo good. Like orgasmic good." Emily licked her lips, closed her eyes, and threw her head back in one hell of a sexy move, which would have been arousing if Sydney hadn't been so concerned about Sue's icy demeanor.

"Are you okay?" Emily asked.

"Fine." Sydney responded without taking her eyes off Sue.

"Hey." Emily held Sydney's chin and turned her head until they were eye to eye. "You don't look fine. Did something happen?"

"It's probably nothing. Sue just didn't seem very welcoming."

"What'd she say?" Emily sat upright and glanced down the bar, like maybe she was getting ready for a fistfight.

"Nothing really. I'm sure I'm just overreacting."

"It's awfully loud in here. She probably couldn't hear you very well."

Sydney nodded, still not quite convinced.

Emily jumped off the stool and grabbed Sydney's hand. "Let's dance."

Sydney's eyes widened. "*You* wanna dance?"

"This sounds like a fun song." Emily flashed the cutest expression ever.

Sydney laughed and followed Emily to the dance floor, where they moved to the rhythm of "Disco Duck." It felt good to jump around and work up a sweat. More than anything, though, it was great to see how happy Emily looked, laughing and cutting loose—something she probably didn't do nearly enough. After a few minutes, the tempo changed, and the Bee Gees' "How Deep Is Your Love" began. They both froze, feet firmly planted on the neon-flashing floor. Sydney was sure the apprehension in Emily's eyes mirrored her own. They glanced around at nearby couples, each in a tight embrace. Jiggling around to a crazy, fast song was one thing, but this was entirely different.

After a few uncomfortable moments, Emily cocked her head and looked at Sydney as though to ask "you wanna?" Sydney couldn't very well say no, so she nodded and stepped into Emily's arms. A sigh caught in her throat when Emily slipped a hand around her waist and tugged her closer. Ahh. That felt nice. Too nice. It'd been far too long since Sydney had slow-danced with a woman. In fact, had she ever? The women she'd gone out with weren't much for love songs. Sydney melted into a puddle of goo when Emily rested her head on her shoulder and lightly caressed the back of her neck. Imagine what it would feel like for those fingers to stroke other parts of her. With that thought, Sydney's legs almost gave way.

What was it about Emily that affected her so? Maybe it was the fact that she was unlike any other woman Sydney had ever dated, not that they were dating, of course. Sydney should just close her eyes and enjoy the moment. She'd probably never be this close to Emily again. As they swayed to the music, everything around them disappeared. It was as though they were the only two people in the room until someone grabbed Sydney from behind, awakening her from a lovely dream.

"What the..." Sydney turned, ready to tell some drunk chick to beat it. Instead, she stared into all-too-familiar eyes. "Monica? What the hell are you doing here?"

"I've been texting you all day." Monica's speech was slurred and she reeked of alcohol. She wobbled and looked back and forth between Emily and Sydney.

"Looks like someone got lucky." Monica attempted to punch Sydney on the arm but missed by several inches.

"You're drunk. Let's get you out of here." Sydney grabbed Monica's arm and peered sideways at Emily. "Sorry about this. We should probably go."

They exited and stood in the parking lot, Sydney supporting Monica so she didn't fall face-first.

"Why are we leaving?" Monica asked and hiccupped once. "Damn. I must've drunk too fast. That always gives me the hiccups."

"Try drank too much," Sydney said. "Where are you staying? We'll drive you."

Monica giggled. "With you, silly. You're in that big cabin all by yourself."

"Christ. You didn't get a hotel?"

Monica leaned close to Emily, swayed back and forth, and whispered, "Don't tell anyone, but Sydney broke into what's-her-name's cabin."

Emily took a step back and placed a finger under her nose, probably to escape the whiskey fumes.

Sydney looked at Emily and shook her head. "I'm so sorry about this. Can she just stay the night? She can crash in Jill's office, and I'll take the sofa."

"Of course," Emily said. "She's certainly in no shape to drive."

Sydney stuffed Monica into the back seat, glad they were in her car instead of Emily's in case she got sick.

"I'm really sorry," Sydney said and opened the passenger door for Emily. "I'll make sure she leaves tomorrow morning."

"It's okay. You don't have to keep apologizing."

Once they were on the road, Emily turned in her seat and faced Sydney. "Is she your girlfriend?"

Sydney shot Emily a quick glance. If she didn't know any better she'd swear she saw disappointment in Emily's eyes. A twinge of joy shot through Sydney at the prospect of Emily being jealous.

"Monica is my straight roommate."

Monica leaned across the seat and hugged Sydney's neck, practically choking her. "If anyone could get me to jump over the fence, it'd be Syd. Isn't that right, honey?"

Sydney pried Monica's arms off. "Why don't you sit back and relax?"

Monica turned her attention to Emily. "I've known Syd since she was seventeen."

"Really? Where'd you meet?"

"On the street corner of…where was that again?" Monica asked and hiccupped.

Sydney stepped on the accelerator. The sooner she got Monica away from Emily, the better, considering she was probably about to spill Sydney's life story.

"I taught her everything she knows about pole dancing," Monica said and collapsed back in the seat.

Good. Hopefully she'd pass out.

"Is that right?" Emily asked Sydney.

"Yes. Actually, she taught me a lot."

Monica held up a finger. "*And* I got her a job at…at"—*Don't say it. Don't say it*—"Leave It to Beaver," Monica said and hiccupped again.

Sydney's heart dropped to the ground, and she visualized running over it with the car, over and over again. She gripped the wheel tight and drove even faster. Out of the corner of her eye she could see Emily staring at her, but she didn't dare look.

They drove in silence, thankfully, until reaching the cabin. Sydney walked Monica up the stairs and tucked her into the sofa bed in Jill's office, certain they wouldn't be hearing from her anymore tonight. She went into the bathroom, put her PJs on, and glanced into the bedroom. Emily was nowhere in sight, which meant she was still downstairs. Maybe if Sydney was super quiet and slipped under the afghan on the sofa feigning sleep, she'd get away with not having to answer any questions.

No such luck. Emily was sitting on the sofa sipping something out of a mug.

"You can take the bed if you want to head up," Sydney said.

"I will in a minute. Why don't you have a seat?" Emily patted the place beside her.

Sydney faked a dramatic yawn and sat. "It's awfully late. We should get some sleep."

Emily placed her cup on the table and faced Sydney. "We're friends, right?"

"Of course."

"So why do I know hardly anything about your past?"

Here we go. Sydney couldn't very well race out of the cabin, although that's exactly what she wanted to do. "What do you want to know?"

"Why did you run away? Where did you go? How'd you support yourself? And what's...what was it called...Leave It to Beaver?"

Geez. No easing into the conversation. Emily got right to the point. Sydney should get this over with in one swift motion, like getting a bikini wax. It'd hurt like hell at first but better not to prolong the pain. She took a deep breath and let it out slowly.

"Probably no surprise from what I told you before, but my mom was verbally abusive, and the multitude of stepfathers parading in and out weren't much better. Being on my own was a more attractive option than staying under her roof. After I left, I lived on the streets for a while, doing whatever I could to survive. Everything *except* selling myself. I'd never do that. When I met Monica, she took me in, got me a job, and we've been roommates ever since. And just roommates. Nothing more. And...um...Leave It to Beaver is a...it's a strip club. I worked as a pole dancer there for five years."

"Why didn't you tell me any of that earlier?"

Sydney studied her clenched hands. "I didn't want you to think badly of me. You'd *really* think I was a stripper then." Sydney looked at Emily. "I never once took my clothes off or had sex with strangers."

Emily scooted closer and put her hand on Sydney's knee. "I believe you. Even if you had stripped, it wouldn't change my opinion of you. Who's to say what I would've done in the same situation? So then you quit the club and went to work at the Little Bird?"

"Not quite. I've had about six jobs the past two years. I have a talent for getting fired." Sydney smirked.

"It's because waitressing, or whatever else you did, isn't your passion. Why did you quit the pole-dancing job at the club?"

"It was demeaning. I hated the entire atmosphere of the place. I want a better life, a respectable life."

"I think I see a little more clearly why you're dead set on the PowerBar job. But like I said before, your self-worth doesn't come from the outside. I'm sure the Beverly Hills position isn't the only respectable pole-dancing gig out there."

"You don't think I'm going to get it, do you?"

"That's not what I'm saying. You're amazing. They'd be crazy not to hire you, but don't put all your hopes on this one position. Maybe something bigger and better is out there, something you haven't discovered yet."

"Maybe you should tell yourself the same thing."

Did I just say that out loud?

Emily raised an eyebrow. "What's that supposed to mean?"

"Nothing."

"Tell me. I want to know."

Sydney gazed into curious brown eyes. She wanted to tell Emily that maybe she should try to find someone more suited for her than Gretchen, someone who could make her happier, maybe even someone like Sydney. Instead, she pulled the afghan under her chin, let her head drop back, and closed her eyes.

"I'm exhausted," Sydney said. "Let's go to sleep."

CHAPTER FOURTEEN

The Love Hormone

Emily should have strategized about meeting Fran later that day, but instead she sat at the bar in the kitchen with her laptop and googled *oxytocin*. She knew a little about the love hormone from studying lovebirds, but she wanted to find out more for reasons she wasn't yet ready to admit.

She clicked on a link and read. "Oxytocin is a neurotransmitter… blah blah…that's boring." She wanted the juicy details, not the technical ones. Emily glanced at her cell phone when it rang. It was Gretchen. She paused, hit the reject button, and made a mental note to call her later. Gretchen would talk too long, and Emily wanted to review the website before Sydney woke up.

She scrolled down the page, stopped when she reached the interesting part, and silently read.

> *People who excite romantic feelings in us trigger an increase in oxytocin levels. It affects the body in a myriad of ways, such as shaky knees, flushed cheeks, racing heart, sharing intimate details, less need for sleep, and sexual arousal.*

That wasn't good. Emily had stayed awake half the night thinking about how much dancing with Sydney had affected her. It'd felt so good to be in her arms, touching in all the right places. She'd never been so turned on by a slow dance before, even with Gretchen. Emily placed her hands on her hot cheeks and felt light-headed. This was probably a heavy dose of guilt and not an overload of the love hormone. She focused back on the screen.

There is a strong correlation between oxytocin and the intensity of an orgasm.

Emily gasped. That hit close to home. She'd never had an orgasm with Gretchen. Emily had always blamed herself, but maybe she just wasn't romantically attracted to her. She vigorously shook her head. That was crazy talk. They were perfect together. Weren't they?

"Whatcha looking at?"

Emily slammed the computer lid shut when she heard Sydney's voice.

"Nothing." That didn't sound believable even to Emily's ears, but luckily Sydney didn't seem suspicious.

Sydney took a carton of orange juice out of the fridge, poured a glass, and sat opposite Emily. "So today's the day."

"For what?"

"Aren't you meeting Fran at noon?"

"Right." Emily waved her hand.

"You okay?" Sydney gazed at her curiously.

"I'm fine." Emily wasn't about to admit that her mind was still on orgasms.

"So what's your lovebird plan?"

Emily chewed on her bottom lip. She hadn't exactly been honest with Sydney about the lovebirds. It's the least she could do after Sydney had opened up about her past.

"I need to tell you something," Emily said. "I sorta lied a little about the lovebirds."

"Wait a second. You're not looking for figs *or* lovebirds?"

"No. I am. But it's"—Emily glanced around to make sure Sydney's drunk friend hadn't walked in—"Madagascar lovebirds."

Sydney stared, stone-faced. What did Emily expect? Sydney didn't know birds. This was going to take some explaining.

"The lovebirds on Fran's farm are extremely rare. They're found only on the island of Madagascar. There have been rumors for years about a flock in Southern California that escaped from an aviary, but no one has managed to photograph them. This is the bird story of the decade, and no one knows about it but me."

Sydney appeared more worried than impressed, rubbing her chin and staring off into space.

"It would save my magazine," Emily added.

"What do you mean?"

"It's in the red. I promised Gretchen and our parents that I'd shut it down and go back to the corporate world if I didn't get this story."

"Shit. This is big." Sydney's eyes widened, in a non-blinking, wild-woman sort of way.

"If it weren't for Owen, I wouldn't be in this place." Emily scowled.

"W-what did he do? I mean...who is that?" Sydney audibly gulped.

"Owen is a competitor. He stole a huge story off my desk and published it as his own. It would have been big enough to secure my magazine's future."

"Why would he do something so underhanded?"

Emily sighed dramatically and rolled her eyes. "He blames me for being deaf in one ear because of an accident that was totally his fault. I stopped at a crosswalk to let someone...you know, walk...and he rear-ended me. So hard that his airbag exploded, which—apparently—can cause hearing loss. He claims I stopped suddenly, but I didn't. If he hadn't been riding my bumper he never would have hit me."

All the color drained from Sydney's face, and she looked like she was about to barf. Before Emily could ask if she was okay, Monica stumbled in looking like hell.

"Please tell me you have a jar of pickle juice here." Monica pressed against her temples.

Emily scrunched her nose. "Pickle juice?"

Sydney nodded. "It's a surefire hangover cure. The salt in the juice replenishes electrolytes."

Sydney grabbed a jar out of the fridge, opened it, and handed it to Monica, who chugged it down. Emily's stomach soured. She couldn't imagine drinking sixteen ounces of pickle juice.

Monica slammed the jar onto the counter and eyed Emily suspiciously. "Who are you?"

"We met last night. I'm Emily."

Monica paused for a full five seconds before she grinned. "Oh, right. You were Sydney's dirty-dancing partner."

Emily's cheeks warmed. "What? No. There was nothing dirty about it. I'm engaged." Emily stuck her left hand out.

"Damn. You must have nabbed a rich one. But I'm sure she isn't nearly as sexy as Syd."

Emily's cheeks grew even hotter, so much so she was sure she looked like a radish. "Sydney is…well…she's certainly…jazzy."

Jazzy? I sound like a 1930s black-and-white flick.

Emily glanced at Sydney, who tilted her head and furrowed her brow.

"What I mean is, yes, of course she's sexy. Anyone can see that. But Gretchen is also—"

"Jazzy?" Monica stifled a giggle.

"All right. Stop teasing Emily." Sydney grabbed Monica's arm and tugged her toward the door. "Come on. I need to ask you something."

"Why can't you ask me in front of your girlfriend?"

Sydney shot Emily a quick glance. "Just come on," she said and pulled Monica through the swinging doors.

The great thing about saloon-style doors is that you can pretty much overhear what someone is saying when they're in the living room, especially when you place your ear in the opening over the door. Not that Emily was the nosy type, but she was curious as to what Sydney and Monica were chatting about in angry-sounding tones.

"I promise to pay you back," Sydney whispered.

"How are you gonna do that with no job?" Monica asked, not quite so whisper-like. "And what do you want the money for anyway? Two hundred and fifty dollars is a lot of dough."

Sydney needed money? She should have asked Emily. She'd have been more than happy to help. Her parents had more money than they knew what to do with.

"I owe a guy," Sydney said.

"Who?"

"Shh. Not so loud. Let's go outside."

Was Sydney in trouble? It sounded suspicious, but Emily was sure it wasn't anything shady. Sydney wasn't the druggie or gang type. More than anything, Emily wanted to wave a wand and make it all better. She couldn't bring up the subject of money, though, or else Sydney would know she'd been eavesdropping.

After a few minutes, Sydney popped her head into the kitchen. "I'm going to drive Monica to her car so she can head back to LA. When I get back we can leave for Bud's."

"You'd go with me?" Emily asked, touched by the gesture.

"Of course. Thanks to you, I passed the GED. It's the least I can do."

Emily couldn't stop smiling. Having Sydney as a friend felt nice. Really nice.

❖

Emily's pulse raced the closer she and Sydney got to Bud's Burrito 'n Bait Shop, which was where they'd meet Fran. Emily had been in Ojai a week, and she wasn't any closer to finding the lovebirds. The only good thing was that she was fairly certain no one else knew about them. Otherwise the press would be everywhere.

"If things get dicey, give her this." Sydney, who was sitting in the passenger seat, pulled the Conway Twitty cookbook out of her backpack.

Emily sighed. "It's going to take more than artery-clogging recipes to warm Fran up."

"Just try it," Sydney said, sounding annoyed.

"I'll see. I really do appreciate you helping me. If you ever need a favor, just ask."

Sydney sat upright in her seat. "Really? Even if it's a big one?"

"Yes," Emily said brightly. "No amount is too much. All you have to do is ask."

This was working out perfectly. Emily thought she'd have to skirt around the topic of money, but it sounded like Sydney was going to come right out with it.

"You mean you'd do *anything*?" Sydney asked.

"Absolutely. Just name it."

Sydney's eyes twinkled, and she rubbed her palms together. "This is awesome. I didn't think you'd accept. We'll start tomorrow."

"It's no problem...wait. What do you mean *start*?"

"The pole-dancing lessons."

"What?" Emily swerved, nearly running off the road. "I never—"

"You said anything."

"Hold on. I thought you were talking about something else."

"Like what?"

Emily paused and decided to ignore the question since she couldn't think of a lie fast enough. "You don't understand. I have no balance, I'm as graceful as an elephant, and I have no rhythm."

"Perfect!" Sydney beamed.

"How is that perfect? You want to see me fall on my ass, don't you?" Emily gawked at Sydney, at least as much as she could do so and still stay in her lane.

"You're just the type of woman I want to teach. Someone who has a gazillion reasons not to try."

"I think you're overlooking an important fact here. I never asked you for lessons."

"I need the practice. For the PowerBar audition, I have to demo how I'd teach a beginner to pole dance. You want me to do well, don't you?"

Emily pulled into the Bud's parking lot, turned off the engine, and faced Sydney. "We're not done talking about this, but I can only deal with one challenge at a time."

When they walked into the store, Fran was standing next to the counter chatting with Bud. They looked good together, and if Emily didn't know any better, she'd think Fran was flirting, the way she coyly smiled and batted her eyelashes. This setup might be easy after all.

The smile on Fran's face fell when she spotted Emily. "It's about time you showed up."

"Sorry that I'm," Emily looked at her watch, "one minute late. I'd like you to meet Sydney. She's a friend of mine."

Sydney held out her hand, pumped Fran's arm twice, and flashed a heart-stopping smile. She was certainly charismatic. Maybe it was a good thing Emily had brought her along.

"It's so nice to meet you," Sydney said. "And good to see you again, Bud."

Bud tipped his hat. "Howdy."

"When did you two meet?" Fran eyed Sydney suspiciously.

Emily's heart stopped, like literally stopped. The jig was up. They were going to get caught for breaking onto her land.

"Here. Bud's got the best burritos." Sydney patted her stomach.

That was easy. Sydney was a pretty good fibber, much quicker than Emily, anyway.

"How was your trip to Santa Paula?" Emily asked cheerfully.

"Dreadful. Ain't nobody wantin' to buy figs no more. And now those dang birds are eating my crop. How do I git rid of 'em?" Fran rested her fists on her hips and faced Emily head-on.

"Well, I know several things you can do, but I can't really recommend anything until I see the lovebirds firsthand."

Fran grunted and immediately turned to Bud. "What's the number for the California Wildlife Association? They could help me."

"No!" Emily said much too forcefully, which scored her a murderous look from Fran.

"Wait a second," Sydney said. "We forgot to give Fran her gift."

Emily rolled her eyes. That freaking cookbook again?

Sydney focused on Fran and displayed a smile even more stunning than before. "We heard from a little bird, no pun intended, that you like a certain country-western singer."

Fran's head jerked to Bud, and she glared at him hard, enough to make him lower his eyes and look like he wanted to dive into the bait tank.

"What's this about?" Fran squinted at Sydney.

"We came across something in Santa Barbara we thought you might like." Sydney reached into her backpack, whisked out the *What's Cooking At Twitty City* cookbook, and held it two inches from Fran's nose.

The varied emotions that crossed Fran's face amazed Emily. She went from pissed to confused to shocked to elated in a matter of five seconds. She snatched the book out of Sydney's hands and looked like she might actually kiss the photo of Conway Twitty on the cover.

"This…how…what…who…" Fran was actually kinda pretty with her face lit up and incoherently babbling. Emily liked this Fran much better than the scary one.

"I'm glad you like it." Sydney shot Emily an I-told-you-so glance.

"I've been searching high and low for this for decades. It went out of print years ago. It's the only memorabilia I don't have." Fran gazed with such wonder and innocence that Emily actually had an urge to hug her.

"Bud, look." Fran showcased the book like a game-show host presenting a new car.

"Would you look at that." Bud whistled through his teeth. "Maybe you could wrangle me up something. I haven't had a home-cooked Southern meal since my mama died."

"That's a great idea," Sydney said. "In fact, why don't we make dinner for all of us?"

We? Was Sydney talking about Emily? Hopefully not, considering all she knew how to make were Pop-Tarts.

"We could come over, if that's okay, of course, and prepare a feast for both of you." Sydney nudged Emily with her elbow.

"Oh. Yes. That's a great idea," Emily said, finally getting the message.

This was perfect. She could gain access to Fran's farm and set Bud up on a date. It'd be a double date, but that was still technically a date.

"At my place?" A dark shadow crossed Fran's eyes, and she frowned. She looked like she wanted to run out the door.

"We could get to know each other better, and I can give you some tips on how to deal with the lovebirds," Emily said, hoping that would sweeten the offer.

"Come on, Frances." Bud poked her on the arm. "These nice girls are offering to cook for us. You can trust them. What happened was three years ago. Ain't it about time you got past that?"

Emily and Sydney exchanged curious glances. What had happened?

Fran's eyes darted around until they landed on the cookbook. "Well, I suppose it wouldn't hurt nothing. And I never was much good at cookin'."

"Great," Sydney said. "We'll buy all the ingredients and make whatever you want." Sydney reached for the cookbook, but Fran pulled it away. Apparently, she was the only one allowed to touch it.

Fran flipped through the pages, stopped in the middle, and pointed. "Could you make this?"

Emily leaned over and read the title. "Chicken-fried steak and hush puppies? No problem." Emily silently prayed Sydney knew how to create such a dish.

Sydney pulled out her cell phone. "I'll take a photo of the recipe so we'll know what to buy."

"Does tonight work?" Emily asked. Everyone nodded. "Perfect. How about we come over at six and eat by seven thirty?"

Emily grabbed Sydney's arm and pulled her toward the door before Fran could change her mind. "We better get going. See you tonight."

"Hold up, little lady," Fran yelled. Emily stopped and reluctantly turned around. She'd almost made a clean break for it. "Don't you need directions to my place?"

"Oh, yeah." Emily nervously chuckled.

Fran scribbled something on a notepad by the register and handed it to Emily. Nodding thoughtfully, Emily pretended to study the address.

"Thanks." Emily waved the paper in the air and practically ran out of the store.

It wasn't until they were in the car that they burst out laughing.

"Oh my God. You were so awesome," Emily said and gazed at her co-conspirator. She felt lighter and happier than she had in a long time. She wouldn't have traded the past week with Sydney for anything.

"I told you the cookbook would get big points."

"You were right. We make a pretty good team. After we leave Ojai I don't want this," Emily motioned between them, "to end."

"Really?" Sydney's blue eyes lightened several shades.

"Of course. We're friends. I'd miss our adventures."

I'd miss you.

"Your wife won't mind?"

Wife? Oh, right. She was getting married in a few months.

"Gretchen is reasonable. She'll understand."

"So understandable that you haven't told her we're rooming together?"

"She'll be okay after I explain everything." Emily wasn't sure if she was trying to convince herself or Sydney. "Mark October fifteenth in your calendar 'cause you'll most certainly be invited to the wedding."

"Uh. I'll pass. Thanks." Sydney motioned toward the keys dangling from the ignition. "We should probably get going. We have grocery shopping to do."

"Why wouldn't you want to come to my wedding?"

Sydney shrugged. "It's just not my thing."

Emily started the car, put it in reverse, and backed out. "You'll be missing out on a fancy affair. Lord knows our parents have probably moved the location to Buckingham Palace by now."

Driving back to the cabin, Emily secretly felt relieved that Sydney wouldn't be attending the nuptials. Something didn't feel right about standing at the altar with Gretchen reciting vows while knowing that Sydney was in the audience.

CHAPTER FIFTEEN

Farm Feast

Once Emily excused herself to shower, Sydney went downstairs to text Owen. She hated borrowing money from Monica, but no way in hell would she keep the two hundred and fifty dollars after what Emily had said. Sydney wouldn't be satisfied until the money was in his hot little hand. Then maybe the hard, painful lump in her stomach could dissipate. If she'd known how important the bird story was and how hateful Owen had been, she never would have agreed to his slimy deal.

A true friend would come clean and admit everything, but Sydney didn't want to risk losing Emily. It was strange how the bird-watcher had wiggled her way into Sydney's heart in such a short time. That had never happened before. But then again, Sydney had never met anyone like Emily.

Sydney propped her feet on the coffee table, grabbed her phone, and typed.

Deal is off. I'm not spying anymore. What's your address and I'll mail your money back.

Hopefully, Owen would respond soon. Then Sydney could help Emily find the Madagascar lovebirds with a clear, almost, conscience. Within seconds, her phone rang. It was Owen. This wasn't going to be pleasant.

"Did you get my text?" Sydney asked into the receiver.

"What the hell is this about? We made a deal."

"I'm done. What's your address?"

"No way. You promised to tell me why Emily is in Ojai, and don't give me another fake lovebird story."

"Look. Get it through your thick skull that I'm not helping you anymore. If you won't give me your address, I'll find out the name of your magazine from Emily and mail it to you."

"So you told her about our deal, did you?"

That was a loaded question. If Sydney said no then Owen would snitch to Emily, but if she said yes that would be yet another lie to add to the already high stack of them.

"Of course." Sydney glanced at the stairs to make sure Emily wasn't coming down.

"You bitc—"

"I'll mail you a check."

Sydney disconnected and googled bird magazines in Southern California. Since there weren't many to choose from, it didn't take long to locate Owen's publication. She'd mail him a check first thing tomorrow morning. This should fix everything, sorta. Regretfully, she'd told Owen about the lovebirds, but luckily she hadn't known they were rare Madagascar ones, and he hadn't believed her anyway. So she had no reason to feel guilty about spying…except that she did.

Sydney obviously knew her way around the kitchen, even one she'd never been in before. She moved at warp speed—mixing, chopping, and frying things Emily had never seen before.

"What exactly are hush puppies anyway?" Emily peered into clumps of something or another sizzling in a pan of hot oil.

"Deep-fried cornbread. Haven't you ever had them?" Sydney glanced at Emily and resumed plopping more balls into a deep fryer.

Emily chuckled. "Are you kidding? My mom was the food police. *Fried* wasn't in her vocabulary."

"What did she cook?"

"Anything that didn't have gluten, dairy, eggs, sugar, or corn in it."

"Wow. No wonder you snuck candy bars."

Emily looked through the kitchen window and spied Fran and Bud sitting in a porch swing. They looked like two teenagers, giggling and flirting.

"I think Fran has a thing for the bait-and-burrito king," Emily said. "I wonder why she turned down his date offers? And what did Bud mean when he said Fran should let go of what happened three years ago?"

"Beats me." Sydney stopped what she was doing and studied the couple. "They do look giddy. Bud might even get kissed if he takes that toothpick out of his mouth for even half a second. Were your parents ever that happy?"

Emily snorted. "Heck, no." When she got a weird look from Sydney, she added, "They weren't the lovey-dovey type. When I was growing up, I rarely saw them hold hands or be affectionate." Emily stared into space and visualized her parents. "Now that I think about it, they weren't that close. But I'm sure they love each other. I guess."

"Hmm. What about you and what's-her-name?" Sydney wrinkled her nose and looked like she'd just bitten into a sour grape.

Sydney very well knew Gretchen's name. Was she jealous? No. She was probably still miffed that Gretchen got her fired.

"She isn't the demonstrative type," Emily said. "But I know how she feels."

Sydney placed breaded steaks into a pan. Emily almost laughed aloud, thinking of the conniption fit her mother would throw if she could see what Emily was about to devour.

"What about you? Are you the affectionate type?" Emily asked, surprised by how curious she was to know the answer.

"Sure." Sydney stuck a fork in one of the steaks and turned it over.

"*Really?*" Emily hadn't meant to sound so surprised. "I mean, considering your anti-relationship stance, I didn't think you would be."

"Granted, most of the women I've dated weren't into cuddling, but if I was with someone special it'd be different." Sydney looked directly at Emily. "Soft kisses in the park, holding hands in the grocery store, slow dancing…"

Emily's body hummed with the recollection of Sydney's strong arms around her as they swayed to the music. She grabbed the edge of the counter, light-headed just thinking about how close they'd been. Was it getting hot in here? Emily resisted the urge to fan herself with a spatula.

"I'm going to set the table," Emily said and headed into the dining room, glad to put some space between them. What was wrong with her? She was engaged. Fantasizing about dancing intimately with another woman wasn't allowed.

Emily put thoughts of Sydney out of her mind and arranged the table setting. After she did that, she stepped into the living room and glanced around. No question that Fran was a Conway Twitty fan with numerous posters, albums, and a glass case with concert memorabilia. Emily grinned when she saw the cookbook safely stored in a plastic bag perched in the center of the case. Sydney had been right about that gift after all.

Emily approached the record player and selected an album, studying the cover.

"That's my favorite one."

Emily spun around when she heard Fran's voice.

"I didn't mean to be intrusive," Emily said, afraid she'd been caught snooping.

"Put it on," Fran said and sat in a recliner. When the music started, she closed her eyes and rested her head back. After a few minutes, she spoke. "My husband used to sing that to me."

Fran had been married? That was surprising. Emily sat on the edge of the sofa, not sure how to respond. She didn't have a husband now, so obviously something had happened to him, either divorce or maybe worse.

Fran opened bloodshot, moist eyes and looked at Emily. "That was a long time ago. He's no longer with us."

"I'm so sorry." Emily reached out and lightly squeezed Fran's hand. "What happened?"

"Farming accident. Three years ago."

That must have been what Bud was talking about before. But that didn't explain all the no-trespassing signs. Why did Fran distrust people so much?

"Did something else happen?" Emily gripped the armrest, hoping she wasn't overstepping her boundaries. When Fran gave her a quizzical look, she added, "If you don't mind me asking, why don't you allow anyone on your farm?"

Fran glared, non-blinking, for a full minute, like they were having a staring contest. Normally, Emily would have backed down and rambled to fill the silence, but she was too curious as to Fran's answer.

Finally, Fran said, "Carl, my husband, had kids from another marriage. They didn't approve of me, and when he died they wanted to take over the farm. After the law sided with me, they were none too happy, so they broke onto the land and vandalized the place several times. Once, they even almost burned it down."

"Oh my gosh." Emily put a hand over her heart. "That's terrible. Did you have them arrested?"

"I couldn't. Carl loved them kids. I warned that if they ever stepped foot on my property again I wouldn't think twice about having 'em thrown in jail."

Who knew Fran had a soft spot? Most people would have immediately pressed charges.

"So that's when you put up the signs?"

Fran nodded. "I know what people think about me. I'm not a cantankerous old woman. I'm just protecting my property. It's all I have."

"I understand. It's the way I feel about my bird magazine. It's everything to me, and I'd do anything to save it, which is why—"

"Dinner's ready!" Sydney called from the dining room.

Emily groaned. Talk about bad timing. She was about to bring up the subject of the lovebirds.

When they got into the dining room, Sydney was poking Bud in the ribs and signaling for him to pull Fran's chair out. Finally, he got the message and jumped into action.

"Why, thank you kindly, Bud." Fran sat.

"Everything looks mighty fine," Bud said and scanned the table.

"Help yourself." Sydney handed Bud a platter of chicken-fried steak and motioned for him to pass it around the table.

They ate in silence for several minutes. Emily was surprised everything tasted so good. She'd probably have indigestion tonight, but it'd be worth it.

"How long you two been dating?" Fran asked and took a swig of beer.

Emily and Sydney looked at each other for a split second before vigorously shaking their heads.

"We're not a couple," Emily said. "I have a fiancée. Gretchen. Why would you think we're together?"

Fran stuffed a hush puppy into her mouth and chewed. "Well," she said through a mouthful. "The way you two look at each other reminds me of the way I looked at my Carl."

Emily's cheeks heated. "We don't look at each other any particular way. I'm marrying Gretchen."

"So you said." Fran cut a piece of steak.

"Sydney and I are just friends." Emily looked at Sydney, struck by what looked like sadness brewing in her eyes. Emily pried her gaze away and focused on Fran. "I'm getting married in a few months."

Sydney rolled her head back and groaned. "We heard you the first time."

Why was Sydney snippy all of a sudden? This conversation was getting way off track.

Emily put her fork down and looked directly at Fran. "Could we talk about the lovebirds, please? The best way I can help is by seeing them myself."

Fran pursed her lips and shook her head. "I dunno..."

"I won't know what solutions to suggest without doing so. I can come over tomorrow, if that's convenient." Emily crossed her fingers under the table, praying Fran would agree.

Fran took a sip of beer and looked at Bud, who nodded his approval. Emily made a mental note to thank him later.

"Well," Fran said and paused for what seemed like an eternity. "I guess it couldn't hurt."

Emily wanted to sing and dance and squeal all at the same time. After a week of waiting, she'd finally know for sure if these were the Madagascar lovebirds.

CHAPTER SIXTEEN

Pole 101

Fran took her straw hat off and scratched her head. "They were right here. See all those half-eaten figs on the ground?" She kicked several pieces of fruit.

"Are you sure it was this tree?" Emily raised the binoculars hanging around her neck and peered through the lens.

"Positive. Maybe they moved on to another one since they got their fill here." Fran looked down a row of fig trees at least a mile long.

Emily lowered the binoculars and sighed. "That's possible."

"I gotta get back to the house." Fran looked at her watch.

"Do you care if I keep looking?"

Fran narrowed her eyes. "You ain't gonna steal any of my figs, are you?"

"Never. I promise." Emily held up two fingers.

"Hmm. All right. Don't get lost out here."

Emily scanned the area. "Can I come back tomorrow, too?" When Fran scowled, Emily quickly added, "To take photos. Or keep looking if I don't find them."

"Well...I gotta go to Santa Paula for the day...but I guess I can trust you." Fran dug into the pocket of her overalls and thrust a key at Emily. "This opens the front gate. Now if anything goes wrong, I'm holding you personally responsible."

Emily smiled. "Thanks, Fran. I swear I'm only here for the lovebirds."

Fran turned to leave and stopped when Emily called out to her.

"How many trees do you have anyway?"

Fran yelled over her shoulder. "Eighty-three."

Emily never should have asked. How was she supposed to find miniscule birds in all that? And to make matters worse, lovebirds are cavity dwellers. They construct their homes in tree holes. Emily would never spot them unless they were flying around. Luckily, Madagascar lovebirds have extra-large wings in relation to their bodies, so they'd be easy to see when mobile.

Emily trekked down a gravel path while peering through binoculars and listening for bird calls. This was going to take forever, since she had to investigate each tree thoroughly before moving on. After traipsing up and down rows for at least two hours, she stopped and wiped sweat from her forehead. She should have brought water but didn't think it'd be this difficult. Fran was supposed to lead her right to the lovebirds. This whole Ojai excursion hadn't turned out the way Emily had thought it would. She'd already been there over a week and no story yet. Emily gazed up at the sky, streaked with reds and purples. The sun was setting, and her feet were killing her. Plus, she was dying of thirst. Feeling dejected, she headed back to the house.

Fran was standing on her porch leaning on the railing. "From the look on your face I'd say you didn't have much luck."

"You could say that." Emily sighed.

"You sure you wanna come back tomorrow? I can call you if I see them again. Maybe they moved on to someone else's farm."

Emily's stomach knotted. That would be the worst scenario possible. No. They were still here. She could feel it. She'd find those little buggers even if she had to search for a month.

❖

When Emily got back to the cabin, Sydney was sitting in the kitchen eating.

"Hey, how'd it go?"

Emily ignored the question, grabbed a bottle of water, and chugged it down without stopping. She slammed the empty bottle down on the bar and drank another full one, wiping her mouth on her sleeve when she was done. Yes, she was thirsty, but all that liquid was more about trying to wash down the lump in her throat. Her emotions were so close to the surface she could easily burst into tears at any moment. That was the last thing she wanted to do in front of Sydney, though, so she swung in the opposite direction and got really angry.

"You wanna know how it went? I'll tell you. I spent all afternoon looking for twenty tiny birds in a buttload of fig trees in the ninety-degree heat. I covered maybe five percent of the land and found absolutely nothing." Emily yelled so loud that even she wanted to cover her ears to muffle the sound.

Sydney stopped chewing mid-bite and stared.

"And to top it all off, what Fran said is probably true. The lovebirds most likely migrated to another crop and aren't even on her farm anymore. I'm never gonna find them. I'll have to go home, close down my magazine, which is the one thing I love in this world, and get a job I hate." Emily paused for three full seconds and then burst into tears—wailing, ugly tears. So much for not crying in front of Sydney.

Sydney dropped her fork and stood, looking frightened and unsure what to do. Finally, she wrapped her arms around Emily and patted her back.

"I'm sorry," Emily said with a sob. "I'm getting you all wet."

Emily tried to pull away, but Sydney held her even tighter. After a few minutes, she released her hold.

"Look at me." Sydney lifted Emily's chin.

"No. I look horrible."

Sydney grinned. "That's not even possible."

No matter what Sydney said, she must look like a sad, dripping poodle. Normally, Emily didn't care what other people thought, but for some reason she wanted to look attractive around Sydney. Would it be suspicious if she slipped away to wash her face, apply a little makeup, and then resume their discussion?

Sydney's smile dropped and she looked suddenly serious, fire blazing in her eyes. "I promise we'll find the lovebirds. If they're not at Fran's, then we'll track them down wherever they are. I won't let you lose your magazine."

Emily cried even harder, but for a different reason this time. Everyone in her life wanted her to shut down *The Tweet*. Most days she felt like a one-woman army, but now she had someone on her side, someone strong and self-assured, someone who wanted her success.

"Thanks." Emily wiped her eyes and attempted to compose herself.

"I won't give up. But the longer it takes, the more chance someone has to find out about the lovebirds. I have to publish the story before Owen or anyone else does."

"Why worry about something that hasn't even happened?"

"I suppose." Emily sniffed again.

"Will Fran let you keep looking for the birds?"

Emily nodded.

"Good. We'll go tomorrow. I'll be your birding assistant. Just as long as I don't have to wear a funny hat and anything khaki. I don't look good in tan." Sydney displayed a lopsided grin, probably trying to lighten the mood so Emily didn't open the floodgates again.

"What about your audition?"

"It's not until Sunday. I still have time to practice."

"Oh. Right. I'm supposed to help you."

The last thing Emily wanted was a pole-dancing lesson, but Sydney needed her assistance, and she wasn't about to let her down.

Emily looked at her phone when it rang. "It's Gretchen. I haven't talked to her in days. I need to take this."

When Sydney backed away, Emily tugged her arm. "You don't have to leave. Finish your dinner."

Sydney sat at the bar and resumed eating. Emily wiped her eyes, which was pointless since Gretchen couldn't see her over the phone, and cleared her throat.

"Hey, Gretchen," Emily said, trying to sound peppy.

"Why haven't you been taking my calls? What's wrong? You sound like you have a cold."

"It's just allergies. Lots of sagebrush here." Emily looked at Sydney and shrugged.

"How's it going? Did you get on that woman's farm?"

"Yes."

"Well? Did you find the birds?"

"No."

"So you're coming home?"

"I need to keep looking. They're here somewhere. They couldn't have gone far."

Silence.

"Gretchen? You still there?"

"You don't want to get married, do you?"

"Of course I want to get married." Emily gazed at Sydney. "I'll be back as soon as I can."

More silence.

Finally, Gretchen said, "I found a buyer."

"For what?" Emily wasn't selling anything.

"For *The Tweet*. I wasn't looking, but an interested party just landed in my lap."

Emily felt like someone had reached inside her chest and squeezed her heart. Not for a moment did she believe that Gretchen didn't seek someone out. She'd been trying to get Emily to sell the magazine since she started it.

"It's a backup plan if you don't find the lovebirds," Gretchen said. "We need to think about our future. After we get married we'll want to buy a house. We talked about something in Beverly Hills, and we can't do that on your current salary."

All the blood in Emily's body rushed to her head. Normally, she'd agree, but for some reason this conversation had her fuming.

"For your information, I'd rather be happy doing something I love, even if it doesn't make a lot of money, than be stuck at a job I hate. You've never supported my dream. From day one you've been against this, and I was foolish enough to allow you and our parents to make me agree to a two-year time limit on something I love."

"Whoa. Where's this coming from?"

"Look. I'm sorry if I'm coming on strong, but it's how I feel. I think we should have a serious talk about our future when I get back. Let's not do this over the phone."

"Fine. I'd rather not talk to you when you're being unreasonable anyway. Good-bye."

Emily couldn't blame Gretchen for being angry. She was the one changing the rules. They'd agreed on what their life together would look like and the fate of *The Tweet* years ago, but for some reason none of that sat well with Emily anymore.

"Wow," Sydney said. "I'm proud of you. What brought that on?"

"I'm not sure. I guess a combination of Gretchen finding a buyer for my magazine and…you."

"*Me?* What did I do?"

"You don't put up with shit. You're going after your dream job, and you won't let anything stand in your way. You'd never allow anyone to plan your future for you. My parents have been doing that my entire life. I never even wanted to go to college and major in business. Christ, I'm even engaged to the woman they set me up with. It's high time I live by my own rules."

Sydney jumped off the stool and looked like she was about to hug Emily but instead gave her a high-five. "That's what I'm talking about! Does this mean you're not getting married?"

"What? No. Of course I'm marrying Gretchen. We're…it's all set." Emily was going to say they were perfect for each other, but for some reason the words stuck in her throat.

"Right." Sydney's shoulders slumped.

"That doesn't mean I'm not going to stand up for what I want. And you know what I want to do right now? I want a God-damn pole-dancing lesson from the best fucking instructor in the state."

Sydney looked shocked. "Really?"

Emily resolutely nodded. They locked arms, then marched into the living room and up the stairs.

"So you curse now?" Sydney asked, peering out of the corner of her eye.

"Damn right," Emily said, feeling like she could conquer the world.

❖

By the time Emily changed and walked down the hall toward the bedroom, her confidence had waned about 80 percent. More than anything, she didn't want to embarrass herself in front of Sydney or show how terribly out of shape she was. Not that Emily was trying to impress Sydney…well, okay, maybe she was.

Emily rounded the corner and suddenly stopped in the doorway, like she'd just bumped into an invisible wall. Sydney looked amazing. Emily had seen her scantily dressed before, but this outfit was even more enticing. She wore high-rising purple and black Lycra shorts that displayed smooth, round hips flowing into incredibly toned legs and a matching bikini top, which showed much more than Emily should be gawking at. Luckily, Sydney was busy adjusting bolts on the pole, unaware that Emily was drooling. She needed to get her act together. Friends weren't supposed to slobber over each other.

Sydney glanced toward the door and did a double take. She stood upright and scanned Emily up and down, obviously suppressing laughter.

"What?" Emily looked at her perfectly acceptable outfit of gray sweatpants and matching long-sleeve shirt. What was the problem? Everyone knew sweats were for working out.

"What's with the outfit?" Sydney bit her lower lip.

"This is what I exercise in." Emily raised her chin and pranced into the room.

Sydney chuckled. "Maybe if you're doing chair aerobics in an old folks' home."

Emily's face heated. She wasn't sure if it was from Sydney's comment or the fact that fleece was awfully hot.

"That will not work for pole dancing," Sydney said resolutely.

"Well, I'm not wearing that!" Emily pointed at Sydney.

Sydney took several steps forward, which were several steps too close considering she was practically naked. Just the thought of Sydney being naked made Emily even hotter.

"You need skin contact with the pole to safely do moves," Sydney said, her tone surprisingly soft. "I know being so exposed is a vulnerable feeling, but that's the essence of pole dancing. It's about letting go, trusting yourself, and taking ownership of your body."

"That's an area I've never particularly felt confident in."

"I know, but maybe it's time to change that."

Sweat dripped down Emily's back, and she stared into deep-blue eyes. Maybe Sydney knew what she was talking about. As scary as it was, perhaps Emily needed to let go for a change and get in touch with her physical side.

"Okay. I'll give it a go. Plus, I'm sweating like a pig in this thing." Emily tugged at her shirt and fanned herself.

"Great." Sydney opened a drawer, grabbed something, and tossed it at Emily. "Wear these booty shorts."

Emily held up the material with two fingers. She'd had shorts bigger than that when she was seven. "Booty shorts? Let me guess how they got their name."

Sydney ignored Emily's scowl and said, "Do you have a sports bra under that sweater?"

"It's a sweatshirt, not a sweater." Emily peeked down her shirt. "Yeah, but you're not suggesting…"

Sydney tilted her head. "I thought you said you'd give this a real try."

"You're right. But you can't think we're the same size." Emily eyed the shorts.

Sydney sighed, looking irritated. "You talk like you're fifty pounds bigger than you really are."

"What's that supposed to mean?"

"It means you lost weight years ago, but you still have an overweight mentality. You're the perfect size and shape, Emily. Now yell when you're done changing. I'll be right outside." Sydney walked out and closed the door.

While Emily stripped, she wondered what she'd gotten herself into. She wanted to help Sydney practice for her audition, but this was way out of her comfort zone. She stuck both legs into the shorts and struggled to shimmy them up and over her hips. They were snug, but surprisingly they fit. She stood in front of a full-length mirror and attempted to pull the hem of the shorts down, but they didn't budge. She turned sideways and examined her backside. Yep. Those were definitely booty shorts, considering her rear end was hanging out.

"You done yet?" Sydney yelled through the door.

"I suppose. You can come in."

When Sydney opened the door, her eyes opened wide. "Wow. You look hot. Those shorts fit you perfectly."

Seriously? Emily had never looked hot before in her life. The compliment seemed sincere, though, so she checked herself out in the mirror again. Even though she was showing almost as much skin as a newborn, she actually didn't look half-bad. Maybe Sydney was right after all and Emily wasn't the size of a small cottage.

"So you ready?" Sydney was much too peppy considering what they were about to do.

"Let's get this over with." When Sydney shot Emily a stern look, she added, "I mean, let's have fun!" and forced a fake smile.

"You might want to take that gargantuan thing off first before you poke your eye out." Sydney pointed at Emily's engagement ring.

Deciding Sydney was probably right, Emily slipped it off. She flexed her finger, enjoying the freedom of movement. In fact, her entire hand felt lighter. She hadn't realized how much the ring had been weighing her down. Emily glanced around, looking for a safe place to store it. She opened a drawer and placed it on top of some shirts, making a mental note not to forget it.

After they stretched, Sydney plugged her cell phone into speakers and fiddled with it until sexy, stripper-sounding music started. Was that supposed to get Emily in the mood? It did nothing but make her feel even more intimidated.

"We're going to start with a few simple moves," Sydney said and grabbed the pole above her head. "First, I'll teach you how to walk."

At least she was starting with something easy. Emily already knew how to do that. She watched as Sydney pranced around several times. Looked easy enough, but no way would Emily be nearly that graceful and fluid.

"Now, your turn. Hold the pole above your head."

Emily did as instructed. "Like this?"

"Perfect. Lean to the side so there's about an inch between you and the bar and keep your feet close to the base."

Emily walked around once and looked at Sydney.

"Good, but relax," Sydney said. "Don't be so stiff. Shake your body out." Emily shimmed her shoulders. "Your entire body."

Emily let go of the bar and gave it all she had, rattling every muscle and bone. Surprisingly, she did feel more relaxed and even had a little attitude in her strut this time.

"Excellent. Let's try a balance trick."

Sydney did a fancy move that ended in her whirling around the pole. Surely she wasn't suggesting Emily try that.

"That's a *beginner* move?" Emily asked, taking a step back.

"It's not as hard as it looks. I'll talk you through it."

Skeptical, Emily stepped up to the pole and held it with her right hand. "What'd you do with your leg?"

"Wrap the back of it around the pole and grab the bar with both hands."

Emily did so, feeling like she was about to tip over.

"Now push off with the leg that's on the floor and lift it up as you spin around the bar."

"So both legs are off the ground? You're kidding me, right?" Emily glared at Sydney.

"All I'm asking is that you try. It doesn't have to be perfect."

"Trust me. It won't be." Emily attempted to whirl around but ended up in a tangled heap on the floor.

"Good try," Sydney said and helped Emily to her feet.

"Now you're humoring me. That sucked."

Sydney rubbed her forehead. "You're so hard on yourself. When I was first learning, I ended up on the floor more often than not. You can't expect to be an expert the first time. Try again."

Emily attempted another turn and landed in an ungraceful thud. The next five tries weren't much better. She stood and rubbed a sore spot on her thigh. She'd have bruises tomorrow for sure.

"You're doing great," Sydney said. "But don't stop mid-turn. You're holding yourself back."

"I'm afraid of falling."

Sydney grinned. "You're already doing that, so why not let go and trust yourself this time?"

Emily took a deep breath and slowly let it out.

Let go and trust.

With a renewed determination, she got into position, pushed off, and did a perfect turn around the bar. It took them both several seconds to realize what had just happened.

"You did it!" Sydney clapped her hands and hugged Emily fiercely.

Emily was so happy she couldn't stop giggling. She'd never felt so proud of herself. So many times she'd wanted to give up and storm out of the bedroom, but she'd stuck with it and had done something she'd never thought possible.

Sydney held Emily at arm's length and looked into her eyes. "You're amazing. It took me twice as long to learn that move."

"It's all thanks to you," Emily said, smiling widely. "What you said about letting go really hit home."

Emily leaned forward and kissed Sydney's cheek, which seemed to surprise them both. As they gazed into each other's eyes, the space between them sizzled like bacon in hot grease. Emily wasn't sure who made the first move, but before she knew it they were kissing. And not a peck on the cheek either. An all-out, full-on, lips-to-lips smooch, one that made Emily's stomach drop and her skin tingle. Who'd have thought Sydney's lips would be so soft and taste like banana cream pie? It was probably her ChapStick, but that didn't deter Emily from wanting to devour her delicious mouth. And devour she did as she melted into silky, moist lips. Somewhere in the middle of it all, Emily felt weightless, like she could levitate off the ground. Sydney was the perfect kisser, just the right amount of everything. Sydney wrapped an arm around Emily's waist and pulled her closer, their bare skin pressed together.

Wait. Emily was feeling Sydney's toned stomach? That wasn't supposed to happen. Suddenly, she was aware that they were nearly naked and stuck together like Siamese twins. Reluctantly, Emily pried her lips away. She shook her fuzzy head and stared into eyes filled with longing. Sydney wanted her. Who knew she'd be just as turned on as Emily had been? They were so close Emily could feel the warmth of Sydney's jagged breath caress her cheek. She took a giant step backward, afraid she'd be tempted to go in for seconds.

"Oh my God. I'm so sorry." Sydney looked like she was about to reach out but then hid her hands behind her back.

"No. It was my fault." Emily cringed at the sound of her voice, hoarse with desire. "I started it with that cheek…thing." Emily couldn't bring herself to utter the word *kiss*, as though saying it out loud would make it too real.

They held each other's gaze until Emily looked at the rug, the curtains, anywhere but Sydney's mouth. She needed to get out of there…and fast, considering every cell in her body wanted to lay Sydney down on the bed and do a lot more than just kiss.

"It's late." Emily snatched her sweats and held them in front of her bare legs. "You can take the bed tonight. I'll sleep on the sofa." She darted toward the door.

"Emily."

Emily stopped but didn't turn around, her back to Sydney.

After a long pause, Sydney whispered, "Good night."

Emily rushed down the hall and into the bathroom. What the hell was she doing kissing Sydney? And even worse than that, how could she enjoy it so much? It was wrong on so many levels, yet it had felt so freaking incredible and so right. Emily lightly traced her lips with her fingertips, still feeling the sensation of Sydney's mouth sliding against hers. She'd never been so affected by a kiss before, not even with Gretchen. Oh, God. Gretchen. Emily covered her face. She'd be devastated if she found out about this. She didn't even know Sydney was staying in the same cabin with her. Emily was a sorry excuse for a fiancée.

Emily peeled off the incredibly short shorts and unhooked her bra. Before putting her sweats on, she caught her reflection in the mirror. She rarely looked at herself nude, mostly because she didn't think it was an attractive sight. Her breasts were too small, hips too wide, and her thighs were the size of Sequoia tree trunks. For the first time in forever she observed herself objectively, with her heart and not her mind. What Sydney had said was true. Emily had an "overweight mentality." In reality, she looked quite beautiful. She ran a fingertip over her breast, down her stomach, and in between her legs, feeling moistness.

How could one single, probably thirty-second kiss make her so wet? Normally, she'd have to partake in a heavy make-out session for that to happen. Not wanting to ruminate about what had happened any longer, Emily jerked on her sweats and headed downstairs, hoping a good night's sleep would fix everything.

Sweat trickled down Sydney's forehead and stung the corners of her eyes. She'd been running in the streets of Ojai in the dark for almost an hour. She'd had to get away from the cabin, the bedroom, Emily. What was it about that woman that made her do such stupid things, like kiss an engaged woman?

God. That kiss.

It'd made Sydney's heart beat faster than it was right now, and she'd barely been able to stand upright, sure that her weak knees would give way at any moment. She'd kissed her fair share of women but never felt anything even close to what she had with Emily. It'd been the perfect mixture of tenderness and passion. When Emily had pulled away, Sydney had resisted the urge to kiss her again, afraid that if she did, she wouldn't be able to stop.

The kiss was bad enough, but Sydney was also getting much too attached to the bird-watcher, considering she looked forward to seeing Emily's beautiful face every morning. In fact, she'd become the brightest spot in Sydney's days, like a sparkling star in the night sky. She felt closer to Emily than anyone, especially after sharing intimate details about her life. And since when did Sydney give a rat's ass about lovebirds? She wanted to find those little creatures almost as much as Emily did. Friends were one thing, but this was getting out of hand. Maybe she should leave. She could sleep in her car until the audition in a couple of days. But the thought of leaving Emily made her heart ache. That was the last thing she wanted to do. Instead, she needed to keep her guard up, protect her heart, and for God's sake not kiss her again.

It was close to midnight when Sydney got back to the cabin. Slowly, she opened the door and peeked inside. It was almost completely dark. She tiptoed across the hardwood floor, trying not to wake Emily. They needed to clear the air, but not tonight—not when Sydney's head was still filled with the taste of Emily's lips.

Ouch! Sydney put a hand over her mouth when she banged a knee against the corner of a table. She must have stood still for at least a minute until the sharp pain subsided into a throbbing ache.

"You okay?" Emily sat up in the couch. Or at least that's what it looked like in the semidarkness.

"Fuck. That hurt." Sydney groaned, happy to finally be able to make a sound.

"Do you need ice?"

"No. It's fine. Sorry I woke you."

"You didn't. Where were you?"

"Running. Had to release some energy."

Sydney squinted, desperately wishing she could see Emily's face. Maybe that would reveal what she was thinking and, more importantly, feeling.

It looked like Emily ran fingers through her hair or maybe rubbed her face. "About the, you know, kiss. It never should have happened. I don't know what I was thinking. I've never cheated on Gretchen before. I'm not the type to do that sort of thing. Really."

"It wasn't all your fault. I don't know if you noticed, but I was doing my fair share of responding."

"I noticed," Emily whispered. "I don't want you to think badly of me, and I don't want things to be weird between us. I really value our friendship."

Sydney's heart sank. Friends. Of course. What else would they be?

"You're important to me, too," Sydney said.

"So we're okay?" Emily's voice quivered.

"Sure. We're fine." Sydney wanted to say so much more, like how much she loved kissing Emily and how much she wanted to do it again. Instead, she went upstairs.

After taking a shower, Sydney went into the bedroom, ready to collapse into bed. She opened the nightstand drawer, her eye catching sight of Emily's engagement ring. She must have forgotten to put it back on after the pole/make-out session.

With two fingers, Sydney picked it up and examined it closely. She couldn't even imagine how much something like that would cost. Sydney could never afford anything more than a plastic ring out of a bubblegum machine. Emily deserved a lot more than that. She deserved a ring like this and a fiancée who didn't live on the wrong side of the tracks.

CHAPTER SEVENTEEN

Love in the Afternoon

"You sure you have time to help me?" Emily asked as she and Sydney zigzagged around fig trees.

"Absolutely. I couldn't be any more ready for my audition. Besides, I want to find the lovebirds as much as you do."

Emily grinned. She had a feeling Sydney wasn't joking. It was heartwarming how supportive she was.

"Do you think they're even still here?" Sydney asked, gazing up into the trees as she walked.

"My instincts tell me they are. They won't be easy to find, though. They're the smallest birds of the species, frighten easily, and nest in tree holes. But they're strong fliers and have large wings. They'll be easy to spot when they're flying around."

Sydney stopped and wiped sweat from her forehead. "It's like trying to find a needle in a haystack."

"Do you want to take a break?"

"I thought you'd never ask."

They both sat under a tree and leaned against the tree trunk. Emily pulled out two waters and handed one to Sydney.

"What happens if you don't find the lovebirds?" Sydney asked and took a swig.

"I'll find them. No matter what happens, though, I'm not giving up my magazine. It's the one thing in my life that makes me happy."

Well, that and you.

Emily guzzled down an entire bottle of water without stopping, not sure if she was trying to quench a thirst or drown her feelings. She'd been attracted to Sydney before the kiss, but now even more so.

In fact, she couldn't even look at her without wanting to do it again… and again.

They both looked upward when leaves rustled. Emily attempted to dodge several figs that rained down and smacked her on the head.

"Ouch," Emily said and rubbed her crown.

Sydney giggled. "You okay?"

"After this I never want to see another fig for as long as I live."

They both ducked when something soared overhead.

"Whoa," Sydney said. "What was that?"

"It was moving so fast. Maybe a hummingbird."

Sydney flinched when something flew straight toward her and landed on her shoulder. Emily froze and her jaw dropped, shocked at what she was seeing.

"Don't move," Emily whispered. "And don't make a sound."

Emily saw Sydney try to peer out of the corner of her eye at whatever was perched on her shoulder. Emily should reach for her camera, but all she could do was stare at the most perfect, beautiful Madagascar lovebird she'd ever seen. The bird cocked his head and looked at Emily as though to ask, *what's your name?*

"I'm Emily. And I can't believe I'm looking at you right now."

The lovebird chirped twice and flew into the tree.

"Was that what I think it was?" Sydney asked, goggle-eyed.

Emily broke out into a smile so wide her cheeks ached. "Oh. My. God. They really did survive! He even had scars on his throat and head."

"Scars?"

Emily spoke fast in one long, run-on sentence. "The man I spoke with at the San Diego aviary said the lovebirds had cuts from an animal attack. That's why they were healing there at the time of the fire. They're really here. And we found them."

Emily jumped up and placed a hand on the tree trunk to steady herself.

Sydney rose and stood beside her. "Do you think they're in this tree?"

"Only one way to find out." Emily dropped her smile when she looked upward. Leave it to Fran to have the world's tallest fig trees.

"You're not thinking about climbing up there, are you?" Sydney arched an eyebrow.

"It'll be dark soon. We don't have time to walk back to Fran's to ask her for a ladder and then back here again."

"I'll do it." Sydney grabbed a branch.

"No way." Emily held Sydney's forearm. "I don't want you breaking a leg."

"But it's okay if you do?"

"I don't have an important audition."

"Oh. Right. I still don't think you should do this without a ladder. We can come back tomorrow."

Emily looked at Sydney like she belonged in a straightjacket. "Are you insane? I'm not leaving." Emily hung a camera around her neck.

"What's that?"

"An Audubon Bird Cam. It's a motion-activated, digital wildlife video and photo recorder with an infrared sensor that detects motion."

"Looks fancy."

"It's top-of-the line when it comes to birding." Emily flipped open the lid and flashed a silver nameplate.

"You had your camera engraved?" Sydney smirked.

"This baby cost me three months' salary. If I ever lose it, I want my name and address on it. Now give me a boost."

"All right. But be careful."

Sydney laced her fingers together and bent down. Emily placed one foot into the makeshift stepstool and catapulted upward, her right hand just missing a branch. After a few more attempts, she managed to attach herself to the tree. Now all she had to do was climb up, which was easier said than done. She'd conveniently forgotten the fact that she was terribly clumsy. She'd spent most of her childhood on crutches due to falls. Even as a bird-watcher she rarely had to actually climb a tree. The majority of fowl could be seen from the ground with the high-powered Bird Cam, but these were no ordinary creatures. She needed to get up close and personal.

Emily placed a shaky foot on a limb, pressed down to test its strength, and reached above her head to pull herself up. She glanced down at Sydney and considered trading places with her. It looked awfully safe on the ground. No. She could do this. She had to do this. After several strategic moves and using every muscle in her body, she was halfway up the tree.

"Don't look down," Sydney yelled, which, of course, caused Emily to look at the ground. Ugh. Her stomach rolled. From this perspective it appeared like she was twenty stories up. One wrong move and she'd tumble down.

"Why'd you stop?" Sydney yelled.

"Because I looked down."

"I told you not to."

Emily adjusted her footing and perched on a solid-looking branch. Maybe she was high enough to see something.

"Are you okay?" Sydney asked.

"Yes. I'm going to use the zoom on my camera."

Emily adjusted the dials and slowly scanned the tree, amazed at what came into focus. At least ten vibrant-green lovebirds with gray heads were perched on branches. Before she could press the shutter button, a gust of wind blew through the trees and knocked her off balance. Fear shot through her gut as she fell backward, scrambling to catch branches. She heard someone scream and realized the sound was coming from her own mouth as she plummeted toward the ground. It was one of those things that happen in slow motion. Wafting downward like a feather, Emily didn't see her life flash before her eyes, but she did remember everything she was thinking.

This is bad. Really bad. It's gonna hurt something awful. I'm not ready to die. I didn't even get a chance to kiss Sydney again.

Thud. She hit the dirt hard and felt like a sword had been jabbed into her lower back. Pain. Intense pain. But that was good, right? That meant she wasn't dead.

Sydney rushed to Emily's side. "Don't move. Are you hurt?" Fear tinged Sydney's voice. And why shouldn't it? Emily had just fallen God knows how many feet out of a freaking tree. How embarrassing. She was the world's clumsiest person ever.

Emily tried to sit up, but Sydney held her down. "I'm fine," Emily said, even though she wasn't completely convinced.

"Are you in pain?"

Emily peered into worried eyes. Not only was this humiliating, but now she'd upset Sydney. "My back hurts, but it's not too bad." Okay. So maybe that was a little white lie. It throbbed something awful.

"You could have a broken bone, a slipped disc, or something worse."

"I'm fine." Apparently, Emily was an expert liar now.

Sydney seemed hesitant but reluctantly released her hold. "Okay, but sit up slowly."

"Oh my God!" Emily patted her chest.

"What's wrong?"

"Where's my camera? It must have fallen off my neck."

"We'll find it in a minute. Let's make sure you're okay first."

Emily wanted to jump up and scour the area. It was the only Bird Cam she owned or could afford. What would she do if it was damaged? Emily raised her torso, probably too quickly, and yelped when a sharp pain shot through her, making her nauseated.

"Seeee. You *are* hurt," Sydney said, sounding halfway pleased that she'd been right. "We need to get you to the ER."

Emily lay back down. "The hospital? No way."

"You just fell out of a tree. You need medical attention." Sydney's voice rose several octaves. "Now you lie here, and I'll go back to Fran's and get something to transport you to the car."

"You're leaving me? What if bears or coyotes are out here?"

Sydney looked momentarily concerned. After a few beats she said, "They'll eat the figs and not you."

"Wait! Find my camera first."

Sydney rolled her eyes but searched the area. After a few minutes, she bent down and picked something up.

"Here." Sydney jabbed the camera into Emily's hands. "Promise me you won't move?"

"I promise."

Emily immediately turned the Bird Cam every which way, inspecting it for damage. She ejected the memory card, blew on it to remove dust, and slid it back in. Everything looked okay, but just to be sure she snapped a few photos of the sky, since she was stuck lying on her back. Relief washed over her when she reviewed the images on the screen. Her prized possession was safe.

With all the ruckus of the accident, Emily had almost forgotten about the lovebirds. She slowly smiled and felt practically giddy. If she wasn't hurt she would have done a happy dance, prancing on her tiptoes and clapping her hands like a court jester.

Emily attempted to sit up but then plopped back down again. Crap. Maybe she really was hurt. She didn't have time for this. The lovebirds were right overhead. She needed to be in the tree taking pictures and video. Well, she couldn't do much now. Hopefully Sydney would be back before dark. Emily felt awfully vulnerable and exposed lying in the middle of nowhere all alone.

After what felt like hours, Emily stiffened when she heard a rattling sound that grew louder by the minute. Were rattlesnakes lurking out here? She turned her head and saw Sydney in the distance, pulling something behind her. What was that? As Sydney came into full view, Emily groaned.

"Seriously? A little red wagon?" Emily asked when Sydney was a few feet away. "You couldn't find a better means of transportation?"

"It's a *big* red wagon and the only thing I could find long enough for you to lie flat in. There's only one problem." Sydney pinched her nose.

Emily hated to ask, but curiosity got the better of her. "What?"

Sydney unpinched it. "This is what Fran uses to carry fertilizer in."

"Manure? You're going to make me lie in crap?"

"No. Well. Sorta. I cleaned it out. But it still kinda smells."

Emily sighed. "Could this get any worse?"

Sydney knelt beside Emily. "How are you feeling?"

"Stupid for falling."

"It wasn't your fault. That was a massive gust of wind. Let's see if you can sit up."

Sydney helped Emily upright, and with some effort she even managed to stand. She was going to protest that she was fine, but considering she still felt like someone had just jabbed a hot poker into her back, she kept her trap shut. Emily mumbled obscenities as she lay down in the wagon that smelled like a horse stable. Talk about feeling like a five-year-old when Sydney pulled her down the path to the car. This really couldn't get any more embarrassing.

❖

Sydney fluffed a pillow and gently placed it behind Emily's back as she sat up in bed. Normally, she wasn't the nurturing type, but she hated that Emily had gotten hurt and wanted to do anything she could to help her. Emily had been a trouper since the fall, not even complaining when they waited in the ER for over an hour when Sydney knew she must be in agony.

"Has your pain pill kicked in yet?" Sydney asked and pulled a blanket over Emily's legs.

"Considering I think I could stick a fork in my leg and not even feel it, I'll say yeah."

Sydney snorted. "Good. You're lucky you didn't break your back or slip a disc. The doc says you'll be up and running again in a few days."

"A few days is forever when I just found the lovebirds. What's that?" Emily motioned to a tube in Sydney's hand.

"It's a muscle-relaxant cream. I use it after a day of pole dancing."

"Thanks. I'll put some on tomorrow."

"You should do it now before you go to sleep."

Emily slouched down in bed. "I can barely lift my arms or keep my eyes open."

Without thinking, Sydney said, "I'll do it. Roll over."

Emily hesitated but then carefully repositioned herself until she was lying on her stomach. Sydney stared into the eyes of two lovebirds on Emily's flannel PJs, realizing that she'd have to expose skin in order to rub the lotion in. Maybe this wasn't such a great idea after all.

"Is something wrong?" Emily turned her head and surveyed Sydney.

"No," Sydney responded, much too quickly. "Is it okay if I, you know, adjust your clothing to get to the area?"

"Sure. Do whatever you have to do to make it stop hurting."

Sydney lifted Emily's shirt and winced when she saw shades of red, purple, and blue.

"What's it look like?" Emily asked.

"Like you fell on your back. It's pretty bruised. Is this where it hurts?" Sydney lightly placed her palm over the injury.

"Yeah. And lover."

"What?"

"Lower! I meant lower."

Sydney chuckled. "Nice Freudian slip."

"These pills are making me loopy."

"Is it okay if I move your pants down a little?"

"Like I said before, do what you want."

Sydney gulped. Actually, she wanted to do a lot, most of which included completely ripping the cute lovebird jammies off. Sydney mentally chastised herself. Emily was hurt. This wasn't a time to get frisky. Sydney ran a finger underneath the waistband and tugged downward, just enough to expose the tops of a perfectly formed rump. Instinctively, she licked her lips. Emily had beautiful skin, smooth and creamy. She couldn't wait to see what it felt like.

"This might be a little cold," Sydney said.

She applied the cream, which caused Emily to flinch, and carefully rubbed in small circles. It instantly melted on Emily's warm body.

"Tell me if I'm pressing too hard." The last thing Sydney wanted to do was cause Emily more pain.

"It feels good. Can you put some on my hips, too? They feel really sore."

Sydney glided her hands around and tenderly massaged the softest skin ever. When Emily moaned, Sydney stalled.

"Don't stop." Emily's voice was deep, at least an octave lower than normal.

Sydney resumed stroking, daring to go deeper to knead tense muscles. "Are you sure this isn't too hard?"

"Not at all. I could let you do this all night."

Now that was an enticing idea. Sydney would love to touch Emily all night, and not just her back. She used both hands to massage one hip and then the other and practically melted into a puddle when Emily groaned in a way that sounded awfully sensual. Was that what Emily sounded like when she was aroused? Was she vocal during sex or the quiet type? And did she cry out when she had an orgasm? It was suddenly scorching in the cabin, like someone had just blasted the heater. Sydney had better wrap up this mini-massage before she got too carried away.

Sydney pulled Emily's shirt down and fixed her pants. "All done. I hope it helped."

"Aww. You're finished?"

Emily turned over and peered up with droopy eyes. She looked utterly squeezable. Sydney wanted to lean down and place a light kiss on her crimson lips and tuck her into bed.

"Thank you," Emily said and yawned. "You've been amazing."

"My pleasure." Emily had no idea how much Sydney had enjoyed touching her.

"I'm going to wash my hands and then hang out here until you fall asleep." Sydney motioned to a chair in the corner of the bedroom. She bent down and kissed Emily's forehead. It wasn't her mouth, but at least it semi-satisfied Sydney's desire to place her lips somewhere on Emily's body.

❖

A sharp stab shot through Emily when she turned over in bed. What the hell was that? Oh, right. Fig tree. Falling. Big ouch. The accident was coming back to her. She halfway opened her eyes and squinted at the clock. It was four a.m. Past time for another pain pill. She grabbed the bottle off the nightstand, popped a pill into her mouth, and took a swig of water. Hopefully it'd kick in fast.

She was about to lie back down when she saw a dark figure slumped in the chair. Sydney. That couldn't have been comfortable. One leg was over the armrest, and her head was drooping at an odd angle, making her look like a stuffed animal with not enough cotton in its neck. She'd been so sweet to take care of Emily—transporting her to the emergency room, waiting for hours, and helping her into bed. Not to mention the massage. God. That massage.

Emily's face heated with the memory of Sydney's hands on her. It had felt amazing and so very sensual. Even injured, she'd longed for Sydney to stroke between her legs and relieve the ache deep within. Though Emily had never had an orgasm with anyone before, she was fairly certain it wouldn't have taken much to climax under Sydney's touch. What was that about? Maybe Emily wasn't so cold after all. Maybe she'd just never been with the right woman before.

"Sydney. Wake up." No response. "Sydney!" Still nothing. Emily took a pillow and lobbed it, jolting Sydney awake when it plopped on her stomach.

"What's wrong? Do you need something?" Sydney was beside the bed in seconds.

"What are you still doing in the chair? It's four o'clock."

"Guess I fell asleep. Are you okay?"

"Fine. I just took another pain pill."

Sydney yawned and scratched her head. "All right. I'll head downstairs to the couch."

"Like that's any more comfortable than the chair. We can share the bed." Emily scooted over.

Sydney hesitated and stared at the empty space beside Emily. The moonlight streaming in from the window cast a pearly glaze over Sydney's face, making her look breathtakingly beautiful.

"I don't want to accidentally kick you or something." Sydney met Emily's eyes.

"It's fine unless you do karate in your sleep. This is a king. We won't even touch."

Sydney's gaze bounced from the chair to the door to Emily. Finally, she slipped into bed.

Emily propped on her elbows and gawked at Sydney. "We don't need another accident."

"What do you mean?" Sydney furrowed her brow.

"You're teetering on the edge about to fall over. Are you scared of me?" Emily grinned.

Sydney inched closer, turned on her side, and faced Emily head-on. "I don't know. Do you plan to kiss me again?"

They both grew suddenly serious, the air between them hot and still. Emily dropped her gaze to Sydney's mouth. She'd give anything to taste her sweet lips again. Before she did something stupid, Emily flipped over—too quickly considering her back—and said, "We should get some sleep. Good night, Sydney."

CHAPTER EIGHTEEN

Three's Company

Whoever said things always looked better in the morning was full of crap. In fact, things were exactly the same, considering Emily's back was still sore and she still wanted to kiss Sydney. Emily stared at Sydney's angelic face as she slept just a few feet away. It'd be so easy to cozy up next to her and nuzzle her awake.

Instead, she sat upright and pressed two fingers against her temples. It was times like this she needed a friend to talk to, or maybe a priest, considering she should probably go to confession. Cheating on a fiancée was most certainly frowned upon. But then again, it wasn't like she'd had sex with Sydney. But God, she'd wanted to.

I'm going to hell for sure.

Considering Gretchen was her closest friend and she had no idea where to find the nearest priest, she'd have to settle for the next best thing: her mom.

Moving slower than a hundred-and-fifty-year-old tortoise, Emily got out of bed and stood upright. She grabbed her phone, went downstairs, and stepped onto the deck. With shaky fingers, she pressed the speed dial on her cell phone, incredulous that she was actually going to do this. Her mother was a great source of information for questions like how many calories are in a bagel or how many minutes of step aerobics does it take to work off a chocolate fudge sundae, but concerning matters of the heart? Not so much.

Her mother answered on the first ring. "Hello, darling. I'm about to head out. You know I have Pilates every Saturday morning."

"Oh. Sorry. I forgot."

"I'll call you when I get back. We need to review the reception menu."

"Wait. Don't hang up. I need to ask you something." Emily paused, not sure where to start.

"Well?"

Emily heard car keys jingling.

"Have you, I mean, were you ever attracted to anyone other than Dad when you were engaged?"

Silence. Lots of uncomfortable silence. This wasn't good.

"Mom?"

"Who have you been talking to?"

"I'm not sure what you mean."

"Did your father say something?"

"No. I haven't...no."

"It was a long time ago, Emily Gail."

Wait. What? There *had* been someone else?

"His name was Troy," her mother said. "I met him around the same time as your father. He was...ahh...a dreamboat..."

Somehow, Emily knew the dreamboat comment referred to Troy and not her father.

"Handsome. Sexy. And reckless. He drove a motorcycle and wanted to travel cross-country, camping and living off the land."

Emily was aware that her mother's voice had drastically shifted. Her usually sharp, grating tone was silky and filled with emotion and reverence.

"Did you date him?" Emily asked.

"For a short time." Her mother's voice was almost a whisper, then grew louder when she said, "Your grandmother absolutely hated him."

"Were you in love with him?"

Fast, shallow-sounding breaths came through the receiver. Why hadn't Emily done FaceTime? She'd give anything to see her mother's expression right now.

"Head over heels." Two beats passed before she added, "But he was completely wrong for me. He was wild and impetuous and actually wanted me to run away with him."

Before Emily could stop herself, she blurted, "You should have!" not realizing she was basically saying that her mother and father shouldn't have gotten married.

Emily's mother chuckled. "Grandma would have had a heart attack. I broke it off with him after your father proposed."

"Did you ever regret it?"

Emily's mother huffed. "What's with all these questions? And now you've made me miss Pilates. You and Gretchen are going to drive me crazy."

"What do you mean? What about Gretchen?"

"It's completely normal to have cold feet before getting married."

"Gretchen has cold feet?" Emily asked, oddly excited about the prospect. "Because I've been thinking maybe we're rushing into this."

"Don't be ridiculous. You two are perfect for each other."

A short time ago, Emily would have wholeheartedly agreed. But now things felt different.

"If I leave now I can catch the second class," Emily's mother said. "You get that story written and hurry back here to your fiancée."

Emily heard a dial tone. Obviously, her mother was finished with the conversation. Emily stood on the deck, astonished. She hadn't had a chance to ask about her feelings for Sydney, but she'd learned that her mom had been—in her own words, head over heels—in love with someone other than her father. Emily's parents had never seemed particularly happy together. Not that they fought. They seemed content, which for some reason made Emily sad. She'd rather be alone than settle.

Emily frowned when she heard someone banging on the front door. They never got visitors. It must be a salesman or maybe even a religious group. If she waited long enough they'd probably just go away. She raised her face to the sky, enjoying the heat of the sun on her skin. Her back was stiff, but it didn't hurt as much as she thought it would. She wouldn't be climbing trees any time soon, but maybe with Sydney's help they could see the lovebirds again today. Emily might even get some photos.

She heard muffled voices when she opened the sliding-glass door and walked into the kitchen. Sydney must have gotten up and answered the door. Hopefully, she wasn't getting suckered into buying a set of encyclopedias. Emily moseyed into the living room and gasped at what she saw. She squeezed her eyes shut for a few seconds and then opened them again.

Nope. It wasn't a mirage. Gretchen was standing in the middle of the room looking like she was ready to kill someone, and unfortunately, Emily knew who that someone would be. Sydney, who was standing beside her, took a step back, looking like she wanted to bolt.

Gretchen put her hands on her hips, her face flushed. "What the hell is going on here?"

"G-Gretchen." That's all Emily could utter.

"What the fuck is *she* doing here?" Gretchen pointed at Sydney.

Emily held up her hands. "This is not what it looks like."

"It looks like you're shacking up with another woman! And someone who ruined my proposal, no less." A vein in Gretchen's neck bulged, so much so it looked like it might actually burst.

"No. No. It's not like that." Emily shook her head. "There's no shacking. We haven't done…" Emily looked at Sydney. She was going to say they hadn't done anything wrong, but they sorta had. Sydney slightly shrugged, sympathy written across her face.

Gretchen rushed toward Emily, so close their noses almost touched. "I thought of all people you'd be the last person to cheat."

"What? I didn't cheat." *Or did I?* "Look. Let me explain. Neither of us knew we'd be here, and with the women's festival there were no other rooms in town. We're roommates and nothing more."

Sydney lowered her head, looking sad or maybe disappointed. Did she want there to be more? Before Emily could consider that possibility, someone knocked and they all turned.

"What now?" Emily muttered and opened the door, shocked to see a policeman.

"Good morning." The officer tilted his hat. "Can I come in?"

"Um. Sure." Emily stepped aside to allow him to enter.

"I'm looking for a Sydney Cooper." The policeman surveyed the three of them.

"I'm her." Sydney weakly raised a hand.

The officer approached Sydney. "You're under arrest for breaking and entering. You have the right to—"

"What? Where?" Sydney asked.

"We had a call from," the officer looked at a notepad in his hand, "Jill Taylor, the owner of this cabin. She said she received notice from an Emily Wellington that you're trespassing."

Geez. Could this get any worse?

"Wait," Emily said, stepping between Sydney and the officer.

"I'm Emily, and there's been a mistake. I reached out to Jill to tell her Sydney could stay here, but she must not have gotten the email. Sydney didn't commit a crime. She belongs here."

"So you two are together?" The officer motioned between Emily and Sydney.

"Yes." Out of the corner of her eye, Emily could see Gretchen fuming. She'd have a lot of explaining to do later, but for now she couldn't let Sydney be arrested.

"I'll need to see some ID," the officer told Emily.

She grabbed her bag off the coffee table, fished out her wallet, and handed him her driver's license.

Seemingly satisfied, the officer faced Sydney and pointed. "You're free for now, but if we find out otherwise, we're taking you in."

Sydney gulped. "Understood."

"I take full responsibility for this mix-up," Emily said. "I'll straighten this out with Jill. I'm sorry for your trouble."

After the officer left, Emily looked at Gretchen, who appeared furious.

"Maybe I should leave," Sydney said.

"Yes. That's an excellent idea," Gretchen said without taking her eyes off Emily.

"I'll just pack my bags and get out of here."

"No! You can't leave for good." That was the last thing Emily wanted.

"It's probably for the best." Sydney peered at Gretchen out of the corner of her eye.

"Definitely not. You have an audition tomorrow, and there's no other place to stay. Just give us some time alone, okay?"

Sydney nodded and raced upstairs.

"Definitely not?" Gretchen said in a mocking tone.

"Can we just please sit down and I'll explain everything?"

Emily slouched into the couch while Gretchen stood and hovered over her like a vulture.

"This is so screwed up." Emily rubbed her forehead. "At first, I did think Sydney had broken into the cabin, but things changed. I'm sorry I didn't tell you she was staying here. I was wrong not to do so. But nothing is going on. In fact, we've become friends. She's been helping me find the lovebirds."

"You're friends with that…that…person?" Gretchen crossed her arms.

"I owe Sydney a lot, Gretchen. She helped me get access to Fran's farm."

Gretchen plopped onto the sofa. "You should have been honest with me."

"You're right. I'm sorry."

Gretchen's eyes widened and her mouth formed a perfect *O*. "Where's your engagement ring?"

Emily looked at her left hand. *Crap.* "It's in the drawer upstairs. I forgot to put it back on after the pole dancing les—"

"The *what*?"

This was getting worse by the minute. "Sydney is auditioning tomorrow for an instructor position, and I was helping her. I didn't want to damage my ring so I took it off."

Gretchen scooted to the edge of couch. "You were pole dancing? With *her*? Oh my God. I don't even know who you are anymore."

"I'm still me."

Or was she? The old Emily wouldn't have come within two feet of a pole, nor would she have had the courage to do a lot of the other things she'd done this past week.

"You're certainly not acting like a fiancée," Gretchen said. "Do you even still want to get married?"

Emily stared into concerned brown eyes. It was a simple yes-or-no question, one to which she should readily have an answer. Why then did her mouth feel like it was stuffed with a hundred cotton balls? Emily really needed to say something. *Anything.* But she hadn't a clue as to how to respond.

"I guess I have my answer." Gretchen looked away, like she couldn't bear the sight of Emily anymore.

Emily swallowed hard. This wasn't going to be easy, but she needed to be honest with not only Gretchen but also herself.

"When I accepted your proposal, I thought we belonged together. I mean, everyone expected us to get married." Emily paused and took a deep breath. "But things changed. I changed. I do love you, Gretchen. But I'm not *in* love with you. I'm sorry."

Emily tensed, awaiting the inevitable outburst of anger, screaming, tears…except that didn't happen. Gretchen sat calmly and stared straight ahead, looking like she was attending a church service. Had she even heard what Emily said?

Emily cleared her throat and asked, "Am I really the love of your life?"

Gretchen turned and faced Emily, her expression impassive. "I thought you were. But now you seem like a stranger to me. You're reneging on everything we planned, like shutting down *The Tweet* and buying a house in Beverly Hills. Is this because of her?" Gretchen nodded toward the stairs.

"I'm not having an affair with Sydney...but we did kiss."

Gretchen's eyes grew two sizes bigger.

"But that's all we did," Emily said quickly. "I should have talked to you before this, but I wasn't even sure of my feelings. Everything happened so fast."

"So you have *feelings* for her?"

"I do."

Emily studied Gretchen. She was taking this awfully well. Gretchen had been more upset about a thirty-dollar parking ticket than she was this. She couldn't possibly be in love with Emily and be so calm right now.

"Can you honestly say you haven't had reservations about us getting married?" Emily asked.

Gretchen pursed her lips and stared at her hands. "I suppose it's crossed my mind. We've been dating so long that I thought it was the next reasonable step, but the closer it gets..." Gretchen looked at Emily. "When we'd talk on the phone and I'd ask you if you still wanted to get married, part of me wished you'd say no."

"Don't you see? This is something we should be ecstatic about and not just because it's what we planned or because our parents pushed us together."

Gretchen nodded. "So, are we breaking up? And calling off the wedding?"

"Yes. I think it's the right thing to do. We both deserve to be with someone that we're totally, completely in love with."

Gretchen rolled her head back. "Oh my God. Our parents. They're going to freak. Our moms have the entire wedding planned already." Gretchen sat upright and pointed at Emily. "You're breaking the news to them."

"Fine." Emily groaned. "Hey, are you okay with all this?" Emily placed a hand on Gretchen's arm when it looked like she might actually cry.

"I'm going to miss you. You've been in my life a long time." Gretchen's lower lip quivered.

"This doesn't have to be good-bye. I do really care about you, Gretchen. I hope we can be friends after some time has passed."

"Me, too." Gretchen lightly squeezed Emily's hand. "Well, I guess I should go."

They both stood, an awkward silence filling the air. Should they shake hands or hug? Emily wasn't sure of the proper protocol in this particular situation.

"Do you want to stay for breakfast?" Emily asked, hoping she'd decline.

"No. I should get back to LA." Gretchen slung her bag over her shoulder.

"Take care of yourself, and keep in touch."

Emily followed Gretchen to the door and watched as she drove away. She should probably feel sad, but she didn't. She felt freer than she ever had before.

Chapter Nineteen

Lost and Found

Emily kicked the cabin door open since her arms were filled with bags. Her back had been feeling pretty good so she'd gone grocery shopping. She wanted to make Sydney a thank-you dinner for taking such good care of her. After stuffing the fridge with salmon and veggies, she stood in the living room and listened intently. Sydney was awfully quiet. In fact, Emily hadn't seen or heard her since she went upstairs when Gretchen was there. Pushing the blinds aside, she glanced outside but didn't see Sydney's car parked on the street. Maybe she'd gone out.

Emily headed upstairs and stopped suddenly when she passed the bedroom. Something was different, something that didn't feel quite right. A chill ran down her spine when she realized what it was. The pole was missing. She rushed into the room and threw the closet door open. All of Sydney's clothes were gone. Aimlessly, Emily walked backward and plopped down on the bed, catching sight of a piece of paper on the pillow. She grabbed it and read.

> *Emily,*
>
> *I thought it best if I leave. I don't want to cause any problems for you and Gretchen.*
>
> *P.S. I left the muscle cream on the nightstand for you to use. Take care of yourself and don't fall out of any more trees.—Syd*

A vise clamped down on Emily's heart. Sydney had left, for good. But where would she go? She had an audition tomorrow. Emily had to find her.

She rushed downstairs, opened her laptop, and searched for hotels. Maybe she'd managed to find a room even with the festival going on. Considering the size of Ojai, it didn't take long to call every place within a ten-mile radius, with no luck. Without pausing, she grabbed her keys and rushed to her car. She had no idea where she was going, but she had to find Sydney. She didn't belong anyplace except at the cabin with her.

❖

Meditation Mount was beautiful at night. The expanse of sky looked like a clear, sparkling sapphire. The temperature was perfect, the sweet scent of nearby roses filled the air, and the cushiony St. Augustine grass was like walking on marshmallows. Sydney laid out a blanket on top of a hill and sat. She hugged her knees and admired the moon overhead. This wasn't so bad after all. It beat being in the cabin with Emily and her fiancée, that was for sure. The thought of leaving Emily made her heart ache, but she certainly wasn't going to stick around and watch them fawn over each other. Just the thought of that made her want to retch.

All right. Sydney could admit it. She liked Emily more than just a friend. In fact, more than anyone she'd ever dated. No. More than anyone she'd ever known. Dammit. Those were the breaks. She would have to fall for an unavailable woman. Every muscle in Sydney's body tensed. *Fall for?* Was she in love with Emily?

Granted, she'd never been in love before, but what else could it be? Sydney had turned into one of those sappy women she used to roll her eyes at, the ones who couldn't stop gushing about their girlfriend. That was Sydney in a nutshell. Emily was all she thought about since they'd met, and any time they spent apart simply and unequivocally sucked.

Sydney lay down and put her hands behind her head. She'd get over this. Tomorrow, she'd ace the audition and then get back to her life in LA. She was a loner. She didn't need anyone. Thoughts of Emily and those damn lovebirds would fly right out of her head. Sydney chuckled. *The lovebirds would fly out of her head.* That'd be just the kind of bad pun Emily would use.

A vision of Emily's sweet face flashed before Sydney's eyes.

Sydney was going to miss her something awful. Maybe getting over the bird-watcher would be harder than she thought, considering it felt like someone was physically tugging on the bottom of her heart.

Sydney bolted upright when she heard a noise that sounded like a car door slamming. Meditation Mount was in the hills with no houses around, so that couldn't have been it...unless...no, it couldn't be. Maybe someone had seen her break in after closing and called the police. That's all she needed, especially after almost getting arrested for trespassing in Jill's cabin. Sydney's stomach dropped when she heard quick footsteps down the gravel path. She was either about to be eaten by a wild animal or arrested. She shielded her eyes when a light shone directly at her. Police officers had flashlights. She was toast.

The dark figure rushed forward and jumped on top of her. Sydney struggled, trying to fight off the attacker until she heard a familiar voice.

"What the hell are you doing here?" Emily hugged her fiercely, let go, and punched her hard on the arm.

"Ow!" Sydney rubbed the sore spot and blinked several times, letting her eyes adjust after being blinded. "What'd you do that for?"

"You scared me. I've been looking for you for hours. I didn't think I'd ever find you...ever see you again." Emily's voice cracked, and she sounded like she was about to cry.

"Didn't you get the note?"

"That was the worst of it!" Emily shrieked. "After everything we've been through, you leave a note? You don't even talk to me? Tell me good-bye in person?"

"I thought that's what you'd want. I figured that'd be easier for everyone."

"Easier for you, maybe." Emily huffed. "Were you just going to leave and never contact me again?" Hurt filled Emily's eyes.

"I don't think your fiancée would like it if I did." Funny how that word, fiancée, left a metallic taste in Sydney's mouth. Or maybe not so funny.

Emily sat back and seemed to relax a bit. She turned off the flashlight, but luckily, in the moonlight, Sydney could still make out her facial expressions. "Gretchen left. I broke it off with her."

Had Sydney heard right? "You mean...as in..."

Emily nodded. "No engagement. No wedding. No nothing."

A surge of energy shot through Sydney, so much so she had to will herself not to jump up and do cartwheels. This was the best news she'd ever heard.

"Wow," Sydney said, trying to look calm. "I'm surprised. What brought that on?"

"It was a long time coming. I care about Gretchen, but I'm not in love with her."

"How'd she take it?" Sydney could care less about Gretchen, but she did want to hear more about how Emily wasn't in love with her. That fact made Sydney extraordinarily happy.

"Really well. She was having doubts about our future together, too."

"How are you doing? I mean, are you okay?"

Emily shrugged. "I'm fine. If anything, I feel guilty that I'm not sad about it."

"So I guess you two weren't lovebirds after all. Otherwise, you'd be depressed and go through that heartbreak syndrome you told me about before."

"You remembered." The corners of Emily's mouth quirked upward. "Yeah. I guess not, since she isn't the one I want to mate with for life."

Emily crossed her legs and thoughtfully looked up at the stars. God, she was cute. Big brown eyes, beautiful face, pouty lips. Sydney would love to kiss those lips again.

After a few moments, Emily said, "I want a relationship that makes me feel alive. I want adventure and fun. I want excitement, desire, and love." Emily chuckled.

Sydney tilted her head. "What's funny?"

"If I had told you what I want in a relationship when I first got to Ojai, it would have been a very different list."

"What changed?"

"I don't want to settle." Emily took a deep breath, let it out slowly, and faced Sydney. "Being with you, getting to know you made me realize that Gretchen isn't the one for me."

Sydney's breath caught in her throat. Was Emily saying what Sydney thought she was saying?

Emily moved closer, until their knees touched. "Tonight when I realized you were gone, I was terrified that I wouldn't ever see you again. You're the one I want to be with."

Sydney's heart swelled. She wanted to whisk Emily into her arms, but something held her back. Could she really fit into Emily's world? Would her rich parents accept their relationship? They obviously had their heart set on Emily marrying Gretchen. Not to mention the fact that Sydney was unemployed and broke.

"Are you sure?" Sydney asked, sounding more skeptical than she'd intended.

Emily's expression dropped, and she averted her eyes. "You're not interested in me. I thought maybe—"

"That's not it. It's just that you're from Beverly Hills and I'm from South Central. We come from different worlds."

Emily looked at Sydney, a glint of hopefulness in her eyes. "I don't care about that."

"I'm sure your parents would."

Emily opened her mouth, like maybe she was about to deny that point, but then paused.

"Aha!" Sydney said. "You agree."

"Nooo. I was just thinking about it. And besides, it doesn't matter what my parents think. The only thing that matters is whether you want to be with me. So do you?" Emily suddenly looked fifteen years old, scared and unsure of herself.

Sydney broke out in a smile. "Yes." She was going to say more, but Emily jumped into her arms and pressed their lips together.

Ahhh. So soft. So delicious.

The desire to fiercely claim Emily's mouth was strong, but she was someone to be cherished, adored. Sydney had never felt such tenderness for another person before. More than anything she wanted to tell Emily how much she cared for her, how important she was. Emily released a slight gasp when Sydney pulled away. Sydney lightly kissed Emily's forehead, her right cheek, her left cheek, and then looked directly into her eyes.

"You are the most amazing woman I've ever met, Emily Wellington. Beautiful, giving, supportive, caring, and the best kisser *ever*. I'd be honored to be with you."

It was official. Sydney had turned into the corniest person in the state of California. But she couldn't help it. She'd meant what she said.

Emily snaked a hand around Sydney's neck and kissed her in a way that made Sydney glad she was sitting, considering her legs felt like overcooked noodles. After not nearly long enough, Emily stopped and rested their foreheads together. They were both breathing heavily, which was a relief to Sydney. At least she wasn't the only one excited by just a few smooches.

"Make love to me," Emily whispered and looked at Sydney with such emotion that it took her breath away.

Sydney laid Emily down on the blanket and hovered over her. She'd certainly been with other women before, but instinctively she knew this would be different. This would be making love whereas before it was just sex. Sydney unbuttoned Emily's shirt, allowing it to fall open to display a lovely sight of plump breasts encased in a lacy bra. She leaned down, letting her mouth sink into the soft crevasse. Emily's breathing increased when Sydney ran her tongue under the material's edge, precariously close to her nipple. Sydney unhooked the front clasp of Emily's bra and tossed it aside.

"You're gorgeous." Sydney wasn't surprised by her crackly voice, considering her throat was as dry as Death Valley.

She lovingly cupped Emily's breast and placed a light kiss on the hard tip. Emily pressed the back of Sydney's head toward her, silently urging her on. Wanting to give Emily what she craved, Sydney encircled her lips and lightly sucked, which caused Emily to moan and run her fingers through Sydney's hair. Emily reached down and tugged Sydney's shirt up and over her head. All of a sudden clothes were flying everywhere. Out of the corner of her eye, Sydney saw her underwear soar into a nearby bush. She'd have to remember that later, but right now she could care less. It was probably some sort of record, but within seconds they were naked and intertwined in each other's arms.

Sydney was torn between wanting to caress every part of Emily's body or lie back and enjoy the sensations of being touched. She couldn't do both at the same time. The feel of Emily's mouth, hands, and tongue on her heated body was enough to make her lose all her faculties. In fact, Sydney couldn't even remember her own name when Emily nibbled on her earlobe. Since when were her ears an erotic zone? Apparently, every part of Sydney's body was highly charged when Emily was involved.

As though reading her mind, Emily guided Sydney onto her back and whispered in her ear, "Let me. Please."

Sydney went limp. She was totally at the mercy of this beautiful woman. Emily planted kisses down Sydney, leaving a trail of tingles everywhere she touched. When Emily reached her stomach, Sydney inched her legs apart.

"Is that a hint?" Emily grinned.

"Yes. And in case you didn't pick up on it..." Sydney spread her legs even farther.

Emily looked down, her eyes clouded with desire. She lightly ran a finger over Sydney's slit, barely entering her. It wasn't surprising that Emily's finger was wet with Sydney's arousal. In one hell of a sexy move, Emily slipped the finger between her lips and sucked.

Sydney swallowed hard. The way her insides were pounding and on fire, if Emily didn't touch her soon she'd possibly combust. She'd read once in *Time Magazine* about spontaneous human combustion. It's when a person ignites for no apparent reason. And here they were nowhere near a fire extinguisher.

Emily positioned herself between Sydney's legs and kissed her inner thighs, edging closer to where Sydney needed her most.

"Is this what you want?" Emily licked the full length of her.

Sydney groaned. Yes. That was definitely a good start. But she wanted more. Much more. Sydney cleared her throat. "Deeper." Not terribly informative, but hopefully she'd gotten the message across.

Emily obliged and thrust her tongue inside, stroking in and out. Sydney's legs immediately tensed. If she didn't know any better she'd think she was about to come. She'd heard about women having vaginal orgasms without clit stimulation, but she'd never been one of them. Actually, she didn't even think it was a real thing. But apparently it was, because when Emily entered her with two fingers, every nerve in Sydney's body exploded.

❖

Emily had thought she'd seen every beautiful expression on Sydney's face, but watching her climax was the most exquisite of them all. She looked absolutely radiant with her head thrown back, eyes closed, and lips parted to release a sensual moan. If Emily wasn't aroused before, she certainly was now. She kissed her way up Sydney's luscious body and held her close as her orgasm subsided. Emily envied the way Sydney could let go like that. It was something she'd never been able to do with anyone. Would Sydney be disappointed if Emily didn't climax? Would she think something was wrong with her?

"Hey, are you okay?" Sydney tucked a strand of hair behind Emily's ear. "You tensed up."

"Well, I believe you just did the same thing," Emily said, trying to lighten the mood. Unfortunately, Sydney cocked her head and gave her an I'm-not-buying-it look.

Emily propped herself on one elbow and chewed her lower lip. Finally she said, "I don't want to disappoint you."

Sydney looked surprised. "What are you talking about? You could never do that."

"It's just that I've never had an orgasm with anyone before." Her face heated.

Sydney's eyebrows shot up. And why shouldn't they? This was just plain bizarre. "Really? But you've had—"

"Yes. I've had them alone but not while having sex with anyone. I know. I'm weird." Emily covered her face.

"You are not." Sydney pulled her arm down. "That's not why I want to be with you. It's about making each other feel good and connecting in the deepest way possible."

"I agree, but there always seems to be so much pressure to, you know…" Emily motioned with her hands, which was somehow supposed to represent having an orgasm.

"No pressure here." Sydney stroked Emily's cheek. "The only thing I want is for you to enjoy yourself."

"I'm already doing that." Emily grinned wickedly.

Sydney laid Emily back and kissed her long and hard. Within minutes Emily's heart pounded and all of her senses heightened. The crickets sounded like they were playing a symphony just for them, and the scent of sweet roses filled her nostrils.

Emily shivered when Sydney ran her fingernails down her back. Sydney reached for the blanket, probably thinking she was cold, but Emily pushed it away. She couldn't have been any hotter.

"I love the way you kiss," Sydney whispered into Emily's mouth.

Emily wanted to tell Sydney she felt the same, but her mind went blank when Sydney's soft, wet tongue touched hers. Emily could never tire of kissing this woman. It made her light-headed, intoxicated in the best way possible. Sydney pried their lips apart and gazed at Emily with arctic-blue eyes that gleamed with adoration. This moment really couldn't have been any more perfect. Here she was with the woman of her dreams under the stars and the moon.

Emily inhaled sharply when Sydney nibbled her breast and caressed between her legs. Considering the way her insides hammered, Emily had no doubt she was wetter than she'd ever been before. Sydney knew just how to touch her, how to excite her, like they'd been making love for years.

"Do you like that?" Sydney asked in the sexiest voice ever as she fondled Emily's slick lips.

All Emily could do was nod.

"How about this?" Sydney easily slipped a finger inside.

"Yes," Emily said in a rush of breath.

"I want to taste you."

Emily's eyes practically rolled back in her head. She wanted that, too—more than she'd ever wanted anything. Sydney caressed her way down Emily's body. Luckily, Sydney didn't make Emily wait for what she ached for the most when she licked up and down. Instinctively, Emily's hips undulated when Sydney plunged two fingers inside and stroked.

"You feel so good," Sydney whispered. "So soft and wet."

Sydney reached deep inside and stayed there, barely moving, which caused Emily to squirm. Emily needed to be caressed. Faster. Harder. She pressed her thighs together and growled. If Sydney didn't get the hint from that, she wasn't beyond begging. Emily opened her mouth to speak but then snapped it shut when Sydney's tongue flicked her throbbing clit. Tingles cascaded up and down her spine, which was weird since that's what always happened right before she had an orgasm. The more Sydney concentrated on the small, hard bundle, the more Emily felt waves of pleasure flow from head to toe. One wave crested so high that when it came crashing down, Emily lost all control. A burst of white light flashed before her eyes, and she jerked all over in a never-ending spasm of bliss.

Sydney rested her head on Emily's stomach and hugged her tight as she slowly came down from the high. As Emily's breathing slowed and her faculties returned, she was astonished that she'd actually let go. Not only had she had an orgasm, but it was the most powerful one she'd ever experienced.

CHAPTER TWENTY

The L-Word

Sydney awoke to a breathtaking sight. A bright golden sun peeked over mountains in the distance, painting the sky in reds and oranges. Even more beautiful than that, though, was the woman lying next to her. Memories of their time together last night on Meditation Mount came rushing back. She'd adored every second with Emily. Being with someone she was attracted to physically *and* emotionally left her feeling completely fulfilled.

Not wanting Emily to miss the gorgeous sunrise, Sydney kissed her cheek and nuzzled her neck. "Wake up, beautiful."

Emily pulled the blanket under her chin and snuggled closer to Sydney. "No," she said adamantly.

Sydney chuckled and planted a kiss on her forehead. "You're missing the sunrise. And besides, we should get going before the center opens. I don't think they'd be too happy to find two naked lesbians on their property."

Emily bolted upright and turned her head every which way, appearing confused as to where she was. Within seconds a slow grin crossed her face, and she focused on Sydney with droopy eyes, her hair sticking up at odd angles.

"What an amazing night," Emily said, her smile not faltering.

"The best." Sydney leaned over and pressed their lips together. The effect one kiss had on Sydney was amazing, melting her into a puddle.

When they pulled apart, Emily said, "Last night was a first for me in a couple of ways. I've never had sex outside…and well, that orgasm thing." Emily looked embarrassed that she'd mentioned it again.

Sydney slid an arm around Emily's shoulders and held her close. "Why do you think you've never done that with anyone before? Aside from last night, of course."

"Definitely last night." Emily grinned. "I had always blamed myself, but now I think it's because I've never been with the right woman before. Until now."

Bubbles of happiness gurgled inside Sydney. Who'd have thought she'd be so excited about a relationship?

"Aside from how much I love being with you and how incredible you make me feel," Emily said, "it comes down to trust and understanding. You're the only person who has ever supported my dream of having a bird magazine. You truly understand how important it is to me."

It was amazing how fast those happiness bubbles burst into nothingness. Sydney absolutely wanted *The Tweet* to succeed, but Emily had no idea she'd lied about Owen. Well, not that she'd lied, but she certainly hadn't been honest. Not only had Sydney spied, but she'd also taken cash from Emily's mortal enemy. She'd returned the money, but Sydney had a feeling that fact would get buried amongst everything else. They couldn't start a relationship with a lie between them.

Sydney cleared her throat. "There's something I need to tell you."

Emily sat up straight and peered at Sydney. "Sounds serious."

"You're going to be really angry." Not the best way to start, but if Emily expected the worst, maybe it'd help soften the blow.

Suddenly Emily's eyes grew huge. Geez. She was freaked out before Sydney even told her anything. What would she do when she found out?

Emily grabbed Sydney's arm. "Your audition! What time is it?"

Sydney was about to ask *what audition*, when it dawned on her. She couldn't believe she'd forgotten all about it. Sydney looked at her left arm, which was bare.

"Crap. Where's my watch?" She'd taken it off at some point during their interlude.

They scrambled, looking under discarded pants, bras, anything they could find.

"Maybe it's in the blankets," Emily said.

They bolted upright and vigorously shook them out. Sydney's watch flew into the air and plopped into a nearby pond.

"Fuck!" Sydney raced to the water and saw the timepiece floating on the surface with about ten hungry-looking koi heading straight toward it. "No way, you guys." She nabbed it, glad it was waterproof, and looked at it.

"Phew. I can take a quick shower, change, and just make it. If we leave now." Sydney pouted. She'd wanted to make love to Emily again and thought they'd have time before the center opened.

"We can be together later," Emily said, as though reading Sydney's mind.

Emily hugged Sydney close, which wasn't a move that made her want to put her clothes on and leave.

Sydney ran her hands up and down Emily's bare back. "Maybe we have time for just a little more, you know…"

In an unfortunate move, Emily pulled away and said, "Later, Casanova. Right now let's get you to the most crucial meeting of your life."

Sydney wanted to tell Emily that nothing was more important than she was, even a PowerBar job, and she'd do just that when they had more time. After they got dressed, Sydney realized she hadn't told Emily about Owen. She'd have to do that later. Hopefully, she'd understand.

Sydney had never seen so many tall, photoshopped-looking, fit models in her life. Well, they weren't technically models, but they certainly all appeared to be. She stood in the corner of a packed room of women all waiting to audition to be PowerBar's next star instructor. She didn't have a chance in hell. All of these women looked like they'd just stepped out of a Beverly Hills boutique, and considering how they chatted they obviously all knew each other. Why would they want to hire an outsider like her?

Sydney looked at her cell phone when it chimed, indicating an incoming text. She immediately smiled, and her stomach fluttered when she saw Emily's name.

Hey. How's it going? I'm about to go crazy wondering.

I'm still waiting…with about thirty buff women. I might as well leave now. Sydney was only halfway joking.

No way! You'll be a hundred times better than all of them. I've seen you in action, and you're amazing.

We are still talking about pole dancing, right?

For now. When you get back to the cabin, well, that's another story.

Goose bumps appeared on Sydney's arms as she thought about what would happen. She was pretty sure there'd be lots of kissing and caressing.

I'll text you later. They're starting to call people in.

Good luck!

Sydney shook out her arms and rotated her neck several times, trying to loosen up. Emily was right. She was good. Damn good. She could beat out any of these women. She closed her eyes and took a deep breath.

"Hey, you!"

Sydney's eyes popped open to see Robin standing in front of her. They'd worked together at Leave it to Beaver until Robin quit to start PoleCat.

"Are you waiting to audition?" Robin asked.

"Yeah. This is the PowerBar job I was telling you about."

"Right. The one you're stiffing me for."

Sydney flushed. "Well…you know…it's…"

Robin lightly punched Sydney's shoulder. "I'm just messing with you. But if things don't pan out, I'd still love to tell you about my studio."

"Okay, but…" Sydney took a step back and bumped into the wall when Robin got two inches from her face.

"My goal is to help underprivileged women be stronger physically, mentally, and emotionally." Robin was as excited as a puppy whose owner had just got home from work. "As you and I have talked before, pole dancing can be so much more than a form of sexy entertainment. My place will be a refuge of growth for women who need it most. The ones who've been abused, living on the streets, in bad situations, you know? I'm sure I can't pay as much as PowerBar, but we'll be doing a lot of good. What do you think?"

Robin stared at Sydney in a non-blinking, maniacal sort of way. Sydney had to give her points for passion, that's for sure.

"That sounds great, but…"

Robin backed away, frowning. "Right. I get it. I can't compete."

"It's not that." Well, maybe it was that. "I have my heart set on PowerBar."

"It's cool. Good luck. I really mean that."

"Thanks, Robin. Take care."

Sydney watched Robin disappear into the crowd. From the little she'd just heard, Sydney did appreciate her focus. The less-fortunate women did need help. Sydney knew all about that when she'd been living on the streets.

Sydney stretched her arms high overhead and tensed when someone yelled out her name. This was it. Audition time. Hurriedly, she grabbed her bag and followed a blond woman down the hall and into a room. Four bored-looking people sat behind a long table. The only one she recognized was Sue.

Sue studied a paper for a few seconds and looked up, expressionless. "And you are?"

What the hell? This was the second time she hadn't recognized, or pretended not to recognize, Sydney. Sue knew good and well who she was.

"I'm Sydney Cooper." Sydney gave a wry smile, trying not to show her irritation.

Sue jotted something down and said, "This is Haley." She flicked her pen toward a girl standing next to the pole. "Pretend like you're giving her a first-time lesson. Let's see what you've got."

Suddenly, all eyes were on Sydney. Beads of sweat formed on her upper lip, and her heart drummed against her chest. She locked her knees in an attempt to stop them from shaking. Why was she so nervous? She couldn't be any more prepared. She glanced from Haley to Sue, who had an I-just-dare-you-to-fail look on her face. Sydney froze, her feet superglued to the floor. She was going to totally fuck this up.

Sue loudly cleared her throat and raised an eyebrow. Sydney needed to move, speak, do *something*.

"We don't have all day." Sue frantically tapped a pen on the desk.

Sydney closed her eyes and visualized Emily standing in front of her.

"You can do this," Emily said. *"You're better than all of them."*

Sydney snapped her eyes open and stared at Sue. "I'm ready to knock your socks off."

❖

Emily's stomach contracted when she looked at the clock. This wasn't going to be easy. She sat on the bed, opened her laptop, and connected to FaceTime. Within seconds her mother appeared on-screen.

"I'm glad you wanted to meet. We need to go over the reception menu." Emily's mom held up a notebook and read from it. "We'll have lobster, vegetable and couscous salad…"

"Mom."

"…mini gazpacho soups, tuna tartare cones…"

"Mom." Was her mother deaf?

"…prosciutto-wrapped persimmons with—"

"Mom!" Emily practically screamed. That did the trick. Her mother's eyes flicked upward. "I need to tell you something."

"I know you're not fond of persimmons, but I think we should—"

"It's not that. There isn't…Gretchen and I…well, really, it was my decision…um…"

"What in the world are you trying to say?"

"There isn't going to be a wedding."

Her mother gasped. "You two are *not* eloping. Not after all the work I've put into this."

"What I mean is, we're not getting married. I broke up with Gretchen."

Gobsmacked. That was the only way to describe Emily's mother. Utterly and completely gobsmacked.

"Mom? Did you hear me?"

"What. Did. You. Do?"

"I'm not in love with Gretchen."

"What's love got to do with it?" Her mother threw her hands up in the air.

"Really? You're quoting Tina Turner songs?"

"Don't you dare make light of this, young lady." Emily's mother wagged a finger at the screen. "I cannot believe you're doing this."

"Don't you want me to be happy?"

Her mother stared, expressionless. It seemed like a simple question. Wouldn't any parent want that for their child? Maybe not, considering her mom pressed her lips together hard and didn't utter a sound.

"I'm in love with someone else," Emily said. "She's a pole dancer and the most amazing woman I've ever met."

If they hadn't been chatting via computer, Emily was sure her mother would have slapped her across the face. She looked mortified.

"A stripper?"

"No. Sydney is *not* a stripper. She's a very talented pole-dancing instructor, and right now she's auditioning for a position at a studio in Beverly Hills."

Her mother put her hands over her ears. "I can't believe what I'm hearing. You're dating a stripper." Suddenly, she disappeared from the screen. Less than a minute later, she returned, breathing heavily into a paper bag.

"Are you all right?" Emily asked, concerned that her mother would faint from hyperventilating.

After a few moments, she lowered the bag. "Are you proud of yourself? This is what you've done to your mother."

Emily sighed and rubbed her forehead. She needed to take a different tack here. "Remember how you told me that you were in love with someone before Dad? Well, Sydney is my Troy. Don't you ever wonder what would've happened if you'd married the love of your life?"

Her mother paused and actually seemed to consider the notion right before she vigorously shook her head. "We accepted your lesbian thing and have learned to love Gretchen like she was our own, but not this. We would never condone you dating a stripper. You're making the biggest mistake of your life, Emily. Gretchen is perfect for you."

"No. She's perfect for *you*. Look. I'm done talking about this. I wanted you to know so you could cancel any arrangements as soon as possible. I'll be happy to pay for anything that isn't refundable. I'll talk to you later."

Emily disconnected and sat back against the headboard. She wasn't sure why her mother's reaction surprised her so much. She should have expected nothing less. Still, though, Emily had hoped she'd have been understanding, especially after the Troy comparison.

Emily looked at the door when Sydney cleared her throat. "Hey. When did you get back? How'd it go?"

Sydney was pasty white and looked like she might faint. The audition must not have gone well. Sydney shuffled into the room and stood by the bed with her arms crossed.

"It went fine. They said they'd call tomorrow with their decision."

"Great. So, you're happy with your performance?"

Sydney nodded but seemed anything but pleased.

"Are you nervous?" Maybe that was why she appeared so morose.

"No. I feel pretty confident."

"Great. Are you tired?" Something was obviously bugging her.

"No."

"Is something wrong? You seem upset."

Sydney paused and looked at Emily's computer. "I didn't mean to eavesdrop."

Damn. She'd overhead Emily's conversation with her mother. Emily scooted to the edge of the bed and looked up at Sydney. "How much did you hear?"

"Enough to know that she doesn't approve of us dating."

Emily placed her hands on Sydney's hips. "Don't let anything she says bother you. It certainly doesn't reflect how I feel."

"I don't want to come between you and your parents."

"You're not. They'll come around."

Sydney took a step back, causing Emily to drop her arms. "Maybe us dating isn't such a great idea."

"What? No. Of course it is."

"Why don't we take some time and think about things?" Sydney spun around, like she was about to walk out of the room.

"Wait!" Emily said. "Did you also hear me tell my mother I'm in love with you?"

Sydney stopped and turned, her expression unreadable.

"I don't have to think about anything, Sydney. I know exactly what I want. And that's you." Emily stood and closed the distance between them.

"You're in love with me?" Sydney's eyes softened, and a slight grin played on her lips.

"Totally and completely."

"I love you, too." Sydney slipped her arms around Emily's waist and kissed her.

A giggle bubbled deep in Emily's throat. Seriously? This was one of the most romantic moments of her life, and she was about to burst out laughing. It wasn't her fault, though. She felt downright giddy. Emily withdrew her mouth. "I think this might be the happiest I've ever been."

Sydney outright laughed. Maybe she'd been holding back a giggle, too. "I never thought I'd ever meet anyone I'd want to spend the rest of my life with. Hell. I didn't even think happily-ever-after was possible. But now I do because I want that with you more than anything."

They pressed their lips together and collapsed into the bed, where they made love well into the night.

CHAPTER TWENTY-ONE

Truth and Consequences

Emily couldn't snap pictures fast enough. This was the most amazing thing she'd ever seen. She and Sydney were on separate ladders just a few feet away from twenty lovebirds perched in a fig tree. This was the first time she'd been back since falling. Emily lowered her camera and looked at Sydney, awestruck by the breathtaking smile on her face. Emily wanted to ask what she was thinking but was afraid the sound of her voice would scare the birds away. And anyway, Emily could tell from the sparkle in Sydney's eyes that she was just as excited as Emily was.

The moment was perfect and got even better when one of the birds flew onto a branch literally inches from Emily's nose. It was magnificent with its emerald wings, grass-green belly, and gray head. She still couldn't believe she was actually looking at the elusive Madagascar lovebirds and that she had a disc full of photos in her camera to prove it. *The Tweet* would be the talk of the birding world for sure. Emily gazed at the incredible creature as it flew upward and landed next to another bird, who was obviously its mate. They rubbed necks and bit and nipped each other's beaks. Emily snapped a few more photos and motioned to Sydney that she was going down the ladder. Sydney gave her a stern be-careful look.

"Wow. That was amazing," Sydney said when they both reached the ground. "I particularly liked the two that were snuggling. They've got the right idea."

Sydney snaked her arms around Emily's waist and kissed her. It was one of those intimate, deep kisses that left Emily weak all over. Finally, they parted but stayed a breath away from each other.

"I've been waiting to do that all day," Sydney whispered.

"All day, huh?" Emily grinned. "I do believe we spent the morning in bed doing more than kissing."

"This morning seems like an eternity ago."

"Why, Ms. Cooper, I do believe you're a romantic."

Sydney's cheeks tinted pink. "That's a side you seem to bring out in me."

Emily was going to suggest they take a break and head back to the cabin, where they could have a repeat of this morning, but she spotted someone approaching.

"It's Fran," Sydney said, as the figure came into view. "Have you told her about finding the you-know-what?" Sydney pointed upward.

Emily shook her head and felt suddenly ill. She hadn't put much thought into what would happen to the lovebirds, mostly because she hadn't even known if they actually existed. She could call the National Audubon Society and have them transported back to the aviary in San Diego, but that didn't sit well with her. They'd survived in the wild for this long; she wanted them to be free. Whatever the plan, it was clear that Fran wanted them off of her property...and fast.

"I had a feeling about you two." Fran wagged her finger.

At first, Emily wasn't sure what she meant but then realized that she and Sydney were entwined in each other's arms.

"Actually, we weren't a couple when you asked at dinner but," Emily gazed at Sydney, "things have changed."

"I'm happy you two finally wised up. I could see it plain as day that you belonged together."

"And what about you and Bud?" Sydney smirked and wiggled her eyebrows.

"Oh...well..." Fran stared at the ground and shuffled her feet. "We...uh...we've seen each other a few times."

"Have you now?" Emily grinned. She wanted everyone to be as happy as she was.

"Any wedding bells in the future?" Sydney nudged Fran's shoulder.

"Now you two stop joshing me. I came out here to see if you've had any luck finding those birds." Fran ducked when a lovebird whizzed over her head. "What the hell was that?"

Emily smiled tightly. "That was a lovebird."

"You found those dang-blasted things and didn't tell me?" Fran spread her legs wide and rested her fists on her hips.

"Just the other day," Sydney said quickly, probably trying to help. "But then Emily fell out of a tree."

Fran scrunched her thick eyebrows together. "Are you okay?"

"I'm fine. Fran, there's something about the birds I haven't told you. They're rare Madagascar lovebirds. They escaped from an aviary two years ago, and it's amazing they've survived. They don't exist in the wild anywhere in the US. What you have on your farm is a huge exposé in the birding world."

"Wait a second." Fran held up a hand. "You never intended to help me, did you? You're just trying to get a story for your magazine."

"No. No. Well, yes."

"If that don't beat all." Fran clenched her fists and looked like she was about to deck Emily. "Is that why some man was asking all sorts of questions?"

Emily and Sydney exchanged curious glances.

"What man?" Emily asked.

"Some stranger come knocking on my door yesterday wanting to know about the lovebirds."

Emily's heart raced. "What did he look like?"

"He was kindly large, bald...oh and he wore a hearing aid and kept talking about it like I should feel sorry for him." Fran snorted.

Every muscle in Emily's body tensed. She turned to Sydney and whispered, "Owen."

"What the hell's going on here?" Fran asked.

"Owen is my biggest competitor." Emily sneered. "What'd you tell him?"

"Nothing. I threw him out for ignoring my no-trespassing signs."

Emily sighed in relief and grabbed Fran's arm. "Please keep the Madagascar lovebirds a secret, Fran. This is too important."

Fran jerked back. "Why should I? Maybe he can help me if you won't."

"Owen is a thief," Sydney said. "He stole a story from Emily and printed it as his own."

"None of that is my concern. It's been almost two weeks, and these little buggers are still eating my figs!"

"I understand how you feel," Emily said. "Just give me another week to take photos, write the story, and send it to press. After that you can tell anyone you want to about the lovebirds. Please, Fran. I'm asking you as a friend." Emily flashed pleading eyes.

"A week? I'll give you two more days. Come Wednesday, I want those birds gone." Fran stomped away.

❖

"How in the world did Owen find out about the lovebirds?" Emily covered her face with her hands.

Little did Emily know that Sydney actually had the answer to that rhetorical question. This was all her fault. If she hadn't made a pact with the devil, none of this would have happened. She needed to tell Emily the truth, but now wasn't the right time. Not when she was so upset.

"Let's look on the bright side," Sydney said, hoping Emily didn't detect the tremble in her voice. "You still have a couple of days to get the article printed."

"I need more time than that."

"Well, Owen probably doesn't know that the lovebirds are Madagascar ones. Otherwise he wouldn't have asked about them. You'll have a huge jump on him."

"I suppose. If I can wrap everything up and put a rush on the print job before he even knows what's going on…"

"Exactly," Sydney said and forced a smile. "Have you written the article yet?"

"No, but it won't take long. I've already done all the research. I just need to get it down on paper. The most important thing is the photos."

"You got a lot of good ones today, right?"

"I did." Emily nodded. "I still can't figure out how Owen found out about this."

"It's getting late," Sydney said. "Let's go, and we can come back tomorrow."

They walked hand in hand down a dirt path through the forest of fig trees, Sydney feeling guiltier with every step.

After a few minutes, Emily stopped in her tracks. "I can't believe I've been so selfish. Have you heard about the audition results yet?"

Sydney pulled out her cell phone. "Doesn't look like I missed a call."

"Are they supposed to let you know today?"

"That's what Sue said. Considering it's so late, I doubt I got it. They want the person to start this Wednesday."

"That soon? You'd have to leave tomorrow." Emily looked terribly sad.

Sydney put an arm around Emily's shoulders. "You'll have things wrapped up here in a couple of days, and we'll be together again before you know it."

"I know, but I'll miss you."

"Me, too." Sydney placed a kiss on Emily's lips.

Tonight. Sydney would tell Emily about Owen tonight. She'd been deceiving her long enough.

Emily reached under the table and placed a hand on Sydney's knee. She seemed upset, probably nervous to find out about the PowerBar job. Emily was tempted to ask her about it but figured that might make things worse. For Sydney's sake, Emily hoped Sue would call soon.

"Thanks for dinner," Emily said. "It was delicious."

Sydney had cooked spaghetti and garlic bread. The bread was so scrumptious, Emily could have filled up on it alone, but she was planning to seduce Sydney later and didn't want garlic breath.

"You're welcome." Sydney pushed her plate aside and turned her chair to face Emily. "Do you remember when we were on Meditation Mount?"

"Vaguely." Emily grinned seductively to let Sydney know she was joking. How could she forget one of the most amazing nights of her life?

"Actually, I meant when I said that I had something to tell you. Something you weren't going to like." Sydney inhaled a shaky breath.

Emily gently squeezed Sydney's knee. "Hey, you can tell me anything."

"It's just…I care about you so much. I would absolutely hate for anything I've done to hurt you." Sydney's hand quivered when she grabbed her glass and swallowed several gulps of water.

"I don't know what this is about, but I'm sure it can't be that bad."

Sydney cleared her throat several times and jumped up. "I'm going to get more water."

Emily watched as she disappeared into the kitchen, curious as to what was going on. A ringing caused Emily to look around the room. It was coming from Sydney's cell phone on the coffee table. She rushed into the living room and looked at the display, noting the Los Angeles area code.

"Sydney, I think Sue is calling you! Hurry. She might hang up."

"Answer it for me," Sydney yelled from the kitchen. "I'll be right there."

Hurriedly, Emily placed the receiver to her ear. "Hello?"

A strange man's voice spewed a jumble of confusing words. "We made a deal. I paid you good money to find out what story Emily is working on, and I expect you to help me."

"W-what?"

"You heard me. Now tell me what's going on."

Maybe that wasn't such a strange voice after all. It sounded familiar. Really familiar.

"Owen?"

"Who is this?"

"Emily. Why…how…what are you doing calling Sydney?" None of this made any sense whatsoever.

Silence.

"How'd you get her number?"

"Ah. She didn't tell you about our little deal after all, did she?" Owen chuckled.

Emily's chest tightened, and she inhaled short, shallow breaths. What the hell was he talking about?

"I paid her to spy on you," Owen said. "You might as well tell me what story you're working on because I'll find out soon enough."

Sydney rushed out of the kitchen and whispered, "Is it Sue?"

Emily stared, the phone slowly slipping from her grasp.

Sydney grabbed it before it fell to the floor. "Hi. Sue?"

It was as though Sydney had been struck by lightning. Her entire body jerked and stiffened, and her eyes bugged. After less than ten seconds, she disconnected and lowered the phone.

Emily had a million questions, but her mind was such a jumbled mess she couldn't form intelligible words. She saw Sydney's lips moving and heard her voice, but nothing she said registered.

"Wait!" Emily held up a hand. "You're in cahoots with Owen? He paid you to spy on me?"

All the color drained from Sydney's face. "It's not like that. I met him when we first came to the cabin. You and I didn't even know each other, and we weren't exactly friendly. He offered me money to tell him what story you're working on."

"Oh my God." Emily couldn't believe what she was hearing.

"After we became friends I sent the money back to him and told him never to contact me again. Please understand. If—"

"*Understand?* I understand that you lied to me and stabbed me in the back."

Emily's head spun. She sat on the couch, afraid she was about to faint. Sydney sat beside her, too close considering the circumstances.

"I'm so sorry." Sydney's voice cracked.

"What did you tell him?"

Sydney rubbed her forehead. "I told him you were doing a lovebird story. That's all. I didn't say anything about the Madagascar birds."

"Wait a minute." Emily looked directly at Sydney. "That's why you started being nice to me. You didn't want to be my friend. You were trying to get information for Owen. You used me." Emily's stomach soured. Where was a barf bag when you needed one?

Sydney opened her mouth but then closed it. It was true. She couldn't even deny it. Emily stood and placed a hand on the armrest for balance.

"I want you out of the cabin before sunrise tomorrow."

Sydney gazed up with pleading eyes. "Please believe me. That may be how it started, but it's not how I feel now."

"Good-bye, Sydney."

Emily ran upstairs and into Jill's office. She closed the door, leaned back against the frame, and slid down until she was sitting. She seemed to have a gaping hole in her heart, a hole that would never be filled again. She wanted to cry and punch something all at the same time. Never before had she experienced such emotional pain. But then again, she'd never been in love.

❖

Regret is a terrible thing, especially when you can't do anything to change what happened. Sydney sat on the couch for God knows how long chastising herself for hurting the person she cared about the most. Sydney hated the way Emily had looked at her as though she'd never seen her before, like she didn't even know who she was. Emily would probably never forgive her, not that she could blame her. Sydney had to try to talk to her again. She couldn't give up on the love of her life that easily.

Sydney turned out the lights, grabbed her cell phone, and went upstairs. She knocked on the office door.

"Emily?" No response. "I'm so sorry I hurt you. When I met Owen I was broke and really needed the money. I know that's no excuse, but you and I were arguing about who would stay in the cabin. We didn't even know each other. Yes, I was being nice to get information, but that changed after I fell in love with you. Please. Can't we just talk about this?"

Sydney put her ear against the door. Complete silence. Maybe after a night's sleep Emily would be more receptive. Sydney shuffled to the bedroom and lay down in the bed. After a few minutes, her cell phone rang. She halfway hoped it'd be Owen again just so she could tell him to go to hell.

"Hello."

"This is Sue from PowerBar."

Sydney sat upright. "Hi, Sue."

"Sorry it's so late, but it's been quite a day. You were impressive in the audition…"

Sydney waited for the "but." When it came to Sue, there always was one.

"And I'd like to offer you a full-time position."

Sydney felt a jolt of adrenaline. "Seriously? Wow."

"Can you start day after tomorrow? I need you to teach three intro classes."

"Um. Sure."

"Great. Get there at seven sharp so we can get all the new-hire paperwork out of the way."

"Will do. And thanks. You won't regret this."

Sydney hung up, completely stunned. She'd actually got the job. The only thing she wanted to do was run and tell Emily. She would have been so excited and proud of Sydney. If things were different, they would have celebrated with champagne and a night of making love. Instead, Emily despised her and would probably never talk to her again.

CHAPTER TWENTY-TWO

Break a Leg

A golden sun peeked over the pine trees, shooting beams of sparkling rays on Emily as she stood on the deck of the cabin. It was going to be a beautiful day, much too beautiful considering how empty she felt inside. She'd cried herself to sleep last night and awoke with burning, itchy eyes and a pounding head. None of that, though, could compare to the pain in her heart. Even though she was hurt and angry, she couldn't simply flip a switch and turn off her feelings for Sydney. Emily still loved her, which made all this even worse.

Emily turned when she heard a noise behind her. It was Sydney. She looked like Emily felt: exhausted and terribly sad. For a moment, she almost felt sorry for her until she remembered the betrayal.

"I asked you to leave," Emily said in an emotionless voice.

"I'm not giving up on us. You're the best thing that's ever happened to me."

"Wish I could say the same thing."

Sydney winced, like Emily had just stuck her with a sharp needle. "Do you think you can ever forgive me?"

"You don't get it. Not only did you spy on me and put my magazine in jeopardy, but worse than anything, you pretended to be my friend. It was all just an act."

Sydney looked like she'd just lost the final game of the World Series. She probably knew better than to say anything more, knowing it would have no effect.

Emily breezed past Sydney and said, "Be gone by the time I get back."

She was tempted to turn around and look into Sydney's soulful blue eyes one last time, but she couldn't. Walking away was hard enough as it was. Instead, Emily grabbed her keys and left.

The drive to Fran's was a quiet one. Every song on the radio reminded Emily of Sydney, so she shut it off. She thought about what Sydney had asked: Could Emily ever forgive her? She wished she could. She wanted nothing more than to turn back time to when everything was perfect with the world. But she didn't see how that was possible. This was a wound that went too deep.

"What the..." Emily screeched to a halt when she saw Owen's truck parked outside Fran's gate. She got out and marched right up to him. "What are you doing here?"

Owen smirked and cracked his knuckles. "It took me a while, but I know what story you're after."

Emily's stomach turned inside out. "Get out of here, Owen, or else Fran will call the cops. She doesn't allow anyone to trespass on her property."

"Oh, yeah? Well, what do you think you're doing?"

"I have a key. Fran and I are friends. I'm serious. You better scram."

Emily opened the gate, drove through, and locked it again. She flashed Owen a dirty, warning glare and headed down the trail to the fig farm. Was he serious? Did he really know about the Madagascar lovebirds? Maybe that was just a ploy to make Emily nervous. Either way, she needed to finish taking photos and write the article fast.

Emily hiked to the fig tree, hung her Bird Cam around her neck, and climbed up the ladder. Strange how seeing the lovebirds didn't excite her as much as before, probably because Sydney wasn't here to share it with her. Would she ever feel as blissful as she had with Sydney? Would her heart ever heal? Funny how breaking it off with Sydney had been a hundred times worse than with Gretchen. Even though Emily was crushed, she couldn't regret meeting Sydney. She'd shown her what true love felt like, even if for a short time.

Emily shook her head, hoping it'd rid her mind of thoughts about Sydney. The lovebirds were all that mattered now. She zoomed in on a bird resting in a tree hole and snapped several photos. Maybe its mate was foraging for food since the species was rarely seen alone. Emily scanned the area and focused on two lovebirds practically necking. They lightly pecked beaks just like the ones Emily and Sydney had seen yesterday.

Amazing how much had changed in just one day. No more than twenty-four hours ago she and Sydney were as close as two lovebirds, and now they couldn't be further apart. A hard lump formed in Emily's throat and tears pooled in her eyes, blurring her vision. She licked her lips and tasted salt. Great. Standing at the top of a ladder was not the time or place to start bawling.

Emily sniffed and wiped her eyes with her hands. Her heart lurched when she swayed backward. Quickly, she grabbed the ladder, but the steel slipped through her wet fingers, and she tipped sideways, losing her balance.

Oh, God. Not again!

❖

Sydney looked at the clock for the zillionth time. She'd been waiting for Emily to get back to the cabin to try to talk to her again. How long could she possibly stay at the farm? She'd left early that morning. Sydney could track her down there, but she didn't think that'd go over very well, considering the chilly reception earlier.

Sydney pressed the speed dial on her phone. She'd texted Monica last night to tell her about the PowerBar job, and she'd insisted on taking Sydney to dinner to celebrate. It'd probably be a night of drinking, even though Sydney had to be at work early, but she'd reluctantly agreed.

"Hey, Monica. It's me."

"Where are you?"

"Still in Ojai. I'm about to leave."

"You better get your ass over here. It's a two-hour drive, and we have seven o'clock reservations. What's wrong? You sound down."

"Nothing. I'm fine." Sydney was glad she hadn't told Monica about dating Emily. The last thing she wanted to talk about was the breakup.

"You should be ecstatic. You finally got the job you've been bitching about for years."

"I know." Monica was right, but the success had little meaning without Emily in her life. "I'll be there by six thirty. See you then."

Sydney hung up, moved the living room blinds aside, and peeked out, desperately wishing Emily would drive up. Ten minutes passed before Sydney's cell phone rang. It was probably Monica again, checking to see if she'd left yet. Sydney's breath caught in her throat when she looked at the display. It was Emily's number. Maybe she was calling to make up.

"Hello?"

"Hey, it's Fran."

Sydney wrinkled her nose. "What are you doing calling from Emily's phone?"

"We're at the hospital."

Sydney's stomach dropped. "Is Emily okay?"

"She's fine. Mostly."

"What happened?"

"Well, I'm not really sure. Maybe you should just get over here, and I'll explain everything."

"I'm on my way."

For a brief second, Sydney paused to let the information sink in. Emily was obviously either hurt or sick. Hospitals didn't hold people unless something was terribly wrong, but Fran had said she was fine... *mostly*, whatever that meant. Sydney grabbed her keys and was out the door in a flash. Luckily, the hospital was only a couple of miles away, so she was marching through the entrance in no time.

Sydney approached the main desk. "Hi. I'm looking for information about Emily Wellington."

A nurse glanced at Sydney, typed something into a computer, and asked, "Are you related to her?"

Ugh. They only asked that when it was serious. Sydney had seen *Grey's Anatomy* enough to know that. "I'm her girlfriend." Well, *was* her girlfriend.

"I'm sorry, but I can only give patient information to a relative."

Sydney's heart plummeted. That sounded life-threatening. "Where's the waiting room?" Hopefully, Fran would be there.

"Down the hall to your right."

Sydney bolted down the corridor and immediately spotted Fran sitting in a chair flipping through a magazine. She looked awfully relaxed, considering the circumstances. Sydney rushed over to her. "What's going on?"

Fran tossed the magazine into an empty chair and stood. "I'm glad you're here. I don't know why Emily told me not to call you, maybe 'cause she's loopy on drugs, but I figured you'd want to know."

Sydney felt an ounce of relief. At least Emily was coherent and talking, even if it was to tell Fran not to contact her. "What happened?"

"I was just minding my own business when I heard sirens and saw flashing lights barreling toward the farm. They said they got a 911 call about someone hurt in the fig trees. At first I thought it was a mistake until I remembered Emily was out there. I showed them where she was, and sure enough she was lying on the ground unconscious. She came to after we got here and said she fell out of the tree."

"Oh my God." Sydney covered her mouth with her hand.

"Don't worry. She's okay." Fran looked like she was going to hug Sydney but then changed her mind. "Except for a mild concussion and a broken ankle."

That's *okay*? Even one scratch on sweet Emily's body would be too much. But this? This was major. "What did the doctor say?"

"She has to stay overnight for observation, but he doesn't foresee any problems."

"Poor Emily. Who did you say called 911?"

Fran shrugged. "I dunno. Maybe Emily did before she passed out. Do you want to see her?"

"Can I? The nurse said only relatives are allowed."

"Balderdash. She's in room twelve. Do you care if I head back to the farm?"

"No problem. I'll take care of things here."

"Call me later and let me know how she's doing."

"Will do. Thanks, Fran."

Butterflies flitted in Sydney's solar plexus as she walked to Emily's room. She stood outside the door and stared at the number twelve for a full minute. Undoubtedly, she was the last person Emily would want to see. Still, though, Sydney had to make sure she was okay. She put her hand on the cold steel handle, turned it, and peeked into the room, her heart melting at the sight of Emily lying helplessly in bed with her eyes closed. She tiptoed into the room and stood beside the bed, wincing at the sight of a cast up to Emily's knee.

Sydney would have given anything to change places with her. She, not Emily, deserved to be in that bed. Sydney's fingers itched to stroke Emily's cheek or hold her hand, but she didn't want to wake her. Instead, she sat in a chair beside the bed and didn't take her eyes off of the woman she loved.

Fifteen minutes later, a nurse walked in. Sydney sat upright, ready for a fight if she was asked to leave. Luckily, the nurse completely ignored her and roused Emily awake.

"It's time for your pain pill, Ms. Wellington."

Emily's head swayed back and forth, and her bloodshot eyes fluttered open. She groaned, popped the pill into her mouth, and washed it down with a few gulps of water. It wasn't until the nurse left that Emily spotted her. Her eyes lit up and a slow smile crept across her lips. She reached out her hand, which Sydney immediately grabbed. Sydney couldn't have been more overjoyed. Emily was happy to see her.

"How do you feel?" Sydney tucked a strand of hair behind Emily's ear with her free hand.

"Like I was hit by a plane. One going a thousand miles an hour."

Emily stared at Sydney, furrowed her brow, and cocked her head. Sydney was sure she was remembering what had happened between them. Suddenly, Emily jerked her hand back.

"What are you doing here? I told Fran not to call you."

"I wanted to make sure you're all right."

"I'm fine. You can go now."

That was absolutely the last thing Sydney wanted to do. "You need someone to help you."

"I can take care of myself." Emily struggled to sit upright and rubbed her forehead.

"Does your head hurt? The doctor said you have a concussion."

Emily ignored the question, closed her eyes, and reclined into her pillow.

Sydney gazed at Emily's beautiful face. Even after all she'd been through she still looked stunning. "Em, I'm not asking you to forgive me or get back together, but at least let me help you."

No response.

"Do you want me to call your parents?"

Emily's eyes popped open. "Absolutely not. They'd be no help at all. I'll contact them after I get home."

"You can't drive with a broken ankle. Let me take you back to LA."

"I don't want your help. I'll Uber or something after I get the story written."

Abruptly, Emily clutched her chest. Was she having a heart attack? Or trouble breathing?

"Where's my camera? It was around my neck when I fell." Fear filled Emily's eyes as she frantically scanned the room. "Do you see it anywhere?"

Sydney opened drawers and closets, and even looked in the bathroom. "It's not here."

"Oh, God." Emily looked like she was about to faint.

"Relax. I'll go ask the nurse if they have any of your possessions."

"Hurry!"

Sydney scurried down the hall to the nurses' station. "I'm with Emily Wellington in room twelve, and she was wondering if the emergency personnel picked up any of her belongings when they found her. Specifically, she's looking for a camera."

The nurse jutted out her lower lip and shook her head. "No. I don't remember seeing anything when they brought her in, and all of her belongings would be in the room."

"Are you sure?"

The woman responded with a raised eyebrow.

"Got it. Thanks."

Emily was biting the nail of her pinky finger when Sydney got back to the room. "Well?"

"They don't have it."

"Damn." Emily clenched her fists.

"Don't worry. We'll find it."

"You don't understand. All of my photos are in that camera. Without it, I have no proof of the Madagascar lovebirds. I have no story."

"But didn't you…"

"No. I didn't download them on the computer," Emily said, reading Sydney's mind. "I was going to do it last night…but…well…I got a bit distracted." Emily glared at her.

"I see. Your camera must still be by the fig tree. It probably came off your neck when you fell."

Emily closed her eyes and shook her head. "I bet it's shattered."

"Maybe not. But if so, you can just take more photos."

"I'm screwed. Owen said he knows about the lovebirds. If he gets Fran to let him on her property, he'll get the story before me. There's no way I can climb a ladder with a broken ankle to take pictures."

"No, but I can."

The muscles in Emily's jaw visibly tensed. "I said I don't need your help."

Sydney raked her fingers through her hair and sighed. "Look. I'm not lame enough to think that my helping you will make you forgive me. I know you don't want anything to do with me, and that'll probably never change. This is about the lovebirds, not us."

Emily narrowed her gaze and studied Sydney for several long seconds. "How do I know you're not still spying for Owen?"

"I swear I cut off all contact with him after I found out how important this story was to you. I know you don't believe me, but I love you, Emily. I wouldn't purposely do anything to hurt you." Sydney swallowed a hard lump in her throat. How she wanted to cradle Emily in her arms and show her how much she meant to her.

Emily blew out a breath. "All right. But once the article is done, so are we."

Ouch. That remark stung even though Sydney was expecting it.

"I understand. It's too late now, so I'll go to Fran's in the morning and look for the camera. Do you think you'll be released tomorrow?"

"Probably. I'll find out after I see the doctor."

"Okay. I'll swing by here after Fran's."

They held each other's gaze for several seconds until Emily looked away.

"I guess I'll be going." Sydney didn't want to overstay her welcome and risk Emily changing her mind. "Do you need anything else?"

Emily yawned and rubbed her eyes. "No."

"Get some rest. And I'm glad you weren't seriously hurt." Sydney reached out to squeeze Emily's hand but then pulled back. "Right. Well, good night."

Sydney exited the room and walked down the hall, feeling lighter than she had all day. They weren't dating again, but at least Emily was talking to her and they'd get a few more days together. Suddenly,

Sydney stopped. What was she thinking? She had to start a new job tomorrow morning. Well, that wouldn't happen. Surely Sue would understand.

Sydney pulled out her phone and called PowerBar. Sue answered on the second ring.

"Hi. This is Sydney Cooper."

"Oh. I'm glad you called. I forgot to tell you to park in the garage across the street and we'll validate your parking."

"Great. But…umm…something came up. A friend of mine is in the hospital in Ojai, and I need to help her out for a few days. Could I possibly start work next week?"

It was so quiet Sydney could have heard a bird feather hit the floor. Her stomach twisted in a knot with the intuitive knowing that this was not going to go over well.

"You're saying you can't come in tomorrow?" Sue spoke slowly and with a razor-sharp edge.

"It's a medical emergency."

"Is your friend in intensive care?"

"Well. No."

"Is it a life-and-death situation?"

"Not exactly. She has a broken ankle and concussion. But she needs help with a lovebird article and someone to drive her back to LA." Sydney mentally bonked herself over the head. She should have kept her big mouth shut after "concussion."

"Are you saying that's more important than this job?" Sue's voice rose several octaves.

"No. Of course not. It's a long, complicated story. She really needs my help. I'm just asking to start a few days later."

"Unbelievable." Sydney could picture Sue shaking her head and rolling her eyes. "I have three classes tomorrow with no instructor because you're too busy playing lovebirds with your *friend*."

"It's not like that."

"I gave you a chance to make something of yourself, and this is how you repay me? All the other instructors have packed schedules, which means I'll personally be teaching your classes."

"I'm really sorry, Sue. If there was any other way, I'd be there."

"This isn't going to work out. Your priorities are skewed."

Sydney couldn't really argue that point. Emily *was* her priority.

"If you're not here tomorrow, don't bother ever coming in." Sue slammed the phone down.

Crap. Crap. Crap.

What was Sydney supposed to do now? She didn't want to quit before she even started. She'd been trying to get this job forever. And she *was* unemployed. The sensible thing to do would be to hightail it back to LA tonight. It wasn't like Emily wanted her there anyway. But she couldn't. It was her fault Emily was up against a deadline and that Owen was lurking around. Sydney couldn't leave her in the lurch. She was more important than a job. Sydney chuckled to herself. She never thought she'd feel that way about anyone.

Now that she'd made her decision, not that there'd been much of a debate, she needed to tell Monica. Text was easier, or rather more evasive, than calling.

Something came up and I'm staying in Ojai for a few days. Sorry about dinner. I'll explain later.

Monica must have had the phone in her hand because she responded immediately. *Why?! What about the job?*

Doesn't look like it's going to work out.

They fired you already?

I quit. I'll explain later.

Two seconds later, Sydney's phone rang. The last thing she wanted to do was talk to Monica, so she let it go to voice mail. She'd deal with her later.

CHAPTER TWENTY-THREE

Payback Time

"Guess three hundred, you fool!" Emily yelled from her hospital bed.

She'd wanted something to pass the time until Sydney arrived so she'd clicked on the TV. Big mistake. *The Price Is Right* was about to drive her insane. The contestants were guessing ridiculously low prices for a fancy, complicated coffee machine like the one in the cabin. She almost shut the thing off when the next person said, "Fifty dollars." It was enjoyable, though, to watch their hopeful little pathetic faces instantly drop when the host revealed the price to be three hundred and fifty.

"Idiots." Emily pressed the power button and threw the remote into a nearby chair.

She didn't usually get this agitated, but she'd been lying in bed for almost twenty-four hours with absolutely nothing to do. She was beyond ready to leave and anxious to find out if Sydney had retrieved her Bird Cam.

Emily sat upright when Sydney walked in. "Well?"

Sydney grimaced. "I looked everywhere. Even within a mile radius, thinking maybe a coyote got ahold of it."

"That's just great," Emily said sarcastically and crossed her arms.

"If anyone finds it, at least it has your name and address inside. Maybe you'll get it back."

"Maybe," Emily grumbled.

"Do you have another camera? I can go out there this afternoon and take pictures."

"It's not an Audubon Bird Cam, but yes, I have another one. I'm going with you, though."

"No offense, but you'd slow me down. Why not stay at the cabin to write the article, and I'll take photos. If you don't like what I get, I'll go back."

Emily hated to agree, but Sydney was right. She needed to stay put and get the story done and off to the printers. Disappointment gripped Emily's insides. Did this mean she'd never get to see the Madagascar lovebirds again? Damn broken ankle.

Sydney stood beside the bed, so close Emily was tempted to reach out and touch her. Luckily, she came to her senses before she did anything stupid. They weren't together anymore, a fact that she'd have to keep reminding herself of.

"How are you feeling?" Tenderness filled Sydney's eyes. If Emily didn't know any better, she'd think Sydney really was in love with her. Maybe she had started out spying but then did fall in love with her. God. How she wanted to believe that was true.

"Sore," Emily said. "I can leave after I fill out some paperwork from the front desk."

"Great. Want me to go grab it?"

"Sure." Emily watched Sydney walk toward the door. "Hey," she said, which prompted Sydney to stop and turn around. "Thanks. You know. For helping me."

Sydney's face lit up. "You're welcome."

"Sorry you didn't get the PowerBar job. They wanted the person to start today, right?"

Sydney's eyes dropped to the floor. "It's not important."

"I know how much you wanted it."

"I'm exactly where I want to be." Sydney looked directly at Emily and flashed a beautiful, heart-stopping smile.

The gnawing feeling that something wasn't right first hit Sydney when she was looking for the camera. She hadn't wanted to express this point to Emily, but its disappearance disturbed her. The EMTs hadn't found it, and the coyote theory sounded plausible, except for the fact that Fran had said she'd never seen one on her property.

Sydney opened the cabin door to allow Emily to enter. She stumbled in, hobbled to the sofa, and plopped down.

"I hate these things." Emily tossed the crutches aside and propped her foot on the coffee table.

"You'll get used to them. Are you hungry?" Sydney stood over Emily.

"I'll make something later."

"How about a sandwich? Turkey? Tuna?"

Emily smirked sheepishly. "Pop-Tarts?"

"You got it. Toasted or out of the package?"

Emily's jaw dropped. "Oh my God. Is that a serious question? I can't believe I actually slept with you." Emily's face immediately turned bright red, probably at the mention of their intimate behavior.

Sydney chuckled. "How could I forget? Toasted until burnt on the corners. Anything else?"

"Just my laptop so I can start on the article. I think it's on the bar in the kitchen."

"Okay. I'll be right back." Sydney took a few steps, stopped, and turned. "Hey, are you the one who called 911 after you fell?"

"No. I was out cold until I woke up at the hospital. Fran must have. Why do you ask?"

"No reason. Just curious."

Sydney made her way into the kitchen and popped the pastry into the toaster. She leaned against the counter and checked her voice messages. Geez. Ten of them were from Monica, all ranting and raving as to why Sydney hadn't taken the PowerBar job. She'd phone her later. Right now, Sydney had a more important call to make.

After getting Emily set up with something to eat and her laptop, Sydney headed upstairs, went into the bedroom, and closed the door to make sure Emily wouldn't overhear. She sat on the bed and called the devil himself.

"Owen? This is Sydney."

"What do you want?"

"I've been thinking about it, and I didn't treat you fairly. After all, we did make a deal." Sydney wrinkled her nose at the sour taste in her mouth. Lying always had that effect.

Owen laughed, one of those evil, spine-tingling laughs. "It's too late. I don't need you anymore. I know all about the Madagascar lovebirds."

Damn.

"I see. So I guess you're friends with Fran now?" Sydney held her breath, hoping that wasn't true.

Silence.

"Just what I thought," Sydney said. "How are you going to get access to the birds without Fran's permission?"

"I have my ways."

"If you mean trespassing, I wouldn't advise it. Fran is serious about prosecuting. Lucky for you I have a key to her farm. I could easily get you in."

"And why would you do that?"

"Like I said, I feel bad about going back on our deal. I owe you." More silence.

"Why don't you meet me up there in half an hour? What have you got to lose?"

Several long seconds passed until Owen finally said, "All right."

Sydney disconnected and dialed the Ojai police department.

"Hi. This is Sydney Cooper, and I'd like to report a robbery."

Sydney sat in her car outside of Fran's and prayed the police would show up before Owen did. This was probably a horrible plan, but she wasn't sure what else to do since she had no idea where Owen was staying. She'd be in big trouble if this gamble didn't pay off, but she had to follow her instincts.

Sydney grimaced when Owen pulled up next to her. She'd hoped to take care of things without having to go onto Fran's property. Reluctantly, Sydney motioned for him to follow her through the open gate. They drove down the dirt road, parked next to Fran's house, and got out. Luckily, it didn't appear as though she was home. Sydney glanced at her watch. Where were the freaking police? They were going to blow everything.

Sydney nodded to Owen. "Hey. So how'd you find out about the Madagascar lovebirds?"

"That's none of your beeswax," Owen said. He grabbed a bag out of his truck and started down the trail. Obviously, he knew where he was going. He stopped and looked back at Sydney. "Aren't you coming?"

"Actually, I should stay here in case Fran gets back. You know, so she knows you're with me."

Owen paused for two beats and then took off. Sydney shook her head and looked at her watch again. She sat on the steps of Fran's porch and waited a full forty-five minutes before a police car came moseying down the path. Apparently, they took their sweet time unless someone was dying or bleeding. Sydney glared at the two officers as they approached.

"Are you Sydney Cooper?" one of them asked.

"Yes. I'm the one that called about a robbery almost *two hours* ago."

One of the officers took out a note pad and pen. "What happened?"

"There!" Sydney pointed at Owen, who was headed straight toward them. "He stole a camera from Emily Wellington."

Owen slowed considerably when he saw the police officers. At one point it even looked like he was about to make a run for it. Instead, he threw his shoulders back and strode purposefully toward them.

"Good afternoon, Officers. What brings you out here?" Owen shielded his eyes from the sun.

Sydney's heart lurched when she saw an Audubon Bird Cam hanging around Owen's neck. It was Emily's. She was sure of it.

"That's the camera he stole." Sydney pointed at it.

Owen's head jerked toward Sydney, and he gave her a go-to-hell look.

"You're the one who called 911, didn't you?" Sydney asked Owen. "You found Emily when you broke onto the farm and took her camera before you just left her out there alone." Sydney should have been happy he'd even called for an ambulance, but she just couldn't muster any appreciation for the guy.

"I don't know what the hell you're talking about." Owen sneered.

"I can prove it," Sydney said to the officers. "Open the camera, and you'll find Emily's name and address engraved there."

Owen put a hand over the camera lens. "This is mine."

"Like hell it is," Sydney said.

One of the police officers stepped between Sydney and Owen, probably since it looked like Sydney was about to strangle the rat.

"Would you mind opening the camera?" an officer asked Owen.

Owen shook his head and grumbled. "This is ridiculous. You're going to believe her over me?" He took the Bird Cam off his neck and handed it to an officer. "Look for yourself."

The lid popped open when the officer pressed a button. Sydney was about to say "aha," but the words stuck in her throat when she didn't see anything.

"Wait a second." Sydney grabbed the camera and turned it every which way.

Owen smirked.

"I know he took it," Sydney said.

"This is ridiculous and a waste of my time." Owen snatched the camera out of Sydney's hands and opened the door to his truck. "I'm outta here."

"Look in his bag." She motioned toward the bulky sack draped over Owen's shoulder.

"This is harassment!" Owen told the officers. "I'll be reporting this behavior to your supervisor."

The two police officers exchanged irritated glances.

"I suppose you wouldn't mind us taking a look since you have nothing to hide." An officer tugged the bag.

Owen blanched and held it close to his chest. "I...you...shouldn't you have a search warrant for this?"

"Is there stolen property in here?" The officer yanked the sack out of Owen's grasp, unzipped it, and pulled out an Audubon Bird Cam.

"Aha!" Excitement bubbled in the pit of Sydney's stomach. They had him now.

The policeman opened the lid, raised an eyebrow, and turned it toward Owen, displaying the engraved nameplate. "Would you like to explain why you have Emily Wellington's camera?"

Owen glared at Sydney, steam practically coming out of his ears. "I'm not saying anything until I talk to my lawyer."

"Why don't you come downtown with us to answer a few questions?" One of the officers grabbed Owen's arm, stuffed him into the back of the police car, and read him his Miranda rights.

Aside from the day Sydney met Emily, this was quite possibly the best day ever.

CHAPTER TWENTY-FOUR

Lovebirds Unite

"Tell me again. Did they cuff him?"

Sydney couldn't help but laugh. She loved seeing Emily so excited. They'd been sitting on the couch in the cabin for the past half hour, with Sydney recounting everything that had happened.

"No cuffs, but they did ding his head when they put him in the police car."

Emily vigorously rubbed her palms together. "I would have given anything to see that. How come you didn't tell me about this beforehand?" She lightly slapped Sydney's arm.

"I wasn't sure Owen had stolen your camera. It was just a hunch. I didn't want to get your hopes up."

"You still should have told me. How long do you think they'll hold him?"

Sydney shrugged. "If it's his first offense, probably not long."

"I bet he only gets community service." Emily frowned. "Hopefully it's a shit job."

"At least you can still get the article in before he does. Did you check out the photos? Are they intact?"

Emily grasped her camera and flipped through the pictures. "They look okay. First thing I'm doing is backing them up on my computer."

"Did you get the story written today?"

"It's done, and I'm sending it to Cole, my assistant, tonight."

Sydney smiled. "That's great. I'm really happy things worked out for you."

"Thanks to you." Emily's expression softened.

It was now or never. Sydney had to try one last time.

"Em, do you think you could ever possibly forgive me?"

Emily's shoulders sagged. "I don't know. You lied to me, Sydney. You spied and pretended to be my friend."

Sydney closed her eyes and took a deep breath. "I know."

"It's not that I wouldn't want to forgive you, but I don't see how we could go back to the way things were. Not after such a betrayal."

Sydney nodded. "I understand."

They sat in silence for a few moments before Sydney stood. "Guess I should pack my stuff. I'll leave first thing tomorrow morning. You can have the bed tonight, and I'll sleep in the study."

"Are you going back to LA?"

"Yeah. I'll stop by Bud's and then Fran's on my way out and tell them bye."

"I'm sure they'd like that. What will you do for a job?"

"I'll find something. Actually, I have an idea that might pan out."

"Good luck in whatever you end up doing."

"Thanks."

Sydney studied Emily's face, attempting to memorize every feature. Since she intended to be gone before Emily woke in the morning, this would be the last time Sydney would ever see her.

"Good night, Emily." Sydney blinked back tears and walked away.

It was one of those dreams where you're trying to run but going absolutely nowhere.

Sydney was at the end of a long corridor, Emily desperately wanting to reach her. The faster she ran, the farther apart they seemed. Her heart beat wildly and her legs ached. Just when she didn't think she could take another step, she managed to do so. Suddenly, a mist surrounded Sydney. Emily's insides twisted, knowing that if she disappeared into the haze, Emily would never find her, never see her again.

"Nooo!" Emily yelled when Sydney turned and walked away, completely consumed in the fog.

Emily awoke with a start and bolted upright. It was a nightmare, but unfortunately one that was quite real. Emily lay back down and listened hard for any signs of life in the cabin, but it was completely silent. Sydney was gone. Emily was torn between being relieved and feeling incredibly sad. The thought of telling Sydney good-bye was unbearable. Maybe it was best she'd left early. Was Emily making the biggest mistake of her life? Forgiveness is supposed to be the key to happiness and healing. What did it say about Emily that she'd forever hold a grudge against the woman she loved?

Emily grabbed her crutches and slowly made her way down the stairs. She needed to check her email to make sure Cole had everything necessary to get the lovebird issue to the printers. She'd sent him the article, photos, and layout late last night. Just when she sat on the sofa she heard a knock. Excitement shot through her gut. Maybe it was Sydney. As quickly as possible, she hobbled to the door and opened it. It wasn't. Instead, it was her drunk roommate. Well, she probably wasn't drunk at the moment, but that's pretty much all Emily remembered about her.

"You're Monica, right?"

"I'm here to see Sydney." Monica pushed past Emily, almost knocking one of her crutches down, and stood in the middle of the living room.

"She isn't here. She went back to LA."

Monica sighed, looking relieved. "Well, thank goodness for that. She must have come to her senses."

What was that supposed to mean? Had Sydney told her about their breakup? Was she glad they weren't together anymore?

"Yes. Well…" Emily motioned toward the open door.

Monica completely missed the hint. Instead, she said, "Can I use your bathroom? I need to pee something awful."

"Sure. It's upstairs to your right."

Emily closed the front door, made her way back to the couch, and turned on her laptop. At least something in her life was going right. Cole had received everything and sent it off to the printers. When the issue hit the newsstand, *The Tweet* would make history. She should be ecstatic—and not that she wasn't happy—but nothing seemed right without Sydney to share it with.

Monica bolted down the stairs. "Phew. That's better. What happened to you?" She pointed at Emily's cast, as though noticing it for the first time.

"I fell out of a tree."

"Ouch. Are you okay?"

"I'm fine. Sorry you missed Sydney."

Monica scowled. "I'm furious with her. She sent me this crazy text a couple of days ago and then didn't even answer her fucking phone. I came here to talk some sense into her. Are you the one who convinced her to go back to LA?"

"I'm not sure what you mean. I didn't *convince* her. I asked her to leave."

Monica cocked her head and gave Emily a weird look.

"I think we might have a communication gap here," Emily said. "I'm not sure how much Sydney told you about us...together."

"You mean you two? As in yowza-bang-bang?" Monica wiggled her eyebrows.

Emily wasn't exactly sure what that meant. "Well. Anyway. We broke up."

Monica sat on the armrest of the sofa. "Oh. Sorry. What happened?"

Emily waved her hand. She wasn't about to explain everything to a stranger. "Just...you know how it goes sometimes."

Monica punched Emily on the arm. "You're a looker. I'm sure you'll find someone else in no time."

Emily lowered her head and whispered to herself, "Not anyone I'd ever love like that again." Or at least she thought it was to herself.

"You're in love with Sydney?" Monica looked shocked.

"Yes. And I thought she was in love with me too."

"Seriously? Wow. Maybe you two can work things out."

"Doubtful. Anyway, I don't really want to talk about it. Could you just look out for her and make sure she takes care of herself?"

Monica nodded resolutely. "You can count on me. And I'll see that she convinces PowerBar to give her that job back. In fact, that's why I'm here. To talk some sense into her."

"Didn't Sydney tell you? She didn't get the job."

Monica furrowed her brow. "Yes, she did. She sent me a text

Monday night telling me the good news and then another one Tuesday saying she'd quit."

That didn't make any sense. Sydney had said something completely different to Emily. Or had she? Actually, Emily was the one who had assumed she wasn't hired.

Monica pulled out her phone, swiped her finger across the screen a few times, and held it up for Emily to see. Emily's eyes scanned the text. Oh my God. Sydney *did* get the PowerBar job.

"I don't understand. Why wouldn't she…" Emily closed her eyes and threw her head back. "She didn't take the job because she stayed to help me."

"I thought you said you two broke up."

"We did. Monday night. She must have gotten the call after everything blew up, and then I had the accident Tuesday." Emily buried her face in her hands. "I can't believe she did that for me."

"Damn. Sydney must really love you. She wanted that job more than anything."

Emily lowered her arms and looked at Monica. "Yes. She must. I really screwed up. I doubted that she cared about me. I thought it was all just an act. I have to talk to her."

Emily looked at her watch. It was still early. Maybe she could catch Sydney. She snatched her phone and dialed.

"Fran? It's Emily. Did Sydney come by your place?"

"Yes. As a matter of fact she's still here. She wanted to see the lovebirds one last time."

"Thank God. Please do whatever you can to keep her there. I'm on my way." Emily hung up and looked at Monica. "Can you drive me somewhere?"

"You guys are survivors like me," Sydney said to the lovebirds as she stood on a ladder propped against the fig tree.

She'd been there for at least an hour, finding it difficult to leave. Saying good-bye to the birds was like leaving Emily all over again. One landed on a branch right in front of her and pecked her on the nose.

"Are you trying to tell me something?"

The lovebird tilted its head and chirped loudly. Sydney followed its line of vision and saw a fast-approaching tractor. It looked like Fran was driving with someone else in the passenger seat.

"Guess I should get going. Whatever happens, I hope you all stay together. You should never be separated from your mates."

Sydney took one last look at the lovebirds and descended the ladder. She stood by the tree and watched the large, yellow vehicle barrel toward her. The person with Fran almost looked like Emily, but it couldn't be. Sydney was just seeing things. She hooked her backpack over her shoulder and watched as Fran came to a halt. Sydney's heart lurched when her eyes locked with the passenger's. It *was* Emily. Fran went to the other side of the tractor, helped her down, and sat back in the driver's seat. Sydney stood motionless as Emily hobbled on crutches and stood right in front of her.

"I'll get out of your way," Sydney said. "I was just leaving."

"I didn't come to see the lovebirds." Emily tossed her crutches aside and stood with both feet on the ground.

"You shouldn't put any pressure on that ankle." The last thing Emily probably wanted was advice from Sydney, but she didn't want her to do more damage to herself.

"The crutches will just get in the way." Emily limped forward.

Sydney was tempted to take a step back, surprised at how close they were. "Still, though, you want it to heal properly."

Emily's eyes twinkled. "You're always looking out for me, aren't you?" Something was definitely different about Emily. Her energy seemed light, almost joyful. "There's something I really want to do, and it just isn't possible with crutches."

Emily slipped her arms around Sydney's waist and kissed her. Sydney was so shocked her lips froze and she tensed all over.

Within seconds, Emily pulled back. "Is this okay?"

"I don't understand. Does this mean you're not angry with me anymore?"

"I know you passed up the PowerBar job for me. You should have told me, Sydney. I never would have allowed you to do that."

"How'd you find out?"

"Monica showed up at the cabin this morning."

"Oh. I didn't tell you because I knew you never would have let me help you, and I needed to fix what I'd done." Sydney looked directly into Emily's eyes. "I do love you."

"I know that now." Emily placed a light kiss on Sydney's lips. "But that was your dream job."

"No," Sydney said. "Nothing is more important than you. You're my dream."

CHAPTER TWENTY-FIVE

Epilogue

One year later

Emily drove a third lap around the lot, looking for a parking space. Normally, she'd be ticked off, but in this particular case it was a positive thing. She put her blinker on when she saw someone pulling out and sped into the spot before anyone else could take it. She looked up at the PoleCat sign and smiled. Sydney and Robin had made a lot of improvements to the place, including new signage and a paint job.

Emily entered the studio and spotted Robin behind the receptionist's desk. "Hi, Robin."

"Hey, you. I haven't seen you in a while. Syd said you've been busy."

Emily sighed. "It's been crazy, but in a good way."

After the Madagascar lovebird article had been published, Emily had experienced more success than she could have imagined. Not only had *The Tweet*'s sales soared, but she'd even been interviewed on several national news and wildlife programs.

"Speaking of busy, you two are doing awesome," Emily said. "The parking lot is packed."

Robin smirked. "Our membership tripled from this time last year. Hiring Syd was the best thing ever."

"I'm glad. So where is the love of my life?" Emily glanced around.

"She's finishing up with a student."

Emily looked at her watch. "I thought her class was over twenty minutes ago."

"You know your girlfriend. She's probably helping a new student feel more comfortable with a routine."

Emily smiled. She was happy Sydney loved her job. Still, though, she wondered sometimes if she'd ever regretted passing up the PowerBar position.

"You two heading to Ojai?" Robin asked.

"Yes. And we're going to be late if we don't get on the road."

The door to the pole-dancing class opened, and Sydney walked out with a woman. Emily's face heated at the sight of her sexy girlfriend. They'd been together a year, but seeing Sydney in short shorts and a crop top still had an effect on Emily. Sydney glanced at Emily and winked, which sent her heart soaring.

"You're doing great," Sydney said to the woman as they approached the reception area.

"Sometimes I don't think I'll ever get it." The woman frowned.

"Stick with it and I promise you will."

"Thanks, Sydney. I'll see you next week," the woman said and exited the studio.

Sydney wrapped her arms around Emily's waist. "Hey, beautiful."

Emily beamed and looked at Robin. "How'd I get so lucky?"

"You two are disgustingly cute together," Robin said. "I'd love to stay and hear all the lovey-dovey crap, but it might make me retch. Plus, I have a class to teach." Robin chuckled and disappeared down the hall.

"You were supposed to be showered and ready to go by now," Emily said.

"Sorry. I got held up. Just give me a minute." Sydney tried to pull away, but Emily held her in place.

"Not so fast," Emily said. "I'm not done with you yet."

Sydney smirked. "No?"

Emily dropped her gaze to Sydney's luscious lips, her pulse rate increasing before they even touched. She inched forward and traced Sydney's mouth with her tongue before plunging into a deep kiss. The sound of Sydney's pleasurable moans caused Emily's heart to flutter. Emily raked her fingers through Sydney's silky hair and pulled her even closer, the length of their bodies pressed together. It was amazing how one kiss could ignite Emily's passions. If they weren't in the studio, she'd lay Sydney down and make love to her.

They quickly pulled apart when someone opened the front door. Emily grabbed the edge of the counter for balance since she was totally limp and resisted the urge to cover her face, sure it was flushed with desire.

Sydney thrust her hands behind her back and cleared her throat several times. "Hi, Sandra," Sydney said to the woman who'd entered. "Go on back. The class is about to start."

The woman smirked and flashed a knowing glance as she passed them. Once she was out of sight, Emily slid her arms around Sydney's waist and smiled.

"Sorry. Guess we got caught."

"Never apologize for kissing me," Sydney said and planted a peck on Emily's nose. "Give me fifteen minutes and I'll be ready to roll."

Reluctantly, Emily released her hold. "Hey," Emily said and grabbed Sydney's hand. "I need to ask you something. Do you ever regret not taking the PowerBar job?"

"What brought that on?"

"I just wonder sometimes."

"I can honestly say absolutely, unequivocally, no. I do not regret it."

"But—"

"No buts. You were right before when you said my self-worth doesn't come from a job but from within. I wanted to work at PowerBar because it was a high-class place in Beverly Hills, and I thought it would mean I was somebody." Sydney chuckled. "Guess I had a lot to learn."

"You're an incredible person, regardless of where you work."

"I know that now. And I was going to save this surprise until later, but maybe I'll go ahead and tell you."

"What is it?"

"Robin wants me to be her partner. I'm going to be a fifty percent owner of PoleCat." Sydney's eyes sparkled with delight.

"Oh my gosh. That's wonderful. Congratulations." Emily gave Sydney a tight squeeze.

"Thanks. I'm really excited about it," Sydney said, smiling widely. "We're really in sync with what we want to accomplish."

"That's wonderful, sweetie. I'm so happy for you."

"So no more wondering about PowerBar, okay?"

"All right." Emily gave Sydney a quick kiss. "Now go get ready so we can get on the road."

❖

"Did you ever think you'd see that?" Emily said with a chuckle.

"Not in a million years," Sydney said. "But then again, I can't blame Fran for succumbing to your powers of persuasion."

They gazed up at the enormous All Are Welcome sign at the entrance to Fran's farm and drove through the open gate.

"Remember when we broke in?" Sydney asked. "You were scared shitless."

"I was not!" Emily protested but with a smile in her voice.

"Come on. Admit it." Sydney teasingly poked Emily in the ribs.

"All right. Maybe a little. You know, that's when I started falling in love with you."

"Really?" Sydney looked surprised.

"When I got stuck in the fence, you made me feel safe and cared for. I would've followed you anywhere that night."

"I was hooked the minute you threw my avocado protein drink on me and jabbed that humongous ring in my face." Sydney laughed.

"You deserved it." Emily smiled. "But I'm glad you broke into the cabin."

Sydney grabbed Emily's hand and held it. "Me, too."

Emily pulled behind a truck and parked, amazed at all the people. It had taken some convincing, but Fran had finally agreed to open her farm to the public. Her failing business was revived by weekend fig fests, when customers picked fruit themselves and paid by the basket. The biggest draw, though, was that folks from all over the world flocked to see the famous Madagascar lovebirds. After Fran's profits soared, she didn't seem to mind so much that the birds were eating her figs. Fran got rich, and Emily secured a safe place for the lovebirds to reside. It was a win for both of them.

Emily grinned when she spotted Fran and Bud standing on the porch. She'd missed them.

"Hey, you two," Sydney said as they approached.

"Well, look what the cat drug in." Fran smiled. "It's been months since you've visited."

"I know," Emily said. "It's been too long."

Sydney and Emily climbed the steps and gave Fran and Bud each a hug.

"I saw you on that there Discovery program the other night," Bud said to Emily. "You've become quite a TV star."

Emily chuckled. "I think the lovebirds are the stars."

"The place is packed," Sydney said, motioning to the crowd.

"Every weekend gets even busier," Fran said.

"And to think you wanted to get rid of the lovebirds." Emily smirked.

Fran's cheeks turned bright red. "Well. I can be pigheaded sometimes, I suppose."

"Not too pigheaded to say yes to my proposal, though." Bud stood upright and hooked his thumbs under his suspenders.

"Wow. Congratulations," Emily and Sydney said in unison.

"We're getting hitched two months from today, so you two better plan on being here."

"We wouldn't miss it." Emily's heart warmed at the tender look Bud and Fran exchanged. She couldn't help but feel proud that she and Sydney had gotten them together during that Conway Twitty dinner.

After chatting a bit, Emily and Sydney meandered through the fig trees. Anticipation swirled inside Emily as they neared the lovebirds. She'd seen them dozens of times, but the excitement never waned. Disappointment settled in, though, when she saw a huge crowd around the lovebirds' fig tree. They'd never get close enough to see the birds, even with Emily's high-powered binoculars.

"Jesus, look at all the people. I can push through for you," Sydney said, undoubtedly seeing Emily's displeasure.

"No. That's okay. Most of these folks have never seen the birds. They deserve to enjoy them."

"Yeah, but they're kinda like...*ours*."

Emily faced Sydney and smiled. "They are, but you know what? There's only one lovebird I care about, and she's standing right in front of me."

About the Author

Lisa Moreau is an ultimate romantic and loves creating lighthearted, happily-ever-after romances. Her debut novel, *Love on the Red Rocks*, is a 2017 Golden Crown Literary Society Debut Award winner, and her second book, *The Butterfly Whisperer*, won a 2018 GCLS Award.

Lisa has a bachelor's degree in journalism from Midwestern State University, Texas, and has completed an indefinitely large number of creative writing courses at Santa Monica College, California. She lives in Los Angeles for the ocean, mountains and totally awesome weather and only occasionally thinks about moving when she feels an earthquake tremble.

Lisa can be reached at www.LisaMoreauWriter.com.

Books Available From Bold Strokes Books

All of Me by Emily Smith. When chief surgical resident Galen Burgess meets her new intern, Rowan Duncan, she may finally discover that doing what you've always done will only give you what you've always had. (978-1-163555-321-5)

As the Crow Flies by Karen F. Williams. Romance seems to be blooming all around, but problems arise when a restless ghost emerges from the ether to roam the dark corners of this haunting tale. (978-1-163555-285-0)

Both Ways by Ileandra Young. SPEAR agent Danika Karson races to protect the city from a supernatural threat and must rely on the woman she's trained to despise: Rayne, an achingly beautiful vampire. (978-1-163555-298-0)

Calendar Girl by Georgia Beers. Forced to work together, Addison Fairchild and Kate Cooper discover that opposites really do attract. (978-1-163555-333-8)

Cash and the Sorority Girl by Ashley Bartlett. Cash Braddock doesn't want to deal with morality, drugs, or people. Unfortunately, she's going to have to. (978-1-163555-310-9)

Lovebirds by Lisa Moreau. Two women from different worlds collide in a small California mountain town, each with a mission that doesn't include falling in love. (978-1-163555-213-3)

Media Darling by Fiona Riley. Can Hollywood bad girl Emerson and reluctant celebrity gossip reporter Hayley work together to make each other's dreams come true? Or will Emerson's secrets ruin not one career, but two? (978-1-163555-278-2)

Stroke of Fate by Renee Roman. Can Sean Moore live up to her reputation and save Jade Rivers from the stalker determined to end Jade's career and, ultimately, her life? (978-1-163555-162-4)

The Rise of the Resistance by Jackie D. The soul of America has been lost for almost a century. A few people may be the difference between a phoenix rising to save the masses or permanent destruction. (978-1-163555-259-1)

The Sex Therapist Next Door by Meghan O'Brien. At the intersection of sex and intimacy, anything is possible. Even love. (978-1-163555-296-6)

Unexpected Lightning by Cass Sellars. Lightning strikes once more when Sydney and Parker fight a dangerous stranger who threatens the peace they both desperately want. (978-1-163555-276-8)

Unforgettable by Elle Spencer. When one night changes a lifetime… Two romance novellas from best-selling author Elle Spencer. (978-1-63555-429-8)

Against All Odds by Kris Bryant, Maggie Cummings, and M. Ullrich. Peyton and Tory escaped death once, but will they survive when Bradley's determined to make his kill rate 100 percent? (978-1-163555-193-8)

Autumn's Light by Aurora Rey. Casual hookups aren't supposed to include romantic dinners and meeting the family. Can Mat Pero see beyond the heartbreak that led her to keep her worlds so separate, and will Graham Connor be waiting if she does? (978-1-163555-272-0)

Breaking the Rules by Larkin Rose. When Virginia and Carmen are thrown together by an embarrassing mistake, they find out their stubborn determination isn't so heroic after all. (978-1-163555-261-4)

Broad Awakening by Mickey Brent. In the sequel to *Underwater Vibes*, Hélène and Sylvie find ruts in their road to eternal bliss. (978-1-163555-270-6)

Broken Vows by MJ Williamz. Sister Mary Margaret must reconcile her divided heart or risk losing a love that just might be heaven sent. (978-1-163555-022-1)

Flesh and Gold by Ann Aptaker. Havana, 1952, where art thief and smuggler Cantor Gold dodges gangland bullets and mobsters' schemes while she searches Havana's steamy red light district for her kidnapped love. (978-1-163555-153-2)

Isle of Broken Years by Jane Fletcher. Spanish noblewoman Catalina de Valasco is in peril, even before the pirates holding her for ransom sail into seas destined to become known as the Bermuda Triangle. (978-1-163555-175-4)

Love Like This by Melissa Brayden. Hadley Cooper and Spencer Adair set out to take the fashion world by storm. If only they knew their hearts were about to be taken. (978-1-163555-018-4)

Secrets On the Clock by Nicole Disney. Jenna and Danielle love their jobs helping endangered children, but that might not be enough to stop them from breaking the rules by falling in love. (978-1-163555-292-8)

Unexpected Partners by Michelle Larkin. Dr. Chloe Maddox tries desperately to deny her attraction for Detective Dana Blake as they flee from a serial killer who's hunting them both. (978-1-163555-203-4)

A Fighting Chance by T. L. Hayes. Will Lou be able to come to terms with her past to give love a fighting chance? (978-1-163555-257-7)

Chosen by Brey Willows. When the choice is adapt or die, can love save us all? (978-1-163555-110-5)

Gnarled Hollow by Charlotte Greene. After they are invited to study a secluded nineteenth-century estate, a former English professor and a group of historians discover that they will have to fight against the unknown if they have any hope of staying alive. (978-1-163555-235-5)

Jacob's Grace by C.P. Rowlands. Captain Tag Becket wants to keep her head down and her past behind her, but her feelings for AJ's second-in-command, Grace Fields, makes keeping secrets next to impossible. (978-1-163555-187-7)

On the Fly by PJ Trebelhorn. Hockey player Courtney Abbott is content with her solitary life until visiting concert violinist Lana Caruso makes her second-guess everything she always thought she wanted. (978-1-163555-255-3)

Passionate Rivals by Radclyffe. Professional rivalry and long-simmering passions create a combustible combination when Emmet McCabe and Sydney Stevens are forced to work together, especially when past attractions won't stay buried. (978-1-63555-231-7)

Proxima Five by Missouri Vaun. When geologist Leah Warren crash-lands on a preindustrial planet and is claimed by its tyrant, Tiago, will clan warrior Keegan's love for Leah give her the strength to defeat him? (978-1-163555-122-8)

Shadowboxer by Jessica L. Webb. Jordan McAddie is prepared to keep her street kids safe from a dangerous underground protest group, but she isn't prepared for her first love to walk back into her life. (978-1-163555-267-6)

Racing Hearts by Dena Blake. When you cross a hot-tempered race car mechanic with a reckless cop, the result can only be spontaneous combustion. (978-1-163555-251-5)

The Tattered Lands by Barbara Ann Wright. As Vandra and Lilani strive to make peace, they slowly fall in love. With mistrust and murder surrounding them, only their faith in each other can keep their plan to save the world from falling apart. (978-1-163555-108-2)

Captive by Donna K. Ford. To escape a human trafficking ring, Greyson Cooper and Olivia Danner become players in a game of deceit and violence. Will their love stand a chance? (978-1-63555-215-7)

Crossing the Line by CF Frizzell. The Mob discovers a nemesis within its ranks, and in the ultimate retaliation, draws Stick McLaughlin from anonymity by threatening everything she holds dear. (978-1-63555-161-7)

Love's Verdict by Carsen Taite. Attorneys Landon Holt and Carly Pachett want the exact same thing: the only open partnership spot at their prestigious criminal defense firm. But will they compromise their careers for love? (978-1-63555-042-9)

Precipice of Doubt by Mardi Alexander & Laurie Eichler. Can Cole Jameson resist her attraction to her boss, veterinarian Jodi Bowman, or will she risk a workplace romance and her heart? (978-1-63555-128-0)

Savage Horizons by CJ Birch. Captain Jordan Kellow's feelings for Lt. Ali Ash have her past and future colliding, setting in motion a series of events that strands her crew in an unknown galaxy thousands of light years from home. (978-1-63555-250-8)

Secrets of the Last Castle by A. Rose Mathieu. When Elizabeth Campbell represents a young man accused of murdering an elderly woman, her investigation leads to an abandoned plantation that reveals many dark Southern secrets. (978-1-63555-240-9)

Take Your Time by VK Powell. A neurotic parrot brings police officer Grace Booker and temporary veterinarian Dr. Dani Wingate together in the tiny town of Pine Cone, but their unexpected attraction keeps the sparks flying. (978-1-63555-130-3)

The Last Seduction by Ronica Black. When you allow true love to elude you once and you desperately regret it, are you brave enough to grab it when it comes around again? (978-1-63555-211-9)

The Shape of You by Georgia Beers. Rebecca McCall doesn't play it safe, but when sexy Spencer Thompson joins her workout class, their nonstop sparring forces her to face her ultimate challenge—a chance at love. (978-1-63555-217-1)

Force of Fire: Toujours a Vous by Ali Vali. Immortals Kendal and Piper welcome their new child and celebrate the defeat of an old enemy, but another ancient evil is about to awaken deep in the jungles of Costa Rica. (978-1-63555-047-4)

www.ingramcontent.com/pod-product-compliance
Lightning Source LLC
Chambersburg PA
CBHW030513020726
47494CB00004B/1081